## JEFFREY SIGER

was born and raised in Pittsburgh, Pennsylvania, practiced law at a major Wall Street law firm and later established his own New York City law firm where he continued as one of its name partners until giving it all up to write full-time among the people, life and politics of his beloved Mykonos.

The *New York Times* described Jeffrey Siger's novels as "thoughtful police procedurals set in picturesque but not untroubled Greek locales." The *Greek Press* called his work "prophetic." *Euro Crime* described him as a "very gifted American author...on a par with other American authors such as Joseph Wambaugh or Ed McBain," and the City of San Francisco awarded him its Certificate of Honor, stating that his "acclaimed books have not only explored modern Greek society and its ancient roots but have inspired political change in Greece."

www.JeffreySiger.com

# TARGET: TINOS

## JEFFREY SIGER

**W❂RLDWIDE**®

TORONTO • NEW YORK • LONDON
AMSTERDAM • PARIS • SYDNEY • HAMBURG
STOCKHOLM • ATHENS • TOKYO • MILAN
MADRID • WARSAW • BUDAPEST • AUCKLAND

*In memory of my parents, Fred and Thelma.*
*Children of immigrants.*

Recycling programs
for this product may
not exist in your area.

ISBN-13: 978-1-335-66141-8

Target: Tinos

Copyright © 2012 by Jeffrey Siger

A Worldwide Library Suspense/July 2018

First published by Poisoned Pen Press

**Printed in U.S.A.**

# ACKNOWLEDGMENTS

Petros and Georgia Alafasos; Clio Andris;
Roz and Mihalis Apostolou; Andreas Arkentis;
Olga Balafa; Tonino Cacace; Jeff and Liz Carson;
Norbert Carstens; Andreas, Aleca, Nikos,
Mihalis and Anna Fiorentinos; Enzio Grasser-Prym;
Maria Grivogianni; Nikos Ipiotis; Nikos Karahalios;
Flora and Yanni Katsaounis; Olga Kefalogianni;
Panos Kelaidis; Nicholas and Sonia Kotopoulos;
Yianni Lagias and Myrna Tzakas; Ioanna Lalaouni;
Lila and Ilias Lalaounis; Linda Marshall; Lisa Maxson;
Giorgos Minardos; Terry Moon; Jeffrey W. Moses;
Nikos Nazos; Lambros Panagiotakopoulos;
Barbara G. Peters and Robert Rosenwald;
Eleni Polukandriti; Christine Schnitzer-Smith;
Beth Schnitzer; Victoria Sharp; Raghu Shivaram;
Alan and Patricia Siger; Jonathan, Jennifer,
Azriel and Gavriella Siger; Karen Siger;
Konstantinos Sougkas; Sparta Public Library
and Carol Boutilier; Ed Stackler; Pavlos Tiftikidis;
Jessica Tribble; Steve Tzolis; Adamantios Vassilakis;
Alejandro Wolff; Susan Xenarios; Barbara Zilly.

And, of course, Aikaterini Lalaouni.

Leave us, proud person!
We are wild and have no laws,
We do not torture or execute—
We have no need of blood or moans—
But we won't live with a murderer...
You are not born for the wild life,
You want freedom only for yourself.

—Aleksandr Pushkin,
*The Gypsies*

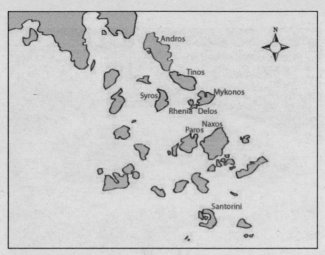

The Cyclades Islands

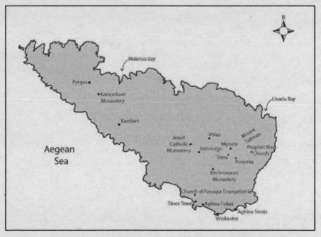

The Island of Tinos

The Church of Panagia Evangelistria

# ONE

*REVENGE OR DEATH.*

That was all that the note said. It was found protected in a cylinder chained to the steering wheel of a van set on fire sometime before dawn. In the rear of the van was another surprise wrapped in chains: the remains of two bodies charred beyond recognition amid bits and pieces of an incinerated Greek flag.

"Freedom or Death" was Greece's national motto and by noon enraged network talking heads relentlessly decried the horror as a national sacrilege, with shouts of justice for the yet unidentified victims and merciless punishment for those "unwelcome foreign elements" tearing asunder the fabric of Greek culture with "their criminal ways." It did not matter that no one knew the truth.

"I'M SORRY, BUT I can't make it," Andreas yelled into his cell phone over the whipping helicopter rotors.

"We must have a bad connection. I could swear I just heard you say you 'can't make it' to the only meeting I asked you to attend with our wedding planner." Lila's voice was in decidedly frosty counterpoint to the heavy, late morning air of July's last days.

Chief Inspector Andreas Kaldis, feared head of the Greek police's Special Crimes Division, cleared his throat as he said, "I thought you'd understand."

"Andreas—" Lila paused. "You can't talk?"

"Yes."

"You better be a hostage."

"Worse."

"You're surrounded by politicians?"

"Just one. I have to go, kisses." Andreas hung up and let out a breath.

"You're a lucky guy," said Andreas' boss, Greece's minister of public order. "My wife would have killed me if I'd done something like that to her less than two weeks before our wedding." He smiled.

"There's still time." Andreas attempted to force a smile. Twenty minutes until they reached Tinos. "You do realize the press will be waiting for us?"

"It is their duty to report this massacre. We're talking about mass murder on the island of the Church of Panagia Evangelistria, the Lourdes of Greece."

Andreas could tell the minister was rehearsing his pitch for the cameras. Andreas preferred listening to the rotors.

*Panagia* was an Eastern Orthodox title for the Virgin Mary and *Evangelistria* referred to the Annunciation when the angel Gabriel announced to the Virgin Mary the incarnation of Christ. Tinos' Church of the Annunciation, Panagia Evangelistria, was the most revered religious shrine in Greece. More than a million pilgrims flocked there each year, many seeking healing from the Miraculous Icon of the Virgin Mary, the *Megalochari*. *Megalochari* meant "Great Grace" and was the Greek people's unofficial name for The Holy Icon of the Annunciation of Tinos kept within the Church of Panagia Evangelistria.

Andreas stared at his minister. "Let's just try not to make any promises we can't keep."

Minister Spiros Renatis glared back, but said nothing. His carefully cultivated public image depended upon Andreas staying on as Greece's number one cop for all things nasty and both men knew that. And being incorruptible gave Andreas a bottom line freedom many in government did not share: knowledge that he could earn far more elsewhere, especially in these days of mandated deep cuts by the European Union, International Monetary Fund, and European Central Bank to every public servant's pay. That gave rise to a simple arrangement: Andreas did things his way and Spiros took all the credit. They hadn't yet worked out who'd take the blame if some day things went terribly wrong.

The helicopter came in from the west, passing over brown-green hills of wild oregano, rosemary, and sage, veined with narrow paths and ancient walls, and on into a valley on the northeastern coast peppered with cedars, olive, and fruit trees. Tinos was a largely undeveloped, narrow arrowhead-shape island pointing northwest. At three times the size of New York City's Manhattan, it was the fourth largest island in the Cycladic chain and had a fulltime population of fewer than 9,000.

The helicopter eased in close-by the edge of a burned out field of wild summer grass. There wasn't a building in sight. As soon as the rotors stopped spinning, Spiros jumped out and hurried off toward the TV cameras. He was wearing his serious face.

Andreas went in the opposite direction, toward a group of men gathered in the middle of a field around a flame-scorched van.

It was the smell that hit Andreas first. Gasoline

mixed with charred flesh. The sort of thing he knew he'd never forget. He tried not to focus on the odor.

*Revenge or Death.* Okay, he could see revenge as the motive for something as brutal as this, but what's the tie in to our national motto and battle cry? And why Tinos for a public execution? The minister was right about that part. Tinos was where desperate pilgrims from all over the world came bearing prayers and offerings to the miraculous curative powers of the *Megalochari*; many crawling the steep half-mile up from the harbor to the church, pushing before them candles they'd vowed to light to the holy icon.

A half-dozen police cars were parked unevenly across a deeply rutted, one-lane dirt road separating an olive grove from the field. Andreas walked toward a cop trying to keep the curious away. "Who's in charge?"

The cop nodded in the direction of a man in plainclothes standing by the open rear doors of the van. Andreas knew him; they'd been together in the police academy.

The odor grew stronger as Andreas approached the van. He struggled not to gag. The man saw Andreas coming and turned to face the van. Andreas stopped next to him and stared inside.

"This tells it all, my friend," said the man. He was Tinos' police chief.

Andreas had been wrong. The odor was not what he would remember for the rest of his life. It was this, an image impossible to fully grasp in the abstract or ever forget in its unfathomable reality. Two shapes entwined in chains. Whatever flesh he could see was charred and blackened to the bone.

Neither man spoke for a moment. Andreas quietly said a prayer.

"Amen," said the police chief. "I've never seen anything like this."

"Me either, and I hope never to again." Andreas swallowed hard.

"This is one for heavy forensics. I called in for help from Athens, but you beat them here."

Andreas waved his hand in the direction of the minister. "Yeah, politics takes precedence over police work. Forensics should have been with us on that helicopter. But he didn't want to wait. They won't get here for hours."

"Same old shit, no surprises there."

Andreas nodded. "So, what do you think?"

"That we've got one hell of a problem and nothing to go on. Two victims chained together amid remnants of a Greek flag. Don't know why the flag didn't burn."

"Probably because someone didn't want it to," said Andreas.

"And then there's that cylinder chained to the steering wheel. We probably shouldn't have gone near it until after the bomb boys had a go at it."

"Not smart. If this was terrorists, that thing could have been set for another surprise."

The police chief shrugged. "Sometimes we Greeks are just too curious for our own good."

Andreas pointed at the ground. "Any footprints?"

"Hundreds. What with firefighters, cops, and the locals, no way to tell what we have, if anything."

"Any witnesses?"

"None so far as we can tell. This area is deserted at night. And the fire started just before sunrise. A farmer over that hill," he pointed southwest, "saw the smoke and called it in. But I've got uniforms talking to everyone who's here." He gestured at the crowd. "Maybe we'll get lucky, find something to go on."

Andreas nodded. "Let's hope so." He patted the police chief on the back. "Be safe, Odysseus. Let me know as soon as you come up with anything."

Andreas walked to where Spiros was holding court and stood just outside the circle of reporters and cameras. He wasn't worried about being drawn into that zoo. Spiros shared the media spotlight with no one. As for the real mess—the one amid the field behind him—Andreas had no idea what Spiros had in mind for him, but he'd find out soon enough because Spiros was just wrapping up his prime time TV performance.

"Ladies and gentlemen, I'm sure you understand I must get on with the investigation, so please excuse me. But I give you and the Greek people my word that the ruthless murderers behind this heinous crime will be apprehended and punished. Greece cannot tolerate such crimes against its citizens."

The reporters kept shouting questions, but Spiros walked toward Andreas, motioning as he did for three cops to keep the press from following him.

"So, what do you think? Sounded pretty good, didn't I?"

Andreas shrugged. "I'm glad you followed my advice."

Spiros' voice bristled. "Sometimes I don't understand you. The van is Greek so we can trace it, but even if it's stolen we have *two* victims. One execution style murder might be hard to solve, but we've got two dead bodies and a message. There has to be an obvious motive for this, one that will point straight to whomever is responsible. And once we start pressing for leads informants will be falling all over themselves trying to make deals and score points with us." He shook his head.

"Frankly, Andreas, I don't understand your negative attitude. I don't want you involved in any of this. The *only* thing I want from you is your opinion on the local cops. Do you think this is something they can handle or not?"

At times Andreas wondered if he and his boss shared the same planet. As Andreas saw it, the bottom line to Spiros' little temper tantrum was one less mess for Andreas to worry about. But, for Spiros, he'd gone so far out on a limb with the media that absent extraordinary luck his career would be toast.

"Odysseus is a good man. He knows his job."

"Good, then I'm leaving this in his hands."

BY THE LATE afternoon the facts, or rather the lack thereof, started rolling in. No identifiable footprints or other signs were found in the area, the van had been stolen that night from the port without a clue as to who did it, and forensics could not identify either victim. Neither the curious present at the scene or snitches had anything to tell. There was not a lead to be found anywhere.

With Spiros having nothing left to feed the press, the media followed its natural instincts and began clamoring for his head.

Spiros' had no idea what to do next. His limb seemed about sawed clear through and his career toasted to just this side of charcoal when two days later relatives of the victims stepped forward and identified the bodies: *tsigani*—known in other languages as Gypsies or *roma*.

And with that the story seemed to fall off the face of the earth.

*Lucky bastard*, thought Andreas.

# TWO

ATHENS GENERAL POLICE HEADQUARTERS, better known as GADA, was across the street from the stadium of one of Greece's two most popular soccer teams, down the block from Greece's Supreme Court, and next to a major hospital. In one way or another, what happened in that neighborhood affected virtually all of the more than five million people who lived in Athens. But at the moment Andreas faced only one Athenian. His boss had surprised him with a mountain-coming-to-Mohammed sort of visit. That usually meant he was in desperate need of Andreas' help.

Andreas wore that glazed look so often seen on those waiting for a politician to get to the point.

"At least that nastiness in Tinos is resolved," said Spiros.

He'd regained Andreas' attention. "You solved the murders?"

Spiros jerked his head up in the Greek gesture for no. "They'll never be solved. You know how blood feuds are among *tsigani*. No one talks to outsiders. Besides, as long as they keep the killing to themselves..." He shrugged.

The *tsigani* were notorious for many things and victimized for far more. They were the objects of Nazi extermination efforts in World War II and a conundrum to the European Union today. Andreas knew that the behavior of a very few had irreparably branded the image of the many, but a solution for that sort of bigotry was not in his hands. He had to accept the reality caused by the few and deal with it.

"Is that what Odysseus thought happened?"

"Tinos police are no longer in charge of the investigation."

"Why is that?"

"It doesn't matter. And their chief is now officially on vacation for two weeks."

"What do you want from me?"

"I want you to close the case."

"And how do you propose I do that?"

"By stating the obvious. They were clan-motivated *tsigani* revenge killings and those who were behind it have fled Greece."

"You're the minister, you can close it." Fat chance of that, thought Andreas. Spiros never put his neck on the line; he always wanted someone to blame if things went wrong. Odysseus must have passed on being his fall guy and I'm his runner-up choice.

"The case is dead, Andreas, and no one cares any more. Let's just officially end it."

To Andreas that translated as the victims weren't anyone who mattered and lacked relatives with political or media clout, so press interest in their murders had evaporated.

"Sorry, Spiros, but Tinos is not within my jurisdiction."

Anger flashed across Spiros' face but he did not raise his voice. "We both know you have jurisdiction across Greece for something like this."

"Yes, but only if it's a matter of national concern or

potential corruption. Don't you think the press might start to wonder why GADA's Chief of Special Crimes made a special appearance to take a case away from local police only to announce that it's closed?"

Spiros paused a few seconds and cleared his throat. "Perhaps I wasn't making myself clear. I'm not asking for you to take personal responsibility, I just thought you might be able to use your influence with your friend to convince him to help us out with this."

I guess we're on to fall guy candidate number three. "What friend?"

"Tassos Stamatos. As chief homicide investigator for the Cyclades, Tinos falls within his jurisdiction and what we're asking him to do isn't something he hasn't done before."

"I can give you his mobile number it you don't have it. I'm sure he'll take your call. After all, you are his boss."

Spiros forced a smile. "I think that suggestion might be better received coming from you."

Andreas couldn't argue with that. Andreas and Tassos met when Andreas was police chief on Mykonos, another Cycladic island, and they'd become fast friends with similar views on many things, including the abilities and ways of their minister. But Spiros had even less leverage with Tassos than he did with Andreas because Tassos was well beyond retirement age and possessed secrets and connections from both sides of the law that guaranteed him lifetime job security for as long as he wanted.

"I would owe him a big time favor. I'd owe you both," said Spiros.

They would be lost on your mountain of other IOUs,

thought Andreas. "Perhaps if you told me what has you so wound up about this case I might be able to help you out. We both know the story is dead in the press."

"I'm not concerned with what the press thinks."

Andreas smiled.

"At least not the Greek press. And it's not just me who's worried. It's my boss."

"Are you trying to tell me that the Prime Minister wants the investigation closed?"

Spiros rubbed his chin. "It's about the money."

"Come again?"

"There are serious people in the E.U. looking for any justification for ending financial aid to Greece. So far the arguments against us are purely financial. That we don't work hard enough, we're corrupt, we don't want to pay taxes. You know the routine. And although you may not think it, that's a problem for those who are willing to let us go under, because more people in the E.U. are sympathetic to us than against us. It's a person-to-person thing. They feel the Greek people are being made to suffer by the E.U.'s big boys in an effort to deflect attention away from their own banks' fiscal mistakes. We don't want to do anything that might give our enemies different ammunition."

"What sort of ammunition?"

"The worst, the hypocritical kind. I don't have to tell you how every country in Europe has its own sort of immigrant issues. Ethnic stereotypes are a convenient, irresistible scapegoat for political failings, especially in hard times, and no one wants to be the first to point a serious finger at another country's shortcomings in dealing with its immigrants.

"But our adversaries would love to switch the focus

of the debate from our country's financial problems to our national character. Paint us as indifferent to the plight of non-Greeks, an intolerant place where only Greeks are treated as deserving of protection, and all others be damned. It's a volatile, irrational, and emotional argument but one that could turn world opinion against us if it found traction in the press. And then it would no longer be just a question of denying us further bailout funds, but whether or not to drum us out of the E.U."

"With all due respect, Spiros, it sounds a bit dramatic to say that the murder of two *tsigani* on a relatively unknown island to non-Greeks could be the cause of getting us kicked out of the E.U."

Spiros shrugged. "Our Prime Minister sees it as a risk and that's good enough for me. Psychos running around the Greek countryside incinerating *tsigani* play right into the hands of those who want Greece to fail. And the longer this case remains open the greater the chance of some foreign reporter seeing glory in a story that shocks the world into action against us by linking Greece to words like 'intolerance' and 'genocide.' We cannot allow that to happen."

Spiros seemed quite satisfied with his speech.

Andreas said, "Don't you think the first thing to do is find out whether there actually are psychos running around out there? And if so, put an end to them."

Spiros faced tightened. "There is no time for that. If the foreign press runs with that sort of story there will be no way to put the genie back in the bottle. We'll be tarred forever. Besides, the only logical explanation for what happened is *tsigani* killing *tsigani*. I'm sure Tassos will agree."

Andreas was surprised Spiros had resisted adding, "even if you don't." He took that as a sign of how desperate Spiros was for his help. What the hell, Tassos was a big boy. He could decide for himself whether or not to go along with Spiros' wished for explanation.

"Okay, I'll talk to him. But, first, I need to see the Tinos police's file on the investigation."

"Why?"

Andreas stared. "If you want me to help you close this case that can't be a serious question."

Spiros bit at his lower lip. "Okay, I'll get it right over to you." He stood up. "But I'm counting on you to do me this little favor and get everything wrapped up before the press gets to thinking there might be more to this than *tsigani* fighting *tsigani*."

Andreas stood. "Thanks for stopping by. Always nice to see you, minister."

Spiros pointed a finger at Andreas' chest. "And I definitely want it closed before the wedding."

"I'll pass along your regards to Lila." Andreas thought that a more politic goodbye than a simple, "So long, asshole."

"*MAGGIE*." ANDREAS FOUND yelling for his secretary far more efficient than the intercom. The door swung open and a sturdy five-foot three-inch ball of energy came bounding into the room carrying a half-dozen file folders.

"You rang."

"I like your hair. It looks very nice today."

"Something really serious must be happening if you're trying to soften me up." Maggie had been a secretary at GADA for what seemed forever. She was its mother superior, knew all its secrets, and was used to speaking her mind. Pure chance landed her as Andreas' secretary when her long time boss retired weeks before Andreas' promotion back to GADA from Mykonos.

"Why do I even bother trying to be nice?"

"The word is 'manipulative,' not 'nice.' And the reason is because you can't help yourself. You're a man. Worse, a Greek man." She put the files on Andreas' desk.

Andreas put his left hand to his forehead and began to rub it. "Okay, I surrender. Please, I need you to pick out a gift for Lila. Something to show her I'm thinking of the wedding."

"Oh boy, you must be in big time trouble."

"You have no idea."

"Unexpected gifts are the sure sign of a guilty conscience. The moment she sees it she'll know something's up."

Andreas stared at her.

"Just call her and come clean."

"Any other advice?"

"Then send the gift. Like a book of photographs showing beautiful weddings in churches. May I get back to work now?"

Andreas drew in and let out a breath. "I really do love you."

"I know." Maggie turned and walked toward the door.

"Have you been able to find Yianni?"

"Yes, he should be here any minute."

"Great, tell him I want to see him as soon as he gets in."

"Will do." Maggie opened the door and pointed back

at the files on Andreas' desk. "They just came from the minister's office." As she closed the door she whispered into the room, "The book will be there by five, so don't forget to call."

Andreas stared at the closed door and shook his head. *I'd rather call Spiros and tell him I quit than make this call. Lila is going to kill me. Calling off the wedding would be too easy on me.*

Andreas was the son of a working class cop; Lila was from one of Greece's oldest, wealthiest families, and the socially prominent young widow of a ship owner. Andreas met her when he called upon Lila's knowledge of ancient Greek art for help in an investigation and things just happened between them. He loved her more than anyone on earth but never expected to marry her; even after she told him she was pregnant. He was certain they had too little in common to form a life together. Lila convinced him he was wrong.

Andreas drew in a deep breath. *Perhaps this call might just prove to her that I was right.* He picked up the phone and pressed a speed dial button.

"Vardi-Kaldis residence."

He let out the breath. "Hi, Marietta, is Lila there?"

"One moment, Chief Kaldis."

It was Andreas who insisted the phone be answered that way. All of Athens knew his soon-to-be-wife as Lila Vardi and, besides, most calls to their apartment were for her anyway.

"Hi, darling. I was wondering when I'd hear from you. What time are you picking me up for our rescheduled meeting with the wedding planner?"

Something in Lila's voice told him this wouldn't be easy. "Uhh, sorry. Things just sort of got out of hand."

"Tell me about it. Remember how cute we thought it was watching Tassaki trying to walk? Well, today he's decided to become a 24/7 sprinter."

Their son was named Tassos, after Andreas' deceased father, but when a well-meaning American friend of Lila's added "aki" to the engraving on the silver frame of a baby photo—thinking Tassaki meant "little Tassos"—the laughs it generated sealed his fate. Greeks were in love with nicknames and little Tassos was now affectionately known by the Greek word for "ashtray." Andreas tried convincing Lila it could have been worse; one of Andreas' sister's boys was called *kremidhas* the other *skordho*, a combination of "onions" and "garlic." Lila still didn't like it, but had come to accept the inevitable.

"What has him so wound up?"

"I think he's waiting for his daddy to come home."

Andreas took that as a warning: MINE FIELD AHEAD.

"I'll try to get home as soon as I can."

"Wrong answer."

"I know. But something's come up and—"

"In other words you can't make it to the meeting."

Andreas prayed for sudden loss of phone service. "Sorry."

There was a seemingly eternal pause.

"Andreas Kaldis, we're getting married in six days no matter how hard you try to convince me otherwise. All I want to know is whether your son and I can expect to see you on Mykonos next Sunday afternoon?"

Andreas swallowed. "I'll try to be home before Tassaki goes to sleep."

"Much better answer. Love you, bye."

It wasn't going to be a big wedding, at least not by Greek standards. Only a few hundred guests. Mykonos was where they fell in love and Lila's family had a home large enough to accommodate the reception. But deciding to hold it on Greece's most celebrated party island only ninety miles from Athens during the peak of the summer had turned it into one of the most anticipated social events of the season. Still, Lila wanted to keep it simple. At least as much as possible.

Andreas remembered Lila's exact words: "We don't need anything else to make it perfect." But now she wanted the bridegroom showing up. Women. Always wanting more from a man than they said. He was smiling at his own stupid joke when a bull of a man about a head shorter than Andreas opened the door.

"Is now a good time?"

"Yeah, Yianni, come in." Andreas pointed to the chair closest to his desk. The men met when detective Yianni Kouros was a brash, young rookie and Andreas the new police chief on Mykonos. They'd been together ever since.

"I had the pleasure of a drop-in visit today from our minister. This just arrived from his office." He patted the pile of folders Maggie had put on his desk. "It's on those two Tinos murders."

"I thought that was your friend's case?"

"No more. Our minister wants us to close it out ASAP based upon what's in the file. He asked me to get Tassos to sign off on it. But no way I'm going to raise that with Tassos until I know what's in here."

"In other words, until I tell you what's in there."

"Smart thinking, detective. Get back to me by this afternoon." Andreas handed him the folders.

"Any ideas?"

"Yeah, let's try not to be as narrow-minded in our thinking as our dear minister."

"Huh?"

"The dead are *tsigani*. Somehow he thinks that's the answer to everything and a reason for closing the case. Understand?"

Kouros nodded and stood up. "So what else is new? Since when haven't *tsigani*, *metanastes*, or for that matter, foreigners in general not been our politicians' fall guys of choice?" He gave a casual salute and left.

Andreas turned his head and stared out the window. There had always been refugees fleeing despots and turmoil in Greece's region of the world, but when Greece joined the E.U. in 1981 it was essentially a homogeneous land of less than ten million. With financial prosperity came Filipinos to serve in domestic jobs no longer done by Greeks and the fall of the Soviet Union in 1989 brought a wave of Eastern European immigrants seeking better lives, but it was after 2002 and the confluence of the euro currency launch, America's wars in Iraq and Afghanistan, and Greece's all-out building boom for the 2004 Athens Olympics, that the floodgates opened.

Romanians, Bulgarians, Albanians, and Poles came to put their much needed construction skills to work for pay far greater than any they could dream of back home, and Greece's porous island and mainland borders became an irresistible magnet for those fleeing Turkey, Iraq, Afghanistan, Pakistan, Bangladesh, and what at times seemed all of struggling Africa. They were the *metanastes*—the foreigners who came to work or simply escape a life in chaos elsewhere.

Greece's population was now almost eleven and a half million of which ten percent were estimated to be immigrants. No one knew exactly how many more were living hidden lives within the country, but with the abrupt change in Greece's financial fortunes virtually every lost job or criminal act now seemed somehow blamed on the *metanastes* or *tsigani*. No one had to tell Andreas how ugly the anger was brewing—on all sides.

MAGGIE'S VOICE CAME over the intercom. "Yianni's here. He said to tell you he's read the file."

"Send him in."

Kouros walked in and sat in a chair across the desk from Andreas.

Andreas looked at his watch. "That was quick. Just a little more than an hour."

"A lot of paper but not much to read. No one saw or heard a thing except for smoke just before dawn. The victims were brothers, one twenty-two and the other eighteen. They were from a *tsigani* camp set up on the southeast part of the island near the port and far away from where the bodies were found. They left the camp the day before they were found. Their family began to worry when they heard about the murders and the two hadn't returned for three nights. The victims were preliminarily identified from jewelry found on their bodies, later confirmed by DNA testing. The Tinos police chief personally interviewed everyone in the camp and came up with nothing. No one had any idea of who might have wanted to kill either brother or of a possible motive. The most anyone had to say was that this was 'not the *tsigani* way' of settling scores."

"What did forensics come up with?"

Kouros leaned in and rested his elbow on the desk. "That's where things get interesting. The victims died of asphyxiation before the fire."

"They were dead before they burned?"

"Looks like it."

"How did they suffocate?"

"Can't be sure, but forensics thinks it might be gas."

"Carbon monoxide poisoning?"

Kouros gestured no. "Nitrous oxide."

"Nitrous oxide?"

"Yes, laughing gas."

"That's the sort of stuff my dentist uses."

"And some use it as a recreational drug. Makes you euphoric, happy. You feel no pain." Kouros shook his head. "They think that's what it was because they found a nitrous oxide cylinder in the back of the van behind the bodies."

"That's not what *tsigani* are known to traffic." Big time drug dealing by some *tsigani* was another mark borne by the many.

"Like I said, it makes things interesting."

Andreas picked up a pencil and tapped it on his desk. "Check to see where you can find laughing gas on Tinos."

Kouros shook his head. "The Tinos police already did. No luck there. It's available just about everywhere, on and off the island. And it's not just used by dentists. Hospitals use it in surgery, motor racers use it to boost engine power, and restaurants use it to puff up whipped cream."

"Whipped cream?"

Kouros nodded. "Find whipped cream and you're likely to find a nitrous oxide cylinder somewhere. And that's the dangerous stuff because it's not mixed with oxygen. If you're breathing pure nitrous oxide—"

"You suffocate. Shit. Anything else interesting?"

"The victims were from a clan that came to Tinos a month before the murders. But their clan wasn't one that usually spent the tourist season working on Tinos or came there to celebrate the Assumption of the Virgin Mary on August 15th."

"August 15th is Tinos' biggest celebration of the year," said Andreas. "And it draws huge crowds, which means major opportunities for what *tsigani* do. Maybe the new boys on the block pissed off another clan who thought they might be muscling in on their action?"

Kouros shrugged. "Could be, but it's not unusual for transient clans to pass through Tinos this time of year. They always did when we were stationed on Mykonos. *Tsigani* revere the Virgin Mary and go there to pay their respects. Besides, why pick those two brothers and this year to make a point?"

Andreas tapped the pencil against his forehead. "Odysseus probably came to the same conclusion. I'll give him a call to see if he had any ideas he didn't put in the file." Cops did that sort of thing, especially with politically sensitive cases. "By the way, is the victims' clan based in Greece?"

Kouros nodded. "Menidi."

"Ouch."

Menidi was an area about three miles west of the center of Athens just south of Mount Parnitha, and perhaps the most dangerous neighborhood in all of greater Athens. Here was where those who gave *tsigani* a bad name threw babies in front of out-of-place expensive cars in the hope of getting a settlement for "the accident," where the poorest of the poor found a place to live, and drug lords and human traffickers ruled. It was a no man's land for cops. But *tsigani* weren't the only bad guys in Menidi. They shared the criminal turf with the *ians*—Russians, Romanians, Ukrainians, Albanians and other eastern Europeans—and the *is*—Afghanis, Pakistanis, Iraqis, etcetera.

"If this involves *ians* or *is* out for revenge I can definitely see the two *tsigani* being fried alive," said Andreas.

"Yeah, but they'd have been wide-awake when it happened," said Kouros.

"I'm not sure what we have here. But it definitely doesn't look like '*tsigani* fighting *tsigani*.'"

"As long as it's what our minister considers non-Greek bad guys killing other non-Greek bad guys he won't give a damn about their ethnicity. He's broad-minded that way." Kouros smiled.

"Spoken like our good friend Tassos. Which reminds me. *Maggie, come in here. I need you for a minute. Please.*"

Maggie popped her head through the doorway. "You're the boss."

Yeah, right. Andreas and everyone else at GADA knew Maggie's mastery of GADA's bureaucratic ways made her more important than any chief inspector.

"Could you find Tassos for me?"

"He's at home."

"On Syros?"

"No, my place."

Tassos was a widower, and Andreas' chance mention of him to Maggie, not knowing of their long ago romantic past, had helped put them back together.

"Do you think you could get him to come in here this afternoon? I need his help."

Maggie smiled. "Don't we all." She closed the door.

Kouros said, "You can't be serious about asking Tassos to sign off on this case."

"I'm not. But the minister said he wants everything 'wrapped up,' and I intend to do just that. Which means I need Tassos' help. No one knows the Cyclades better than he does. I want to know if bad guys are killing bad guys and, if so, who and why. And if it's something else…" Andreas waved his hand in the air. "We'll cross that bridge when we come to it."

"And no doubt burn it to ashes in the process."

# THREE

Tassos was in Andreas' office by four and up to speed by five. That was when Maggie swung in with coffee, a *meze* selection of food, and a quick apologetic, "Sorry to interrupt, but I must keep up my men's strength."

"Stick around," said Tassos. Kouros and Tassos were sitting on chairs next to Andreas' desk. "We're about to start guessing at what has our fearless minister so hot to close an investigation into two murders."

"Which ones? Things are happening so quickly these days that I'm losing count," said Maggie.

"The ones on Tinos while we were at your grand-niece's baptism in Thessaloniki. You're probably better qualified than we are at guessing what's on a bureau-crat's mind."

Maggie set the tray on the desk in front of Tassos. "Make that on any man's mind." She dropped onto the couch.

"Okay, let's start with what's on yours," said Andreas nodding at Tassos.

Tassos picked up a *spanakopita*. "Your friend, the police chief, has been on Tinos for only a little over a year, but he got the interviews right. *Tsigani* don't take revenge that way." Tassos pointed the tiny spinach pie at his chest. "I know the *tsigani* very well and they know me, but I wouldn't have gotten any more out of those interviews than Odysseus did. The two were killed to deliver a very specific message. Any response had to come from the one who received it. No other *tsigani* would dare make that decision. Certainly not by talking to cops. Besides, *tsigani* know from experience that cops don't care what happens to them."

"Some of us do," said Andreas.

"We know that, they don't." Tassos popped the *spanakopita* into his mouth.

"So, what do you suggest we do?" said Kouros.

Tassos finished chewing. "Find a *tsigani* who can get us answers. My money's on this not being *tsigani* revenge killings, but since the victims were *tsigani* that's where I'd start."

"Have anyone particular in mind?" said Andreas.

"A few. Even the *tsigani* king owes me some favors. He shows up on Tinos every year a few days before August 15th to join in the celebration of the Assumption of the Virgin. Makes quite an entrance."

"I bet," said Andreas.

"What does our minister have to do with all of this?" said Maggie.

"He implied the Prime Minister is all over him to close the case," said Andreas.

"Do you believe him or is it just more of that name-dropping bullshit he thinks gets us to do what he wants?" said Tassos.

Andreas shrugged. "I reached Odysseus on vacation. He said everything he knows about it is in the file and that if we want to call it closed, 'be my guest.' But he told Spiros he wouldn't be the one to do it."

"I always liked Odysseus," said Tassos. He looked at Andreas. "If it's not the Prime Minister pushing him, why do you think Spiros is so anxious to end the investigation?"

"I hope it's not because he's trying to protect someone," said Kouros.

Maggie shook her head. "Spiros isn't an idiot. He just treats everyone like he thinks they are. No way he'd be dumb enough to bring you guys into this if he wanted to pull off a cover-up."

"I don't know," said Kouros. "Our politicians are so arrogant these days at all they've gotten away with that I think they believe they can do just about anything they damn well please."

"What do you think has Spiros so anxious, Chief?" said Maggie.

"I think he's honestly afraid that something might turn up along the lines of *tsigani* being victims of a hate crime. And he knows if that happens at least he, if not the whole country, will be back in hot water with the press."

"I can see his point," nodded Maggie. "Remember how fired up the international media was when the crazy French started deporting *tsigani*? Just imagine how they'd tear us apart, the E.U.'s bad-boy, if they could run a story that has Greece addressing its immigration problems by declaring open season on *tsigani*."

"I'd rather not," said Andreas.

"Me either," said Tassos. "We don't deserve it." He stood up. "If you'll excuse me, folks, I have a *tsigani* to find."

"Happy hunting," said Kouros.

Andreas stared at Kouros. "At times your sense of humor is worse than his."

"Then buy me a beer. I'll try to be funnier."

"Deal."

BEER WAS A big seller in Greece. Ouzo and retsina surely were too, and plainly the romanticized choice of tourists, but beer was the day-to-day staple. Andreas and Kouros were in plainclothes alone at a table in the back of a rundown taverna in a graffiti-covered, 19th Century, two-story neoclassical building. It was tucked away on one of the narrow commercial streets at the western end of Alexandras Avenue by the Victoria metro station. As shabby as the place was it had a certain old-world charm definitely not present in any of its late 20th Century, anonymous concrete neighbors.

"How the hell did you find this place?" said Andreas.

"A buddy brought me here a couple weeks ago. Said his father used to take him here. There aren't many places like this left in Athens, what with all the old neighborhoods changing. I thought you might like it. Besides, it's even cheaper than the ones across from headquarters. I figured that since you're paying I'd help save you some money for the wedding."

Andreas lifted his beer. "*Yamas.*"

Kouros lifted his bottle and clinked on Andreas' bottle. "*Yamas.*" He took a sip. "Less than a week to go. Bet you're nervous."

Andreas shrugged. "Only about the dancing. Not the getting married part."

"Come on, you have to be scared just a little bit. You know, one woman, the rest of your life."

Andreas gestured no. "As crazy as it may sound, I feel strangely at ease." He smiled. "Doubt you'd understand, youngster."

"You bet. I like my life just as it is."

"Some day, if you're lucky, you'll know what I mean. Until then just keep playing your *kamaki* games, but be careful where you put your spear, you wouldn't want to dull it permanently." *Kamaki* was the Greek name for the little trident used in hunting octopus—and slang for the Greek man's real or imagined skills at pursuing women.

"Safe sex lecture duly noted." Kouros took another swig of beer.

The bar area in the front of the taverna was filling up with what seemed mainly foreign workers, but the man behind the bar was Greek and spoke only Greek to his customers.

"So, what do we do while Tassos looks for a lead?" asked Kouros.

"Exactly what I planned to do before the minister popped into my office. Get ready for my wedding."

"Terrific. But don't forget about your bachelor party."

"What bachelor party?"

"The surprise one on for the night after tomorrow. Remember to act surprised."

"Anything else I should know?" said Andreas.

Kouros paused and smiled. "Your world, as you know it, is about to change."

Andreas finished his beer. "Let's get out of here. I want to get home before Tassaki goes to sleep." He threw five euros on the table and headed toward the door.

"I have to take a leak," said Kouros.

Outside the street was surprisingly quiet. Then again, it was August and that meant Athens was deserted by anyone who could get out of town. As Kouros came through the front door a man ran past them on the sidewalk screaming in a language neither cop understood at another man running fifteen yards behind him.

When the second man reached the two cops he abruptly turned and pointed a gun at them.

*"Dose mou to porto foli su!"* It was heavily accented Greek but he'd made his point.

Andreas and Kouros immediately reached for their wallets. The man held the gun in his right hand and kept waving it back and forth between Kouros to his right and Andreas to his left. Andreas held out his wallet in his right hand and Kouros did the same with his left. The man hesitated as if deciding which to take first. He reached with his left hand for Andreas' wallet, taking his eyes off of Kouros for a split second.

Kouros' right hand shot up and caught the barrel of the gun between his thumb and forefinger and drove it up and into the man's forehead as he stepped in to put his right hip behind the man's right side and force him backwards into the ground. There was the dull thud of the back of a head striking concrete.

Andreas leaned over the unconscious gunman and took back his wallet. As Kouros checked him for other weapons, Andreas walked to the front of the taverna and picked up a chair. There was the high-pitched whine of a motorbike coming up fast alongside the curb.

Andreas stepped to the edge of the sidewalk and swung the chair into the face and chest of the oncoming helmetless driver, sending both bike and driver sprawling onto the street. As the driver stumbled to his feet, Andreas delivered a Champions League quality soccer kick to the man's midsection, putting him back on the ground. The man tried to stand again. This time Andreas hit him with a roundhouse right that put him out cold.

Andreas dragged the driver onto the sidewalk and

dropped him next to the gunman. He gestured for Kouros to handcuff them both and punched in the code on his phone for "officer needs assistance."

"What the hell was all that about?" said Kouros. "The guy you just beat up was the one the other guy was chasing."

Andreas smiled. "Obviously, you've not kept up with your reading, detective." Andreas looked at his right hand and flexed it. Nothing seemed broken. "There was a bulletin this week on a new urban crime technique. It takes advantage of our natural curiosity. One guy runs by the mark screaming at another guy, the mark stops to see what's going on, the chaser robs the mark, the screamer returns on a motorbike, the chaser jumps on behind him, and they're off and lost in traffic."

"Christ. What will they come up with next?"

"Wish I knew. But there will always be something." Andreas leaned down and checked the handcuffs as a blue and white Athens police car screeched to a halt in front of them.

"Do me a favor, Yianni. Take care of the paperwork on this. I want to go home and hug my kid."

"No problem. Besides, I think I'll go back inside. I could use another drink. Or three."

Andreas put his arm around Kouros' shoulder and smiled. "That, my friend, sums up the difference between your life and mine."

ANDREAS, LILA, AND TASSAKI lived where no one existing on a cop's pay could possibly afford, certainly no honest cop. It was Lila's home when they met and, despite Andreas' initial *macho* discomfort at the thought of moving into his girlfriend's apartment, the reality of their potential living choices prevailed: either an entire, sixth-floor penthouse at perhaps Athens' most exclusive address, next to the Presidential Palace, with unobstructed breathtaking views of both the Acropolis and its majestic sister hill, Lykavittos, or his one bedroom, slight view, maybe the elevator is working, fourth floor apartment.

Andreas was crawling on the nursery room floor watching a diaper-clad Tassaki run around him in circles. Every once in a while Andreas reached out to catch him, put him on his back, and tickle his belly until he laughed. Lila was standing at the doorway smiling.

"One of you is definitely having a good time."

"The one with the diaper is wearing me out." Andreas pinched Tassaki's bottom, making him laugh even more.

"Maybe you should take him with you to your bachelor party?"

"You mean the secret one?"

"Yep, I cleared the dancers."

"If you cleared them, I'm not sure it's worth going." He picked up Tassaki and handed him to Lila. "Give mommy a kiss to make up for daddy's bad sense of humor."

"I'll put him to bed. Go away or he'll never go to sleep."

Andreas kissed Tassaki and went to their bedroom. He kicked off his shoes and plopped on the bed. He shut his eyes and his mind wandered back to that taverna. He wondered if Kouros was also thinking of how close they'd just come to being another random, street crime fatality statistic.

He'd almost fallen asleep when he heard, "Thanks for coming home early."

He opened his eyes. Lila was standing at the edge of the bed holding a book. He wasn't about to tell her how he almost didn't make it home. Ever. "I figured I'm already in enough hot water with you."

"Smart choice."

"You trained me right."

She smiled. "Just keep working on the 'don't worry I won't miss the wedding' part."

"Remind me again, why do you love me?"

"Because of your wonderful mind, compassionate nature, big—"

"Finally, the truth comes out."

"Sorry to disappoint you, stud. It's your big understanding heart. As represented by the wonderful surprise you sent me."

God bless Maggie. "You mean those photographs of church weddings?"

"You did pick it out!" She held up the book.

"Maggie had a hand in it."

"Sometimes, Kaldis, you're too honest a cop." Lila smiled and lightly patted him on the belly with her book. "So, what has you so distracted?"

It always amazed him how Lila sensed his moods. Still, he wasn't going to talk about the taverna. It would only upset her. Besides, he wanted to forget it. He'd take the easy way out. "I thought we agreed no more involvement in my cases." Involvement in one had almost cost Lila her life.

"I'm not trying to get involved, just curious. I think Tassaki's having one parent at risk everyday is more than enough of a gamble on his future."

"No reason to get heavy on me."

She stared at him. "I'm just letting you know why

you have no reason to worry about me getting involved. Our child means more to me than solving your cases."

He wondered if that was meant as a jab at him, but decided to let it drop. After all, it was their wedding week and he was a missing-in-action participant.

Andreas reached up, took her hand, and kissed it. "I'm such a lucky guy."

Lila poked him with her finger. "Don't you ever forget it."

Andreas kissed her hand again. "And you're smart, too."

Lila smiled. "Then why am I marrying a cop?"

Andreas grinned. "My impressive credentials."

"What credentials?"

Andreas pulled her down onto the bed and proceeded to present his credentials to Lila's very vocal satisfaction.

# FOUR

FINDING THE SPECIFIC *tsigani* you're looking for wasn't as difficult as it once was, provided you had his cell phone number. Not all were poor and itinerant; many were well off and some very rich. Stefan fell somewhere in the middle but had major connections among them all. When Tassos finally reached him it was nearly midnight and Stefan said to meet at one of the lowest end *skiladika* clubs in all of Athens. *Skiladika* derived from the Greek word for "female dog" but it was a matter of debate whether applying that name to that sort of club was because of its relationship to the English-language connotation for "bitch" or the notorious howl of some female performers.

*Skiladika* were dark, cavernous places, filled with hardcore Greek *bouzoukia* music sung by third-rate singers playing through a haze of cigarette smoke to crowds of heavily drinking men, and bosom thrusting women prone to breaking into belly-dancing. To some, the places seemed more eastern than Greek and to others the Greek equivalent of an American, redneck country western bar. *Skiladika* were out of touch with the times on almost every level, which was precisely what made them so very popular.

This one was just off the National Road in a run-down area where you'd expect to find a *skiladika* but not a *tsigani*. It wasn't their sort of neighborhood, or for that matter, neither was a *skiladika* their kind of place. Tassos figured that's why Stefan picked it: he wanted to be anonymous, a hard thing for a man of Stefan's girth to achieve. Tassos pulled into the parking lot and sat for a few minutes watching the people heading inside. He wanted to get an idea of the crowd before going in. It looked much as he expected. Mostly working class types dressed up for a night out, and a mix of twenty-somethings slumming it from some of Athens' wealthier parts.

Tassos trailed a group of kids up to the front door. They walked right in and he started to follow in behind them when a bouncer held up his hand. "Twenty euros to get in."

Tassos pointed in the direction of the group in front of him. "You didn't ask them to pay."

"They're regulars. Twenty euros or find another place."

Tassos was tempted to use his badge, a guaranteed get-in-anywhere-for-free card, but that meant a sure-fire loss of anonymity for Stefan. Cops drew attention in these places. He pulled a twenty out of his pocket and handed it over. He thought to ask for a receipt but knew that request would likely target him as a taxman, an even less welcome visitor.

Directly inside the front door was a large bar area separated from the rest of the room by a ledge lined with bar stools. A six-foot wide break in the ledge was the only visible access to a main floor lined with long tables aimed directly at the stage. The tables were filling up fast. A man and several young women stood by the opening directing people to their tables, or at least their share of a table. No one was singing at the moment, which probably was why Tassos heard his name being called from the far end of the bar by the *tsigani* equivalent of Sydney Greenstreet's "Fat Man" character in *The Maltese Falcon*.

"Tassos, over here."

It was Stefan and he looked as if he'd been saving a barstool for Tassos by sitting on two, but when Tassos reached him he found Stefan place-holding a third stool with his foot. "Here, I saved you a seat."

It was rare that Tassos felt slim, but as he adjusted to fit on one barstool this was just such an occasion. "Thanks, Stefan."

Stefan gestured for the bartender to come over. "What would you like?"

"My twenty euros back from the gorilla at the front door."

Stefan smiled. "Done. What else?"

"What do you mean 'done'?" Tassos looked at the bartender. "I'll have a beer."

"I have an interest in this place."

"You do?"

"You seemed surprised that a *rom* would be in this business?" *Rom* was the name *tsigani* preferred to be called.

"I am," said Tassos.

"If you think about it, this sort of place is a natural fit for a lot of what I do."

"I'd rather not."

Stefan laughed. "Well, just so that I don't ruin all your notions, I own only a very small part. What you might call a 'rooting interest' in its success courtesy of the other, more traditional owners."

In other words, a payoff for God knows what he

contributed. "Frankly, Stefan, unless you're about to start naming your partners in this undoubtedly squeaky-clean taxpaying enterprise, do you mind if we get on to another subject?"

Stefan laughed. "This is why I always enjoy doing business with you. No pretenses, no courtesy." Stefan's laid-back, professorial style was beguiling to many, but Tassos knew it for what it was: elaborate camouflage for hustles and scams as ruthless and cunning as any run by the stereotypical worst of his kind.

"And no bullshit please. I need your help finding someone for me."

"Who?"

"Don't know, but somebody who knows something about those murders on Tinos."

"The two *rom* from Menidi?"

Tassos nodded yes. It didn't surprise him that Stefan knew so much about the victims. Knowing things about *tsigani* was his business. That was why Tassos was here. "What do you know about them?"

"Only that their *rom* name was Carausii."

*Tsigani* had at least two names, one for the outside world and another for use among themselves.

"And that there's an older brother, Punka. He runs a crew of beggars around Syntagma." Syntagma was Athens' central square, directly across from Parliament. "Last I heard they were living in that cardboard, plastic sheeting, and scrap wood piece of shit camp just off the highway on the road to the airport."

"Venizelos International?"

Stefan nodded. "By marker forty-five. But he could be long gone by now."

"What's he doing living out there? I thought his clan was from Menidi."

"It is, but he had a falling out with them."

"Just how serious 'a falling out'?"

"If you're asking me if it was serious enough for Punka to roast his brothers, I have no idea. But it was serious enough for him to break off from his clan and go out on his own."

"Do you think you could find him for me?"

"I should be able to. That is, if he's still in Greece. What do you want me to tell him?"

"Just find out where he is. And try not to tip him off that I'm looking for him. Make it so that I find him somewhere he wouldn't expect."

"I assume that means he has reason to be worried about the police. No problem, many of us do. I shall be discreet."

"Which is why I called you," said Tassos.

"And because I owe you several, rather large favors."

Tassos picked up the beer from the bar. "That too. And with your life style I expect you'll be needing more."

"I've reformed."

"And Greece's financial crisis is all a bad dream."

Stefan laughed. "Funny you should say that. Each night I sit here watching people come and go. Almost all are miserable about their prospects and some are in actual fear, but that kind over there," he pointed to a table, "they are the children of the rich, each coddled and protected by mommy and daddy. Most will never work except in family businesses. They come here much like dancers on the edge of a volcano poised to erupt. They see the smoke, smell the sulfur, but still don't get it. And when everything goes boom…" Stefan let his voice trail off.

"Are you trying to convince me you actually care what happens to them?"

"Me? No, I'm trying to figure out how I can work an angle on separating them from whatever the eruption misses." He slapped Tassos on the back and laughed.

Tassos put his beer down on the bar. "On that bit of wisdom, my friend, I'm out of here. When do you think you'd be able to hook me up with Punka?"

"I assume it's urgent, so I'll start working on it right away. With any luck, I'll have an answer for you tomorrow, or the next day at the outside. That's assuming the *rom* is still around."

"Thank you. Night, Stefan."

Stefan reached over and shook Tassos' hand. There was something in it.

"Your money. I'm a man of my word."

Tassos nodded as he thought, at least where only twenty euros was involved.


AT BREAKFAST THE next morning Andreas announced to Lila that he'd be staying home to help her prepare for the wedding.

"Not on your life," was her reply. Which was why Andreas ended up back in his office to the surprise of everyone but Maggie.

"I didn't think she'd want you hanging around. Future husbands have a habit of getting brides nervous by trying too sincerely to act as if they really cared about more than their buddies getting a good table at the reception."

He stared at her. "And don't forget the right brand of beer."

"You get the idea."

"Okay, hold my calls. No one expects me to be here, so let's act as if I'm not."

"Will do."

About an hour later Maggie stuck her head in the doorway. "It's Tassos."

Andreas picked up the phone. "Morning."

"I think we have a line on the brother of the two murdered *tsigani*. An informant just told me where we could find him." Tassos repeated the substance of his conversation with Stefan the night before. "The brother is supposed to be in a taverna out by the airport at three this afternoon and he's not supposed to know we're showing up."

"Do I sense you're not totally comfortable with your informant?"

"He's reliable when it comes to information. That's how he earns his living. But he'd also sell out his mother if he thought it in his perceived self-interest to do so. So, just to be safe, let's assume Punka is expecting us."

"Meaning?" said Andreas.

"Carry heavy and wear a vest. It would be a shame to lose a groom so close to his wedding day. I'll pick you up downstairs at two."

IF ANDREAS DIDN'T know better he'd have thought the taverna was an abandoned shack in the middle of long ago exhausted farmland. A few cars about as beat up and ancient as the place were parked outside. You could hear traffic buzzing by on the highway between Athens and the airport. Though built for the 2004 Olympics, it was still known as the "new road."

Tassos parked the unmarked car away from the building where it gave them a view of the perimeter.

"Keep the engine running, I'll be out in a minute."

"And just what do you have in mind?" said Tassos.

"I'll let you know once I figure it out. Let's just hope if it's an ambush it's not supposed to start until we're both inside." Andreas got out and headed toward the taverna.

He focused on the windows and edges of the building as he walked, and his hand touched his crotch as if adjusting his family jewels, but he was just reassuring himself that the pistol in the holster covering those parts was still in place. The front door to the taverna was open and as he drew closer he saw three occupied tables, one with six men, another with two, and the last with a customer alone. All of them looked to be *tsigani*. A young girl was serving coffee to the table of six. She smiled at Andreas as he came through the door.

Andreas walked in as if he knew exactly where he was headed. He stopped in front of the lone customer, a dark, thin man in his late-twenties. "Punka?"

The man looked up. "Who's asking?" His upper lip curled as he talked. Like an angry little dog.

"Are you Punka or am I wasting my time?"

The man stared at Andreas. "I'm Punka."

"And your last name?" This wasn't the time to be hooking up with the wrong Punka.

He kept staring at Andreas. "Carausii."

"Good, let's go."

"Go? What do you mean 'go'?" Punka sounded frightened and looked toward the table of six.

"I'm a cop and I'm not going to have a conversation with you about what we have to talk about in a place like this."

Punka looked again at the table of six. Two of the men stood up.

Andreas raised his left hand toward the six without looking at their table. "Don't even think about it. Sit down and nobody gets hurt. Move and everybody does."

The two men paused. Andreas turned his head slightly and stared at them. They sat down. "Good," he said.

He turned back to Punka. "Now, let's take a walk."

"Fuck you."

Andreas smiled. "Perhaps you misunderstood me, I'm the cop in charge of investigating the murder of your brothers. Test me and I'll toss you down a shit hole like—" Andreas snapped his fingers. "And you'll never be seen again. Now, do you want to take that chance or do you want to take a walk and talk about things of mutual interest?"

Punka looked nervously at the six.

"Your friends are smart enough to know better. Are you?"

Punka pushed himself back from the table, stood up, and walked toward the door. Andreas followed, nodding to the six as he walked by their table.

Outside, Andreas led him to the car. "Get in."

"I thought we were taking a walk?"

"We did. To the car." Andreas opened the rear door. Punka hesitated.

"Do I have to make another speech?"

Punka got in and Andreas slid in next to him. "Drive," he said to Tassos.

Punka started asking questions the moment the car moved, but Andreas and Tassos ignored him. Tassos drove around for about twenty minutes until it was clear no one was following them. He pulled off onto a dirt road and parked amid a grove of olive trees hidden from the road.

The first words Punka heard were, "Get out," delivered by Andreas after Tassos had opened the rear door on Punka's side. Andreas slid out behind him.

Andreas held out a pack of cigarettes. "Smoke?"

Punka took a cigarette and waited for Andreas to light it.

"Light your own," said Andreas handing him a lighter.

Punka's hands were shaking as he lit the cigarette. "You guys really are cops, aren't you?"

"Yeah, we're cops," said Andreas.

Punka seemed to relax.

Why does that make him feel better? He must be really frightened of someone.

"I want to see some identification. I should have asked for it before."

"Yes, you should have." Andreas smiled, but reached into his shirt and pulled out his credentials.

Punka's lips moved as he struggled to read. "Jesus, you're Chief of Special Crimes."

"And you don't think he's here just to talk about your two pieces of shit dead brothers, do you?" said Tassos.

Punka glared at Tassos. "Don't talk about my brothers that way."

"Stop blowing smoke up my ass," said Tassos. "You're the reason they're dead. You know it and we know it."

"I had nothing to do with what happened to them."
His left eye was twitching.

"Convince me," said Andreas.

"Fuck off. I have the right to a lawyer."

"Yeah, right," said Tassos.

"We're going to bury you in Kordydallos as an accessory to the murder of your brothers," said Andreas.

Kordydallos Prison Complex was Greece's main prison, housing maximum security and other prisoners in the suburbs of Piraeus, the southwest port city of greater Athens. It was repeatedly cited as one of the worst prisons in Europe for overcrowding and alleged inhumane treatment of detainees.

"You can't prove that," said Punka.

Tassos laughed. "Who cares? How long do you think you'll stay alive inside once those friends of yours that you're so afraid of find out why you're in there? What do you think the odds are that they'll let you live a week with what you know?"

"You're dead meat the moment you step inside those ugly gray walls," said Andreas.

Punka was shaking. "I told them not to get involved."

"Yeah, sure, you did," said Tassos.

"I told them I didn't care how much our clan stood to make on the deal, it was pure suicide. But they wouldn't listen. I said, 'stay out of it' don't get involved. You don't live very long crossing the Albanians."

Greeks had a habit of referring to any group that controlled an industry, legal or illegal, or a government of any sort as "mafia." But they didn't mean the cinematic *Godfather* kind who broke legs and chopped off heads—equine and other—to make their point. At least not until recently. Now, they had the real kind to worry about. And of all the organized crime finding its way into Greece, by far the most feared and dangerous hailed from Albania. Virtually every aspect of Greece's organized crime activity somehow fell within the Albanian gangs' spheres of influence and bore their violent imprint. They might partner with *tsigani*, Russians, Greeks, or others, but they came from a land of blood feuds and possessed of a view on the value of life far different from the Greeks.

They did not represent all Albanians, of course, no more so than Italian, Russian, or Irish mobsters were indicative of their cultures. But on any list of European gangsters, Albanians ranked *numero uno*.

"What deal?" said Andreas.

"I don't know, but it was something big on Tinos."

"Stop messing with us, Punka. Don't tell me you 'don't know.'" Tassos stepped toward Punka.

Andreas put out his arm to stop him. "Like the man said, 'Stop messing with us.'"

"Honest, not even our clan leader knew. He got paid to move the camp to Tinos with the promise there'd be a lot more if we 'behaved' and did as we were told."

"What do you mean 'behaved'?" said Tassos.

"Not get in any trouble on Tinos."

"Who made the deal with your clan?" said Andreas.

"No idea. But I heard he wasn't *rom*."

Tassos said, "You expect us to believe your clan made that kind of deal with a total stranger?"

"It's like our leader said, 'the money's real, so who cares who's paying?' Besides, times are tough and it wasn't as if we were giving up anything."

"How about living? Remember, you said you were crossing the Albanians," said Andreas.

"The deal to move to Tinos was made before I knew anything about the Albanians. It wasn't until I heard about *metanastes* crews making similar deals that I realized Albanians weren't included."

"Similar deals?" said Andreas.

"Yes, to move to Tinos."

"And behave?" said Tassos.

Punka nodded. "Yes."

"And that's why the clan booted you out?" said Tassos.

"Yes, because once I realized the Albanians were cut out of whatever was going to happen on Tinos, I tried getting my brothers to stay out of it, not get involved."

"Who killed your brothers?" said Andreas.

"No idea."

"Who do you think might have wanted them dead?" said Andreas.

"No idea."

"For someone supposedly so upset about the murder of his brothers you don't seem to care much about finding their killers," said Andreas.

"As if you'd ever find them."

"We found you, didn't we, asshole?" said Tassos.

Andreas shook his head. "Here's the deal, Punka. It's a one time take it or leave it opportunity for you to live longer than a week. Get us the name of whoever ordered the hits and if we find that you're right you walk. If you don't come up with a name, you're the one who goes inside for the murders."

"And by the way, don't try to run," said Tassos. "We'll find you again and next time…you'll simply disappear."

Punka looked at the ground.

"Do you understand?" said Tassos.

"Yes."

"Good," said Andreas. "Now, I want you to tell us everything you know about your brothers and Tinos, starting from the beginning. And I mean *everything*."

It took an hour, but Punka didn't tell them anything more than he already had or was in the Tinos police reports. Nor did he tell them anything that conflicted with what they knew. It was just a more embellished telling of the same message: I told my brothers not to cross the Albanians.

When they finished they drove Punka back to the taverna. He didn't say a word this time. Not even a goodbye when they dropped him off.

"I THINK HE'S SCARED," said Andreas. They were back on the highway heading toward Athens.

"Yeah, when the Albanians want revenge against one part of a family, they don't care who else they take out to get it."

"No, I meant of you," said Andreas. "You practically scared the hell out of me. That was some chance you took going after him for his brothers' murders."

"The worst he could have done was tell me to 'fuck off.' But we lucked out. He had a guilty conscience."

"I call it good police instincts," said Andreas.

"It comes with thinking like a crook."

Andreas laughed. "I'll get Yianni to make sure Punka is covered 24/7 and that we pull all his phone calls and messages."

"What do you think the chances are of him coming up with a name?"

"Who knows, but he's our only lead," said Andreas.

"Maybe not," said Tassos. "If somehow Albanians from Menidi are involved in this, I might be able to set something up with them."

Tassos had been making influential friends since his days as a rookie cop in Greece's dictatorship years guarding political prisoners at an island prison. Those prisoner friendships were his hedge against the inmates' return to power and had served him well. If anyone could set up a meeting with the Albanians it was Tassos.

"I'm not exactly thrilled at the thought of sitting down with those guys if they're behind the murders."

"Why? The worst thing that could happen is they refuse to meet," said Tassos.

"No, the worst thing that could happen is they agree to meet and then try to whack the cops who are trying to prove they did it," said Andreas.

"Stop worrying. Once they know you're involved they probably won't agree to meet anyway. You have a reputation as a straight shooter. They don't trust guys like you."

"As opposed to…"

"Hey, what can I say? I'm old school."

Andreas rolled his eyes.

Tassos smiled. "Ingrate."

# FIVE

IT WAS NEARLY MIDNIGHT, and for most civilized people past their bedtime. But for many Greeks it was just the beginning of their evening. Andreas was lying on top of the bed covers watching the news. Lila sat at her dressing table looking through some sort of chart for the wedding. Andreas couldn't believe that in four days they'd be married. It was almost Wednesday.

Andreas' cell phone rang.

"Who would be calling at this hour?" said Lila.

Andreas looked at his phone. "Tassos. Hopefully with good news." He pressed to answer.

"I told Lila you'd only be calling at this hour with good news. If not, please hang up and call back tomorrow."

"All I can say is that it's news. Whether it's good or bad depends on your view of things," said Tassos.

"What are you into, Zen or something? Just tell me."

"I was able to set up a meeting with the Albanians. But they'll only see us tonight. It's now or never."

"You're kidding." He instinctively looked at his watch. And Lila looked at him.

"It looks like our only chance to meet."

"Okay."

"I'll pick you up in front of your building in fifteen minutes. Bye."

Andreas put down his phone.

"Honey…"

"Try not to stay out too late."

"I don't want to go but there's no choice. It's very important."

"I'm sure. Just remember. Sunday."

Andreas kissed her on the cheek and left the room to get dressed to meet Tassos. He didn't want her to see him putting on his ballistic vest.

TASSOS PULLED UP alone in front of Andreas' building in a blue and white police cruiser.

Andreas got in next to him. "We're taking a marked car to this?"

"The ones we're meeting know we're cops. I want to make sure everyone else in the neighborhood knows it, too, and that we're there on official business."

Andreas shrugged. "It's your call, but I wouldn't think the Albanians would appreciate the idea of other bad guys in their neighborhood knowing they're entertaining cops. Might start too many rumors."

"Not a problem tonight. They picked a place in Athens, outside their neighborhood. A club in Gazi. The cruiser will get us a parking space." Tassos grinned.

"Which place?"

"Dionysios' Sin. How do they come up with those names?"

"I never knew that place was connected to the mob?" said Andreas.

"It isn't, that's why they picked it. And at this hour it's just getting busy. We'll be lost in the crowd."

Andreas stared out the window. Any meeting with that sort was dangerous, but picking a club in the heart of Athens' busiest nightlife district was about as safe a place as he could have hoped for them to choose. And it was quantum levels safer than a meeting on their home turf in Menidi. Cops rarely went there, and rarer still in a marked car. Andreas let his mind wander to other things, not pouncing on any one thought in particular.

"Here we are," said Tassos. It was a narrow street jammed with cars parked on both sides. Tassos pulled into a space cleared for the entrance to the club. An attendant held his hand out for the key.

"Get serious," said Tassos as he locked the doors and pocketed the key.

Andreas scanned the street to see if anyone was watching them. Everyone was. No wonder, with that grand entrance.

"Where are we supposed to meet them?"

Tassos shook his head. "Don't know. We're supposed to find some guy named Robert and ask for the 'White party.'"

The place was mobbed, the music loud, and the décor classic French bordello from that country's glory days of its greatest decadence. Not bad if you liked that sort of thing. Tassos whispered something in a waiter's ear. The waiter turned and pointed to a man by the end of the bar studying the room. He had to be at least seven feet tall and as broad as the back of a truck.

"That's our Robert," said Tassos.

"Oh boy. They win, I quit," said Andreas.

"He's probably quite gentle."

"Let's hope we don't get the chance to hear him say, 'I'll be gentle.'"

Tassos laughed.

Andreas patted his crotch. His nine-millimeter was right where it should be. "Okay, let's go."

Tassos walked over to the giant and motioned for

him to lower his head. Tassos whispered in his ear and Robert's face lit up in a broad smile. He waved one of his huge hands at Andreas to follow and began moving through the sea of people. It was like two *caïques* following the *Queen Mary*. He led them to a doorway at the rear, opened it, and pointed down the stairs.

"Down there, they're waiting for you." He smiled, patted Tassos and Andreas on their backs as they passed, and closed the door behind them.

"Christ, it's like a tomb in here," said Andreas. "Can't hear a thing from outside or downstairs."

"And vice-versa I'm sure. Probably not even a gun shot," said Tassos.

"Stop making me feel better." Andreas touched his holster again. "Just how sure are you of the guy who set up this meeting?"

"He's a friend of a friend."

"Great. Like I said, stop making me feel better."

At the bottom of the stairs stood two bulky guys, obviously Albanian. They didn't smile, just stared at the new arrivals.

Tassos stared back. "We're here for the White party."

The two men pointed to a door at the end of the hall.

As they walked toward the door Tassos whispered, "Don't shoot until you see the whites of their eyes."

Andreas smiled, but braced for the worst. Just then the door swung open and a tremendous shout came roaring out of the room.

"SURPRISE!"

IT TOOK ABOUT an hour of hugged congratulations, got-chas, backslapping, and *svenaki* shots of vodka from what seemed every guy he'd ever known before Andreas could corner Tassos. "You son-of-a-bitch, this was supposed to be tomorrow night."

"You mean your 'surprise' bachelor party." Tassos was smiling from ear to ear. "We knew you'd be expecting some sort of party so it was Lila's idea to misdirect you into thinking it was tomorrow."

"I guess I should take that as a warning of what life will be like after Sunday."

"Yeah, someone always caring that you have a good time."

"If you want me to have a really good time you'll tell me that your bit about being able to set up a meeting with the Albanians was all part of an elaborate ruse to get me here and that there's absolutely no truth to it."

"Sorry, wish I could. But that part's all real, though it did give me the idea for making sure you'd be surprised when the door opened."

"Remind me of that tomorrow, when I'm sober. What about the two Albanians at the door? Nice touch."

"Hey, not all Albanians are bad guys. They're cops from the western suburbs. It was Yianni's idea. He thought they would lend authenticity."

Andreas felt a sharp slap on his back. "Andreas, Andreas." It was Spiros, the minister of public order.

"*Yiasou*, Spiros."

"I am so glad to be here. After all we've been through together I feel as if we're brothers."

"Thank you, I've had similar thoughts at times," said Andreas thinking of certain well-known biblical siblings.

"I've arranged a little surprise to commemorate the end of your bachelorhood. Enjoy." Spiros winked at Tassos and walked away.

Andreas stared after him. "Why does the thought of a surprise from Spiros not make me happy?"

Tassos waved to Kouros to join them. "Forget about him. At least he didn't ask you for a report on what's happening with the Tinos murders." He put his arm around Kouros. "Yianni, we pulled it off. Congratulations."

Andreas stared at Kouros. "Bastard."

"I love you too, Chief."

Andreas smiled and hugged him.

The food, music, and drink had been running nonstop since they got there, all in a mix of modern and old Greek styles. Now the lights flickered, a disco ball hanging from the ceiling in the middle of the room began to turn, and splashes of colored light darted about in pace with the music. Spotlights splashed about the room before abruptly fixing on three figures shrouded in black beneath the disco ball. Every eye was drawn to the objects caught in the lights. At that instant the music gained a sudden intensity and from beneath each cloak a bare white arm shot straight into the air followed a moment later by a second bare arm.

Andreas had a pretty good idea of what was coming and was certain it did not involve any dancers approved by Lila.

First one then another dancer dropped her cloak, followed by her dress and bra, while the deejay did his masterful job of pumping up the music and virtually every man in the room. It wasn't that hard to do. Tall, blond, blue-eyed, big-busted young women, undoubtedly Eastern bloc, dancing naked down to their g-strings before two hundred drunken men generally did the trick every time.

One woman danced over to Andreas, teasing him to

join her in the middle of the floor. He smiled, but refused. She tried pulling him onto the dance floor. He kept smiling, but refused again. His second refusal met with friendly shouts from around the room of "*pusti*," and other names questioning his manhood. Andreas laughed and smiled but did not budge. When the practically naked woman again tried pulling him onto the dance floor, Kouros smoothly lifted her off her feet and carried her back to beneath the disco ball, smiling all the time, amid a barrage of men yelling offers to take Andreas' place. Everyone seemed to be having a terrific time.

Kouros walked back to where Andreas and Tassos were standing.

"Thanks, Yianni," said Andreas. "I can't believe this."

"My guess is that this is our distinguished minister's surprise," said Tassos.

"What planet is he on?" said Andreas. "Doesn't he realize these girls are part of the sex trafficking trade? The man is an idiot."

"A complete idiot," said Kouros.

Tassos shook his head. "No, my friends, I'm afraid he's just a man. Look around you. The place is filled with cops. They know what's going on. How many do you think even care? They'll say 'Hey, it's not child porn, it's dancers at a bachelor party. Chill out. What's the harm?'"

*What's the harm?* Oh yes, the unofficial mantra of Greece for all the corrupt practices that had brought his great country to its knees.

"Yeah, 'what's the harm?'"

"I GUESS I don't have to ask if you had a good time last night."

Andreas heard the words through the pillow pulled

tightly over his head. "I don't remember," he mumbled into the pillow.

"You could have slept in our bedroom, or a guest room. You didn't have to sleep on the sofa in the elevator foyer."

"It was the only room I could find."

Lila laughed. "Well, my love, it's one in the afternoon. When exactly did you get in?"

"It was light out, that's all I remember. And someone putting me into the elevator."

"That was Tassos. Maggie called a few hours ago. She said he wasn't in much better shape but at least he could walk. What I want to know is who drove?"

"A sober Albanian cop. Who now has lifetime job security. As long as he doesn't talk."

"About what?"

"I don't remember. And that's my story and I'm sticking to it."

Lila laughed again. "That reminds me, Maggie said for you to call Tassos when you're up. Something about a meeting with Albanians."

Andreas pulled the pillow off his face. "Oh no, not that again. I was hoping it would pass, along with the spinning of the room." He sat up and looked at his feet. "At least I took off my shoes."

"Nope, Marietta did that. Come, darling, time for the shower."

He lay back down on the sofa. "Not yet. Please not yet."

Lila grabbed his hand and tugged. "Sorry, big boy. When you play you pay. Time to get up and get to work. Our country needs you."

"In other words, you don't want me hanging around."

"Good, your mind is functioning again."

Lila tugged again at his arm. This time Andreas let her pull him up, but swung his other arm around her waist as he stood. "That's not all that's functioning again." Andreas pulled loose of her grip, slid that now free arm behind her knees and lifted Lila off the floor. "Now, where is that bedroom?"

Lila smiled, put her arms around his neck, and whispered in his ear. "Follow the bed crumbs."

Andreas laughed all the way home.

IT WAS AFTER three when Andreas reached Tassos at Maggie's.

"Thanks for getting me home. Lila would have been very unhappy had I been misplaced so close to our wedding day."

"No problem, but there's still time."

"Why do I think that means you've set up a meeting?"

"I had to call in some serious favors but the one who set it up 'guaranteed' our safety."

"Meaning?"

"It's a better than fifty-fifty chance no one with a grudge against you or me will take the opportunity to whack us. At least inside the room."

"And where would that room be located?"

"Menidi."

"Fantastic, great, couldn't pick a better place. Greece has the lowest violent crime rate in all of Europe and we get to do the equivalent of running through the streets of wartime Baghdad waving an American flag shouting 'Bush is great.'" Andreas drew in and let out a breath. "What if we don't go?"

"To me that's the smart move. Let it go. These bad guys won't budge. They're only comfortable in their own neighborhood. Don't trust us. Like I said, they know your reputation and worry we might be setting them up for a major bust, what with the new government clamoring for a crackdown on organized crime."

"They believe all that nonsense?" said Andreas.

"They're not as cynical as we are on the topic of reform. The exact message was, 'Menidi or fuck off.'"

"Well, glad to hear that we're at least getting off on the right foot."

"So, what do we do?" said Tassos.

Andreas paused. "Wear vests."

"Thick ones."

# SIX

OF THE THREE cops in the unmarked, beat-up van only Kouros was familiar with Menidi. That's what made him the designated driver. He had an aunt who lived north of Menidi in Thrakomakedones, a lovely area with large villas winding up Mount Parnitha's hillsides. It was as different from Menidi as night was to day, but Menidi was where anyone from his aunt's village with government business had to travel. His aunt, like many of her neighbors, kept a beat-up second hand car and nondescript, well-worn clothing for just that purpose; but not all had a bull of a nephew to accompany them on their adventures.

"Do you think we look seedy enough?" asked Tassos.

"I thought you were going to ask if the Kevlar vest made you look fat." Kouros smiled.

Tassos reached over from the passenger's seat with his left hand and popped his middle finger in front of Kouros' face.

Andreas leaned forward from the back seat. "How much longer?"

"About ten minutes, I think. Amazing how much traffic there is. Wouldn't expect it at this hour," said Kouros.

"It's nine o'clock, when all the gremlins start coming out of their hiding places," said Tassos.

"I'd have liked it better if we could have set this up for a daytime meeting," said Andreas.

"Like I said, they wouldn't budge. They wanted every advantage." Tassos tugged at his vest.

"How do you want to handle this, Chief?" said Kouros.

"Play it by ear and pray for inspiration."

"I get it, like always."

"I just want to make sure we come out of this alive. That's the 'prime directive,'" said Andreas.

"Wasn't that a line from a movie?" said Kouros.

Tassos gestured no. "Television. 'Star Trek.'"

"Did they all die in the end?" said Kouros.

"Just drive," said Andreas.

The streets turned to gravel and the van slowed to less than fifteen miles per hour. Beggars appeared from everywhere. Kouros kept pressing forward, ignoring the tapping on the windows, and forcing those who tried to block his way to jump aside.

"I see you've done this before," said Andreas.

"If I slow down too much we'll have to stop to identify bodies."

The building they were looking for was in the middle of the block on a busy street for Menidi. That seemed to the cops' advantage, but not really; for in this neighborhood a busy street was about the same as walking down a dark alley. If someone wanted to whack you they just started shooting. It was up to everyone else to duck.

Kouros circled the block twice before parking directly across the street from the building. It was a run down, four-story, post-World War II apartment building in the ubiquitous concrete-slab-balcony style that had forever tarnished Athens' beauty.

"No telling how many creeps hanging around here might be waiting for us," said Kouros.

"Let's assume all of them," said Tassos.

Andreas cleared is throat. "One more rule. No matter what happens we *never* give up our guns. If this is a set-up, no way we make it easy for them."

Kouros nodded. "No argument from me. I've got three."

"So, which door do we choose?" said Tassos. There were two, one on either side of a central concrete pillar.

Kouros said, "The one on the right looks like it's for the upstairs apartments, the other for whatever's on the first floor." The first floor windows were painted black. "No way to tell what's inside."

"My guess would be the storefront. Ready?" said Andreas.

The others nodded. Three van doors opened, three men got out and headed directly for the central pillar. They were five feet away from it when the storefront door swung open. A man the size of Kouros stood in the doorway staring at them. "In here."

They stepped inside into a tiny foyer leading to a second doorway. The man pulled the outside door closed and all street sounds vanished. It was a *déjà vu* moment for Andreas: another tomb and another two men waving for them to enter a second doorway. Another surprise? For sure, thought Andreas. He adjusted his crotch. *It's show time.*

THE ROOM WAS about the size of a four-car garage turned sideways. A beat-up wooden bar ran along the front left wall just far enough to take five mismatched bar stools. Past the bar, four rectangular tables covered in white linen tablecloths and looking decidedly out of place sat lined up across the middle of the room, while two scratched and marred wooden tables along each side-wall took up the rest of the space. On the rear wall, a door to the left was marked WC and a door to the right stood open, revealing a small kitchen. A dull, uneven glow of orange light struggled to reach the floor from three very dirty and ancient overhead fixtures.

Above the bar sat a television set. Next to it on a wall hung an out of date calendar showing a huge pair of tits surrounded by a woman.

Seven men sat at the tables in the middle of the room, a total of ten bad guys, plus however many more might be hiding in the kitchen and the woodwork.

The three cops stood at the end of the bar facing the tables. None of the bad guys said a word. They all stared at Andreas, as if they knew he was in charge.

Andreas smiled. "And a very good evening to all of you."

A heavily bearded man in sunglasses and sitting off to Andreas' right said in perfect Greek, "What do you want?"

Andreas pointed over his shoulder toward the front door. "For starters, have your friends join you where I can see them. I think ten to three are good enough odds for you. Besides, it would be very bad manners if one of my colleagues had to stand with his back to you while we talked."

The bearded man paused for a moment before nodding for the three to come forward. They brushed by the cops and stood along the back wall, behind the men at the linen covered tables. Andreas looked at Kouros and jerked his head toward the front door. Kouros walked to the bar, picked up a barstool, and wedged it snug against the door.

"Just so we're not disturbed by any unexpected patrons," said Andreas.

"So, like I said, what do you want?" said the bearded man.

"You already know," said Tassos.

"Tell us again."

"It's not about you," said Andreas. "At least I don't think it is. For all our sakes I pray it's not."

"What does that mean?" said the bearded man.

"Hate crimes against *tsigani* aren't popular these days with the E.U. They lead to investigations by Europol."

"What's that got do with us?" said a fat but muscled bald man sitting at the center of the seven men.

"I don't care about you. I care about me. I'm in charge of what happens in Greece, not a bunch of foreign pricks. But if they give me a hard time, I give you a harder one, because you boys are suspects *numero uno*." Andreas had found you could justify almost anything by claiming ego when talking to *macho* types.

The bald man nodded. "As long as you understand there's a price."

Andreas gestured no. "I don't think so. I'm here to get information, not make a deal. I'll owe no favors for anything you tell me."

The bald man bristled. "That's not the way we do business."

Tassos said, "Sorry to tell you, but today's payback time for past favors owed." He turned his head toward a slim, gray-haired man on the far left. "Right, Aleksander?"

The gray-haired man looked surprised. "Didn't think you'd recognize me, Tassos."

"It's good plastic surgery, but you still have that habit of tugging hard on your right earlobe when you're under stress. You ought to work on it."

Aleksander smiled. "Thanks for the tip." He looked at the bearded man. "Tell him what he wants to know."

The bald man said, "But—"

Aleksander raised his hand, the bald man instantly shut up, and Aleksander nodded at the bearded man.

The bearded man cleared his throat. "We had nothing to do with the two on Tinos."

Andreas nodded. "I'm sure. But what can you tell me about what happened there?"

"Nothing more than you already know."

Andreas bit at his lower lip and counted to five. "I get it, you had us come all the way out here just so you could whisper those three lovely little words in my ear, 'we know nothing?' Don't take me for an idiot. Two *tsigani* from a clan in your backyard are incinerated in an execution that made headline news across Greece and you expect me to believe that *if* you knew nothing about it before it happened you simply ignored it and went merrily along without the slightest concern over who might be next? No, my friend, I don't believe that for a minute."

The bearded man glared at Andreas.

Andreas glared back. "I'm still waiting for an answer."

"Okay asshole." It was the bald man. "Aleksander wants you to know the truth, so here's the truth. We would have killed those two if we thought they were behind what's going on."

"What does that mean?" said Andreas.

The bald man looked at Aleksander, waited until he

nodded, then turned to Andreas. "Someone is organizing something big. And whoever it is doesn't want us in on it."

Smart thinking, thought Andreas. Let these guys inside your tent and you're history.

"*Ians* and *is* from all over Athens are involved. But we can't get a line on who's putting it together. If we could—"

The bearded man cut the bald man off. "We wouldn't allow such a potential threat against our country to go forward."

Who's this guy think he is, their lawyer? thought Andreas.

Tassos shook his head. "Guys, I just want to know who whacked those two *tsigani*. And, frankly, so far I haven't heard anything to convince me it wasn't you."

Bald man said, "We live in Menidi among *tsigani*. We need each other, and besides, they're only a small part of whatever's going on. Singling out *tsigani* over this gets us into a war with everyone involved. We're better off biding our time until we find out who's behind it, then we'll do what has to be done to put an end to it once and for all."

He smiled. "And I can assure you that when that time comes the responsible ones will be wide awake and *feel* the end coming."

How the hell did he know the two brothers were dead when they were incinerated? thought Andreas.

"I'm still not convinced," said Tassos.

The bearded man nodded. "I can understand why you might think that. After all, that *tsigani* clan was going against our interests, so it's only logical we would want to make an example of them."

He paused.

"But the trouble with your thinking is that those two murdered *tsigani* were on *our* side. They have an older brother who sided with us against his clan, and a few days before his two brothers were killed one of them got word to us that they should have listened to their brother. They said they thought they were on to who was organizing everything and would let us know as soon as they knew for sure."

"Why their sudden change of heart?" said Tassos.

"They said they didn't want to go against the church," said the bald man.

"The church?" said Andreas.

"Yes, a church on Tinos, and they wanted no part of it."

"Which church?" said Andreas.

"Panagia Evangelistria."

"What's supposed to happen?" said Tassos.

"All we heard was it involved robbing Panagia Evangelistria. They died before getting us any more information."

"They used those words?"

"Yes, 'robbing Panagia Evangelistria.'"

"And that's all you know?" said Andreas. "No idea of when it's supposed to go down or what they're after?"

"Yes, you got it. 'No idea,'" said the bald man.

Andreas looked at the bearded man.

"Yes," said the bearded man.

Andreas looked at the others in the room. "And you?"

Each man nodded yes.

Aleksander cleared his throat. "Tassos, gentlemen, have your questions been answered?"

Tassos looked at Andreas.

Andreas nodded. "Yes. For the moment."

Aleksander said, "This is the only moment you will have. Ask now, because there will never be another chance. The slates are now wiped clean." He looked at Tassos.

Tassos nodded yes.

"Good, thank you." He motioned for Tassos to come over to him. When he did Aleksander pulled him down to whisper in his ear. Tassos laughed and Aleksander did the same.

Tassos turned and said goodbye to the bad guys and, still laughing, took Andreas and Kouros by their arms, swung them around, and headed toward the front door. He kicked the bar stool out of the way, stepped into the foyer, and said, "The second that door opens head left into the apartment building next door, down the stairs to the right, and out the back door. *And move.*"

Andreas and Kouros asked no questions. They were out one door and though the other in three seconds.

Tassos yelled as they ran toward the stairs, "Outside to the left there's a grey Fiat with a Blue Star ferry sticker on the driver's side rear window. Keys are under the floor mat. Yianni, you drive."

They went through the downstairs door and out into the parking lot. "What the hell is going on?" said Andreas.

"Bomb in the van."

"Maybe in the Fiat, too," said Kouros.

"Sure as hell hope not," said Tassos.

They'd just reached the Fiat when they heard the downstairs door crash open, followed by the unmistakable sound of a Kalashnikov.

Andreas pulled his gun and ducked behind the front end of a tiny pickup. "Yianni, get the car moving."

It was the three men who'd been standing in the back throughout the meeting, one with an assault rifle and two with handguns. All were using the spray and pray method of marksmanship. Andreas was more focused, kept his eye on the front sight, and squeezed. He caught the one with the Kalashnikov in the throat. Not quite where he was aiming, but close enough. The abrupt silence startled the other two shooters, and before the one closest to the AK-47 could reach it, Andreas had put a round in his thigh. That's where he was aiming, because he assumed they were also wearing vests. Shooter number three turned and ran back into the building. Andreas heard Kouros and Tassos yelling for him to get in the car.

Andreas jumped onto the back seat and Kouros spun the wheels on the gravel getting out of the parking lot. "What the hell were you doing back there? Couldn't you hear us screaming for you to get in?" said Kouros.

Andreas leaned his head back against the seat. His heart was pounding. "As a matter of fact, no." It was instinctive. His hearing had shut down at the sudden life or death confrontation. All his senses focused on eliminating the threat and nothing else. Andreas shut his eyes, drew in and let out a deep breath. "Anybody following us?"

"Not yet," said Tassos.

"Yianni, call for backup," said Andreas.

"I'm a little busy driving at the moment, Chief," said Kouros.

Andreas opened is eyes, pulled out his cell phone,

and hit the code for officer needs assistance. "Let them track us on GPS."

"Tassos, what the hell did that guy tell you?" said Kouros.

"He said that no matter what he told me I should laugh all the way out the door. He said that the bald guy was a real hothead bad ass and only agreed that nothing would happen to us in the meeting. Once outside we were on our own and Aleksander was certain that by now whatever we'd come in was wired to explode. The Fiat was his final payment on a major favor owed."

"Which was?" said Andreas.

"Let's just put it this way, if I told you who he is—or from the way he now looks was—I will have reneged on a promise that just saved our lives."

Andreas sat quietly for a moment. "Sometimes you are a very difficult man to understand." He paused again. "But thanks."

"You're welcome."

On the trip out of Menidi no beggar stepped in front of the Fiat. They were too busy diving out of its way as Kouros swerved, sped, and slid like a drunken tourist on holiday to the Greek islands.

About a half-mile from the National Road, two police cars were waiting on the shoulder, and the cops inside were waving for them to pull over.

"Finally, reinforcements," said Kouros.

"Don't stop," said Tassos. "They may not be friendly."

"What are you talking about? We sent out a GPS distress call," said Kouros.

"I know, but we're no longer in distress and no reason to risk it." Tassos looked back at Andreas. "The bearded guy in the sunglasses, he's a cop."

Andreas opened his eyes. "I thought he might be."

"I don't know him but I'm sure I've met him before," said Tassos.

"Son of a bitch, I thought I recognized his voice," said Kouros. "The beard's a phony."

"That's how bald guy knew the *tsigani* were already dead when they were incinerated," said Andreas.

Tassos nodded. "He's owned by the Albanians. They probably had him here to watch out for 'cop tricks.'"

"Then why didn't they search us?" said Kouros.

"They were cocky," said Tassos. "They didn't care if we had weapons because there was a guy at each table holding a gun on us from the moment we walked in, probably shotguns and that AK-47."

"That was the reason for the tablecloths," said Andreas.

"Okay, but why wouldn't the cop have them check us for a wire?" said Kouros.

"Same cocky, *macho* bullshit," said Tassos. "They probably had a jammer working in case we were transmitting to someone on the outside and figured any recorder we had on us would go up in the explosion."

Andreas leaned his head back against the seat. He drew in a breath. By now his pulse had returned to normal and his thoughts to what really counted. Lila and Tassaki foremost.

But something else, too: Punka. Son-of-a-bitch had to know more than he claimed about what was going on. His brothers must have told him something. Punka's time on the outside was over.

"Yianni, who's on Punka?"

"Angelo and Christina."

"Fine, call them and tell them to bring him in *now*."

# SEVEN

ANGELO WAS NOT free of prejudices. He never claimed to be. He just tried to keep his from interfering with his professional responsibilities as a cop. But Punka was making it very difficult. Angelo and his partner, Christina, had been staked out in Syntagma for hours watching Punka orchestrate a petty-crime wave in the heart of their city.

The Athens that Angelo remembered as a child had changed dramatically. Its innocence was gone. Residents no longer dared leave their front doors open, or any door or window for that matter. His mother and everyone else's mother now rode the metro clutching their purses. That included immigrant mothers, for they were among the most preyed upon. Many feared that with Greece in economic decline for the first time in decades, there was worse crime to come, and all prayed that whatever came would not get out of hand.

To Angelo, Punka already was way out of hand. Cute, innocent-looking three-year-olds, five-year-olds, seven-year-olds, eleven-year-olds and every age in between raced around smiling and touching as they begged tourists and locals alike for money, and cursing those who did not give. Then there were the babies sleeping in the laps of older girls begging, but not really sleeping: drugged, so they couldn't move or cry. And into this mix dropped the pickpockets, the opportunists. All run by Punka from a park bench and all watched as closely as a distrusting casino pit boss would his dealers.

"I really can't take much more of this," said Angelo into his transmitter. "What do you say, Christina, want to help me kick his ass?" He glanced across the square toward his partner.

"I can do it myself, thank you."

"I bet you could." He looked at his watch. He despised Punka even though he'd never met him. It wasn't a matter of race or the notorious *tsigani* crimes and hustles that played out every day almost everywhere in Europe that bothered him. After all, separating suckers from their money was a time-honored tradition practiced by many groups, including businessmen and politicians. What drove his anger were the children, their exploitation.

He looked at his watch again. "Twenty minutes until our relief gets here," said Angelo.

"Thank God," said Christina. "This is worse than boring. Having to watch that bastard—"

"Christina. Someone's heading toward Punka. Male, late twenties, five-six, thin, dark blue zippered jacket…"

"I see him," said Christina.

"Hold off until contact is made then you follow the new guy. I'll stay with Punka in case it's a diversion."

The new guy walked over to Punka and smiled. They didn't shake hands, but talked for a minute. He offered Punka a cigarette. Punka stood up, stretched, and took it. New guy reached into his right jacket pocket and pulled out a lighter. Punka leaned in for a light and new guy transferred the lighter to his left hand and…

Angelo thought, left hand? Why would he switch

it to his left hand to light the cigarette? "*Move in now, something's wrong.*"

The stiletto was out of new guy's right jacket sleeve and in Punka's heart before Punka could draw a puff. It was a smooth, quick thrust with just enough twisting force to ensure Punka would not survive. He eased Punka back onto the bench and turned to walk away, the stiletto no longer in sight.

It was Christina who reached new guy first, her gun drawn. "*Stop*, police. Drop the knife."

He nodded, and let the stiletto fall from inside his right sleeve.

"On the ground, hands behind your head." It was Angelo coming up behind him.

New guy dropped to his knees.

That was when the shot came. It entered dead center into new guy's forehead.

The cops scrambled for cover.

The shot had to come from a building across the square, down by Ermou Street. But which building?

"Christina, call for assistance and stay with the bodies."

Angelo ran toward Ermou, looking for something, anything. He ran into buildings, tried doors, grabbed anyone who looked suspicious, and did whatever else he could think of to make himself believe he had a snowball's chance in hell of catching the shooter. But he knew it was a waste of time.

Just then his phone rang. It was Kouros.

"Busy night." Andreas' elbows were on his desk, his head in his hands, and his fingers rubbing his forehead. He dropped his hands and stared at Kouros and Tassos sitting across the desk from him. The three of them had just spent two hours with Angelo and Christina going over what happened in Syntagma.

"That was no mugging," said Tassos. "No matter what the guy with the stiletto might have hoped to make it look like."

"And not a sign anywhere that a shooter was ever there, except for the bullet through stiletto guy's forehead," said Andreas.

"Can't wait to see how the papers play this one," said Kouros. "'Today in Syntagma a target under surveillance by the Greek police was the victim of a professional hit and, although the killer was immediately apprehended on the scene without a fight by police, in a matter of seconds after his capture he was taken out by an unknown sniper.'"

"So far, the only good news tonight was that we didn't get whacked," said Tassos.

Andreas rubbed his eyes. "Don't forget the call I got from our distinguished minister screaming about doing something to stop 'foreign criminal elements' from 'slaughtering' each other in 'the heart of our beloved Athens.'"

"Is that supposed to be more good news or bad?" said Kouros.

"I wasn't quite sure if he was upset about the 'slaughtering' or the fact it was done in Syntagma instead of somewhere else," said Tassos.

"That may be a bit harsh," said Andreas. "I think that's just Spiros' way of spinning things to minimize heat from the press. Bad guys killing bad guys always seem to work. The good news was that he didn't make the connection to the Tinos murders. And with any luck nor will the press."

"Yeah, dead *tsigani* are all alike," said Tassos.

Andreas starred at Tassos. "You're incorrigible."

"Thank you," said Tassos. "As a matter of fact, a member of Parliament once told me that if you wanted to understand the Greeks, think one word. 'Incorrigible.'"

Tassos stretched his arms out over his head and yawned. "Whoever arranged this had to know we were interested in Punka. It's just too much of a coincidence. He was never in hiding, so if he were a threat to someone before we were on to him, he'd have been taken out long ago."

"Where's our leak?" said Andreas.

"Maybe it was Tassos' *tsigani* contact, the one who hooked you up with Punka?" said Kouros.

"Stefan is capable of anything. But that would be a very risky play for him. He knows that if I even thought he double-crossed me…" Tassos waved a hand in the air.

"Maybe when the boys from our meeting tonight realized we were pressing the investigation into Punka's murdered brothers they decided to take him out, too?" said Kouros.

"And us along with him," said Tassos.

"Or it could be that Punka said something about the two of you busting his balls and it got back to someone who decided he was better off dead," said Kouros.

Andreas leaned across the desk and stared at Kouros. "You just gave me another candidate. When I was playing hardball with Punka in that taverna, if someone overheard me telling him I was a cop who wanted to talk to him about his brothers' murders it would have made headlines on the *tsigani* gossip network." Andreas slammed his right hand on the desk. "*Damnit.*"

"That might mean whoever whacked Punka knows who you are," said Tassos.

"I never said my name."

"Punka might have told someone who you were after we dropped him at the taverna," said Tassos.

"Or with the way your face keeps popping up in gossip columns about the wedding, someone might have recognized you," said Kouros.

"I doubt if the *tsigani* in that taverna read *Espresso*," said Andreas. "But I get your point. Send Christina and Angelo out there to see if they can locate anyone Punka might have talked to after we dropped him off. Tell them to get the names of everyone inside when I was there and, when they're told no one remembers, to get the names of all the regulars." Andreas paused. "And have them find out if that young girl working there yesterday is into gossip magazines."

"Any ideas on who might be behind this?" said Tassos.

"The Albanians are high on my list," said Kouros.

"They're high on everyone's list all the time," said Tassos.

Andreas ran his fingers through his hair. "If what the Menidi crew said tonight about something major going down on Tinos ties in to what happened in Syntagma, and I can't imagine it doesn't, that church on Tinos is facing some very serious trouble."

"Uhh, speaking of 'serious trouble' could we focus for a minute on a rather immediate, personal problem?" said Kouros.

"What are you talking about?" said Andreas.

"We just pissed off some of the meanest motherfuckers in Greece. They're not going to just walk away from this. How do you suggest we deal with them?"

"Aleksander wasn't happy about what happened tonight," said Tassos. "Going after us disrespected him in a very public way. Worse yet, the ones who disrespected him failed. Don't worry, Yianni, they'll 'work things out among themselves.'" Tassos emphasized his last words with finger quotes morphed into the universal thumb and forefinger sign for a gun.

"Let's hope so," said Kouros. "After all, I'd prefer attending a wedding to a funeral this weekend."

Andreas tapped a pencil against his forehead. "Maybe it's not such a bad idea to put the Menidi boys away. At least the ones from the meeting until after the wedding. Give them a chance to cool down. After all, we don't want them getting so worked up over what we might have in mind for them that they decide to come after us first."

Tassos nodded. "Yeah, I'd rather see you dodging rice than Molotov cocktails."

AMONG THE HARDEST things to find in Athens when you're looking for one is a big time mobster to arrest. They seemed to sense when it was time to disappear. Or perhaps it was a service included with their monthly envelopes stuffed with euros to Athens' not so finest: the "it's time to get out of town" call.

But after the debacle in Menidi no one at that meeting had to be told to disappear. There'd be no way to find any of them unless you knew where to look. That's why Tassos called Aleksander in the middle of the night with a simple proposition: "Tell me where your colleagues from the meeting are hiding, and I'll put them away until things calm down."

Tassos wasn't surprised when Aleksander agreed. Tassos' suggestion temporarily ridded Aleksander of his rivals, giving him breathing room and time to regroup. What surprised him was the list Aleksander rattled off. He named twice the number of bad guys at the meeting. Tassos didn't bother to ask what Aleksander had in mind. It was the price of the deal. Besides, Tassos never cared what garbage did to garbage.

By noon every mobster on the list was in custody. Not a shot had been fired. It wasn't worth it to them. They all had lawyers. The lawyers were lined up outside Andreas' office in what looked to be a bakery line. He'd worked out an informal procedure with the prosecutor. The lawyers came in one by one and ranted for a while about "discrimination by the police against hard working immigrants" until finally getting around to asking about the charges.

That was Andreas' favorite part. Watching the expressions on the faces of the lawyers while he listed the charges. Not one carried a risk of more than thirty days' jail time at most.

"What the hell's going on?" was the most common response, followed closely by "You must be kidding!" The sharp lawyers knew there was a reason, there had to be, and they patiently waited for the other shoe to drop. Only the inexperienced suggested Andreas did not know what he was doing and threatened what would happen to him if the client wasn't released "at once."

Those moments gave Andreas great joy.

"Counselor, you're absolutely right. Your client does not deserve to be in jail on these charges. So let me make a proposal to you. I will withdraw them and bring these instead." Andreas slid a document across the table charging the client with the attempted, pre-meditated murder of three police officers, and a plethora of related crimes.

"As you've no doubt noticed, the crimes charged took place less than forty-eight hours ago, which means your client stays in jail until trial, no bail." That wasn't quite true in all situations, but it was a risk the lawyer knew he must tell his client.

That brought on a volley of protests, claiming "trumped up charges" and the like.

Andreas raised his hand for the lawyer to stop. "Counselor, the situation is simple. Tell your client to relax, spend a few days with old friends in a place that's like home to him, just until things 'cool down.' He'll know what I mean. Or, if he wants to test me, to see if I'm serious about bringing the new charges, tell him about the risks he faces if he doesn't take my deal, and I'm not just talking about the new charges. Remind him I'm one of the cops your client and his buddies tried to murder last night."

Each lawyer's client chose the short vacation option.

That was fine with Andreas. He wasn't ready to arrest any of them yet for what happened in that parking lot. With their connections and money none was likely to be denied bail. Not for just the attempted murder of a cop. Great system.

At least the worst were off the streets for now. All but one. The crooked, bearded cop. No way to arrest him.

But the fates were Greek and once more they stepped in and took a hand. Well, actually broke a hand, two legs, three ribs, and a jaw. The bearded cop was mugged

coming out of a whorehouse just before dawn. He was
found and taken to a hospital next to GADA where he
was under twenty-four-hour police protection, on Andreas' orders. Rumor had it he decided to accept early
retirement. Miraculously, his unbroken hand was the
one he needed to sign the necessary papers, scheduled
for that afternoon in his hospital room.

"Maggie, where's Yianni?" Andreas had just said
goodbye to the last of the lawyers. He was exhausted
and wanted to go home. He'd never made it there last
night.

Maggie stuck her head through the doorway. "He's
in his office, with Tassos."

"Tell them to come in here."

Maggie stepped inside and closed the door. "I think
you should go to his office, Chief. There are still lawyers in the hallway."

Andreas was about to ask why that mattered but if
Maggie said it there must be a good reason. Kouros'
office was on the same floor as Andreas' but windowless. The door to his office was closed. That was unusual. Andreas knocked.

"Come in," said Kouros.

Andreas opened the door and looked in. "Another
surprise party?"

"No, just little old me and mister ex-*lokazides* here,"
said Tassos pointing to Kouros lying across his desk
with a towel over his head. *Lokazides* was the nickname
for the special ops brotherhood of Greece's equivalent
of U.S. Navy Seals.

"A little less noise if you please," said Kouros.

Andreas didn't have to ask what happened. "Looks
like you've been in a fight."

"*Mano a mano*," said Kouros.

"From what I understand about the condition of the other guy I don't think he'd agree." Andreas smiled. "More like man versus bull."

Kouros pulled the towel off his face, one eye was swollen shut and his nose appeared broken, though it was hard to tell if that would be an improvement over the results of its past breaks.

"I'll ask Lila if perhaps she has another veil for you to wear to the wedding." Andreas patted Kouros on the arm. "So, what happened? I thought you were just going to talk to him?"

"I didn't go there to beat him up, it just turned out that way."

Tassos said, "I was there and we tried to talk to him. We gave him the choice you suggested, take early retirement or become your number one target for investigation. He raised various questions about our parentage and yelled to some of his colleagues in the brothel for help." He looked at Kouros. "It was a joy to watch our young friend here at work. There were three of them plus the dirty cop and I was able to assist with one."

"A lead pipe to the back of the head was more than an assist. Where did you find that thing anyway?"

Tassos shrugged. "By the end of the exercise our cop friend saw the light."

Andreas said, "Glad everything turned out okay, good job."

Kouros stared at Andreas. "I don't consider being stretched out on top of my desk as 'okay.'"

"Stop complaining," said Tassos. "You know you enjoyed yourself." Tassos looked at Andreas. "So, what do we do now?"

"It's off to Tinos. We've got to get a handle on what's happening over there."

"Does Lila know?" said Kouros.

"I'll tell her when I get home. She won't mind. Tinos is next to Mykonos." Andreas smiled. "It's an easy commute for the wedding. Let's all plan to leave for Tinos this afternoon."

Kouros and Tassos looked at each other. Tassos said, "Are you sure you can leave today? You do know it's Thursday?"

Andreas smacked his forehead with his hand. "I forgot all about tonight."

Tassos said, "Don't worry. I know who to talk to on Tinos. I'll catch the next fast boat and be there in a couple hours. You stay here and keep your bride-to-be happy. No need to start a war with Lila so close to your wedding day."

"Yeah, getting one going with the Albanians was enough of that sort of thing for me for one day," said Kouros.

Andreas smiled. "Think positively, Yianni. How could things possibly get any worse?"

Maggie opened the door and popped her head inside. "Chief, it's Lila. Something about you keeping a promise to pick up your mother ten minutes ago for the final fitting for her dress."

Kouros put the towel back over his face. "Guess you have your answer, Chief."

# EIGHT

WHEN ANDREAS' MOTHER asked him to come along with her to the final fitting, his first reaction was, "Why me?" He knew as much about fashion as he knew about rocket science, probably less. But, his sister couldn't come and, as the only other child in his mother's life, Andreas went because he knew how anxious she was to look just right. His mother said she'd never bought a dress "this important" before and wanted it to be "perfect."

Her home was not far from his office. She'd moved there as a young bride, it was where her son and daughter were born, and her hero cop husband died. The old neighborhood was unrecognizable from when Andreas grew up there. Greek was no longer the dominant language. No language was. It was a hodgepodge of languages, people, and cultures. It was also dangerous.

Andreas and his sister had begged their mother to move but she refused to leave her home, even to live among her grandchildren. All Andreas could do was ask the local police commander to keep a special eye on his mother's place, and the word on the street was "stay away, it's protected." But new trouble moved into the neighborhood every day, and it took time for them to get the word.

Andreas sat at a traffic light two blocks from his mother's place. The colors and faces passing by were very different from his childhood memories. He guessed at their nationalities. As a cop he was pretty good at that. Profiling some would say. Self-defense said others. Members of certain groups just seemed to commit certain crimes. They specialized. Cops knew that but couldn't say so publicly.

Perhaps we should, thought Andreas. Bring it all out into the open. Let everyone know the truth, that every group had its special sorts of predators—and that they preyed worst upon their own kind. It's not helping anyone ignoring that reality. The scum of a group always makes the news, making it easy for the rest of the country to classify everyone in the group as bad. No way that was true. No more so than that all Greeks were…

The blaring of the horn from the car behind him jolted Andreas out of his daydream. "Okay, I get it, the light's green." He drove through the light and saw his mother standing on the sidewalk. Enough about saving the world, he thought. Time to focus on what really matters. Andreas smiled. "I'm back to thinking like a Greek."

It was turning into a beautiful late afternoon. No Albanian gang war and no more lawyers. Andreas even got to surprise Lila when he walked into their apartment.

"My God, were you fired?" Lila kissed him on both cheeks.

"Not that lucky."

"Then maybe my watch is broken. It reads five-fifteen."

"That means I've only been up for a zillion hours."

"How did the fitting go with your mother?"

"Fine."

"How does the dress look?"

"Fine."

"Boys. You're all alike. Are these the sort of one word answers I can look forward to from our son?" Lila smiled.

"Yes." Andreas stretched his arms and yawned. "Where is he?"

"I put him in for a nap. But if you want to—"

"No, don't wake him, I'm too exhausted to be much fun to play with. I better take a nap myself."

"Good, I'll make sure you're not disturbed until the first guests arrive. You need to get some sleep. Our flight to Mykonos is first thing in the morning."

Andreas thought this might be the right opportunity for mentioning that as soon as they landed he'd be catching a boat to Tinos. *Wrong move, stupid*, said a little voice inside his head. *Take the nap and keep your mouth shut*.

On the Thursday evening before a wedding, close family and friends traditionally gathered together at the home of the bride and groom for *to strosimo tou krevatiou*—the preparation of the wedding bed. Amid food, drink, much joy, and playful teasing, the unmarried girls (alleged virgins all) attempted to make up the bed while the young men waited around to undo it. It was a playful match, with a young man interested in the attentions of a particular girl making care to undo her handiwork. That undoing ritual took place three times before it was on to tossing gold coins and jewelry on the wedding bed amid a shower of confetti, rice, and money.

But the most precious commodity tossed upon the bed, and the truest indicator of the real purpose of the practice, was saved for last: children. Giggling, laughing children, carefully bounced about by giggling, laughing parents. Tradition had the first child on the bed a boy, for superstition held that a male child symbolized good luck. Perhaps as a sign of changing attitudes—or intrigues yet to come—it was not unheard of in modern days for a future bride to coordinate the efforts of her girlfriends at assuring a girl child landed first.

The tradition was rarely practiced when the couple already had a child, but holding it was not forbidden from any religious perspective and Lila wanted to observe it "for Tassaki."

The party went on until three in the morning, and though Andreas had far less to drink than at his bachelor party, the combination of all the toasts he'd been cajoled into joining and no sleep for two days had him feeling about the same. He wasn't even sure if he slept at all before their early morning taxi ride to the airport, and could barely remember their flight to Mykonos. He was also fuzzy about precisely how he'd told Lila on landing that he was going to Tinos and "should" be back that night. But he distinctly remembered her response.

Lila clutched the front of Andreas' shirt, pulled him down to her eye level, and said a single word, "*Sunday!*"

"HOW ARE YOU FEELING, CHIEF?" were Maggie's first words when Andreas called her in the office.

"Not as bad as I'd thought I'd be."

"Where are you?"

"On a ferry from Mykonos to Tinos. Should be there in twenty minutes. Just checking to see if Christina and Angelo have anything to tell me."

"Just a minute, I'll check."

Andreas looked at his watch. It wasn't even ten yet.

"Chief?" It was Christina.

"Can you talk?"

"Yes. We're on our way into the office. Just left the taverna."

"How'd it go?"

"We found the girl. She was there with her uncle. It's his place but he said he didn't know any Punka Carausii and couldn't remember the names of any of his customers. We showed him a photograph of Punka and he said he didn't recognize him."

"My, what a surprise."

"I tried to speak to the girl but he told her to 'shut up' in Romanian. He didn't realize Angelo's girlfriend was Romanian and she always told him the same thing."

Andreas heard "fuck you" from Angelo in the background.

"Angelo told the uncle that since he couldn't help us, we'd have to justify our visit by having him prove to us that he was a law abiding taxpayer. Angelo had him pulling invoices for every item in the place. That shut him up. Also got him away from the girl."

"And?"

"She was scared. I showed her Punka's photograph and she said she'd never seen him before. I said, 'Do you remember the man who came into the taverna the day before yesterday to see Punka?' She acted like she didn't know what I was talking about. I asked her if she'd like to meet 'that man,' and tell him personally that she 'never saw Punka before.' She looked like she was going to cry. That's when I said, 'I'm wasting my time here. Get your things you're coming with us to police headquarters.'

"She burst into tears, said her uncle would 'beat' her if she told us anything. I said, 'He's going to beat you anyway.'"

"Glad to see you're so understanding," said Andreas.

"Thanks, Chief. That got her to talking. She told me Punka was a regular and, yes, he'd come back into the taverna after you dropped him off, but he didn't speak to anyone. Her uncle tried to get him to talk about what happened but Punka wouldn't tell him a thing."

"Why was the uncle so interested?"

"She said he's 'a gossip.' Like every other taverna owner in Greece."

"Did she know I was a cop?"

"Yes, she overheard you."

"Dammit."

"Uhh, Chief."

"Yes."

"You were right about the girl and the tabloids. She scavenges them from the rubbish to look at the pictures. Seems your upcoming wedding made two of the biggie magazines this week, and after you left she realized where she'd seen you before."

Andreas cleared his throat. "And, of course, she told her uncle."

"He likes to be a big man with the gossip. It made her look good to him when she pointed you out in the magazines. One magazine gave your title and the uncle told everyone in the taverna and anyone else he could find that the head of GADA Special Crimes was in his place questioning Punka about the murder of his brothers."

"What did the lying son-of-a-bitch say when you confronted him?" Andreas made no attempt to hide his anger.

Christina paused. "We didn't confront him."

"*You didn't what*?"

"Chief, we figured the uncle wouldn't tell us anything anyway, and if he knew the girl had talked to us he might do her some really serious harm."

Andreas shut his eyes, drew in a breath, and let it out. "You did the right thing. See you at the wedding." He hung up.

Andreas stared out the window. The ferry was preparing to pirouette up to the dock.

It was my screw-up. That's why Punka's dead. No reason for someone else to get hurt because of me. Besides, with Punka gone there'll be no more leads coming from that direction. Andreas slammed his fist into the back of the empty seat in front of him.

We have to find another place to start.

"Welcome to Tinos," came over the loud speaker.

THE HARBOR OF TINOS lay northwest and virtually equidistant from the old and new ports of Mykonos. How long that port-to-port, nine-mile trip took depended on whether one traveled by freighter, ferry, or fast boat. Almost every regularly scheduled commercial passenger vessel in or out of Athens' port cities of Piraeus and Rafina that stopped on Mykonos also stopped on Tinos. That wasn't just because Tinos lacked an airport, but because it was home to the Church of Panagia Evangelistria and the extraordinarily influential earthly power behind it which in less than two hundred years had established what many called The Vatican of Greece: The Panhellenic Holy Foundation of our Lady of the Annunciation of Tinos, better known simply as The Evangelistria Foundation.

Tassos met Andreas at the quayside.

"How was the trip?"

"Uneventful. Except for the part where I told Lila I was leaving her for you."

"As long as you show up for the wedding all will be forgiven."

"She sort of said the same thing. But not as sweetly."

Tassos pointed to a stream of women dressed in black heading in the direction of Megalochari Avenue leading up the hill to Panagia Evangelistria. "Bring her back a candle from the church."

"Not sure they have one big enough to save me." He watched some of the women drop to their knees and begin crawling along the three-foot wide, rose-color carpet running up along the right edge of the road. "Amazing how dedicated people can be to their faith."

Tassos smiled. "Until you know what they're praying for. Not all are crawling with saintly thoughts."

"What are you talking about?"

"On the boat over from Piraeus I was sitting behind three normal-looking church-ladies. They were carrying on about the reason for their pilgrimage. Seems they all hated the same neighbor and were coming to Tinos with prayers and offerings to have their neighbor done in."

"You must be kidding."

"Just because you pray doesn't mean you have a good soul. A lot of very bad people are big-time church-goers. And I'm not just talking about politicians." Tassos smiled. "But at least my little old ladies are leaving their neighbor's fate in God's hands."

Andreas shook his head. "Any luck on who did in the *tsigani* brothers?"

"Nothing specific, but this being Greece everyone has an opinion. Most blame it on *metanastes*."

"So what else is new? Greece's usual suspects for anything bad, foreigners."

"That's about what I said when the Tinians started in on them. But they insisted it's not like that. They said that this season there are more foreign workers on Tinos than they can remember in years. *Tsigani*, too. 'They're everywhere.'"

"Times are bad in Athens and Tinos is one of the cheaper places to live in the Cyclades," said Andreas.

"But there's hardly any work here, and the foreigners are undercutting each other to get whatever work there is."

"Employers must love it."

"Even they're worried. With so many *metanastes* competing for so little work, they're afraid crime will go off the charts."

"Tell me about it. Have you seen what's going on in Athens?"

Tassos nodded. "In the Cyclades, too. But here's the strange thing. I checked with the Tinos police. Got the real figures, not the ones for tourist consumption. If you pull out the two murders, crime actually is down on Tinos."

"That's what I call a real miracle," said Andreas.

"I mean way down. And I'm talking break-ins, robberies. The sorts of things you expect to go off the charts when times are tough."

Andreas shook his head, "Never thought I'd be wishing for crime to be up, but it seems like the bad guys are doing exactly what Punka said they were told to do, 'behave.' Any idea why?"

"No, but I've set up a meeting with someone who knows as much about what's going on here as anyone.

She works for the Evangelistria Foundation. All I told her was that I wanted to talk to her about a 'sensitive' matter. I figured I'd let you decide if you want the Foundation to know that their church might be some sort of target."

"If I recall correctly, two of our kings believed they owed their lives to the curative powers of the *Megalochari*, and at least one of our prime ministers considered that holy icon the source of his political power. How many milliseconds do you think it will take after we share our little theory with your Foundation lady before our Prime Minister gets a call from the Foundation and I get one from Spiros screaming, 'What the hell are you doing?'"

Tassos smiled. "Just tell him 'we're closing the case.'"

Andreas rubbed his eyes. "When's the meeting?"

Tassos looked at his watch. "Fifteen minutes."

Andreas nodded toward the Church of Panagia Evangelistria. "Well, I guess we should head on up there."

Tassos gestured no. "When I told her it was 'sensitive' she suggested we meet at a taverna out of town."

"Guess it's not just cops who worry about their walls having ears."

"Who knows, it might just be her cousin's place and she wants to throw him some business."

Andreas smiled. "But we're cops, we don't pay."

"Could be it's a cousin she doesn't like." Tassos pointed to a marked police car. "That's our ride. You drive."

# NINE

Andreas once had a teacher who said Tinos resembled "a haunting, second millennium BC Mycenaean fortress." It was easy to see why. The island's high-ridged backbone ran northwest-to-southeast above the sea like some ever vigilant guardian of the shoreline while, at its narrow, eastern sea border with Mykonos, Tinos' tallest peak, Mount Tsiknias, loomed down from the clouds and across its foothills toward the port city to the southwest.

His teacher would go on and on about how the true beauty of Tinos lay in its surprises. None of that had changed. To foreigners, virtually everything about the island was a revelation for so few had even heard of it. But it was native-born Greeks, those raised on wondrous stories of the *Megalochari* and perhaps even a daylong pilgrimage or two, who were most surprised at what they discovered outside the harbor town.

Fifty villages as quiet and undisturbed as a dreamer's quaint fantasy of Greece; brilliant vistas at every turn; a meandering two-hundred-mile network of cobblestone trails and old farm paths running from hillside to hillside and dipping into valleys in between; and a history of fabled marble quarries and artisans linked to some of Greece's greatest artistic achievements.

Tassos said they were looking for a taverna in a mountain village in the northeast region of the island.

Locals called that district Kato Meria; the southeastern part of Tinos, including the port, they called Ano Meria; and everything to the west was Exo Meria. The "lower," "upper," and "other" parts, respectively.

The taverna was around a bend on a twisting mountain road and, but for a large sign screaming TAVERNA OMORFI THEA, Andreas would have missed it. The place was practically invisible from the road. Tables inside led to many more on an outside terrace with still more arranged amphitheater fashion along a hillside filled with deep purple bougainvillea and wild fruit trees. It all ended at a fence line of pink and white oleander. Far beyond, out past the valley and port town below, a deep blue sea shimmered toward the islands of Delos and Rhenia on its way to the horizon and a cloudless, robin-egg blue sky.

"The sign was right. This is a beautiful view," said Andreas.

A woman sitting alone at a table under a fig tree waved at them.

"That's Eleni." Tassos waved back and they walked to her table.

She looked about Andreas' age and had the Greek woman's traditional fancy for *décolletage* revealing dress, in this case a white sleeveless blouse. Aside from that national custom she was discreetly dressed in a knee-length dark-navy skirt and mid-heeled navy pumps. She was virtually indistinguishable from any other serious Greek businesswoman. With one exception: her hair was the bright copper color of an Irish setter and curly as a Shirley Temple doll.

Eleni stood. "Hi, uncle." She exchanged kisses with Tassos on both cheeks and shook hands with Andreas.

"Uncle? She's your niece?" Andreas pointed at two men standing by the kitchen. "Let me guess, those two are your cousins."

Tassos gestured no. "The one to the right is Eleni's father, and the other is her brother."

"He's not really my uncle. He's just such close friends with my father that I've called him 'uncle' all my life."

As they sat down Andreas mumbled to Tassos, "You're paying."

The father and son came over with water, biscuits, and coffee, and after exchanging hugs and introductions left them alone to talk.

"So, uncle, what is the 'sensitive' subject you want to discuss with me?"

Tassos smiled. "I see your career has made you all business. Whatever happened to, 'Hello, how are you?'"

She laughed. "I know how you are. My father told me all about Maggie, and since I know you're here with the famous Chief Inspector Andreas Kaldis, who's marrying Lila Vardi this Sunday on Mykonos in the wedding of the season, I assumed you're both anxious to get to what's on your mind."

Andreas looked at Tassos. "I take back what I said before about Eleni being your niece. She must be your daughter."

"I should have only been so lucky." Tassos leaned over and pinched Eleni's cheek. "Andreas, tell Eleni 'what's on your mind.'"

Eleni sat back in her chair and focused on Andreas.

"If you'll excuse me I'm rather new to your family. I don't mean to sound rude, but could you give me a little background on what you do at the Foundation. It might make it easier for me to explain what I need to know."

Eleni looked at Tassos. "He's trying to decide whether he can trust me." She smiled. "But that's fair. I'm personal assistant to the vice-president of the Evangelistria Foundation's commission."

"Who's the President?"

"The Bishop of Syros and Tinos. Whoever is bishop is president by reason of his position. There are ten members of the commission. The other nine are all Orthodox Tinians elected to serve without compensation, and the vice-president runs the day-to-day affairs of the Foundation. You do know what the Foundation is, right?"

"Sort of."

"That's the answer I generally hear, second only to 'not a clue.' And to be honest, that's the way we like it." Shirley Temple flashed a glorious smile.

Andreas smiled back. "Okay, let's start from 'not a clue,' just so that I don't have to interrupt you with questions by having mistakenly opted for the more advanced lecture."

Eleni took a sip of water. "First let me give you a little background. In ancient times, a temple to the Greek god Dionysus stood on the present day site of the Church of Panagia Evangelistria. When Christianity came to the Cyclades the temple was transformed into a Christian church dedicated to the Virgin Mary and Saint John the Precursor. It was in those early Byzantine years that the Holy Icon of the *Megalochari* came to the island of Tinos to be kept and venerated within that church.

"However, the *Megalochari* dated back to long before Byzantine times. It belonged to the early Christian era and those who've studied it unanimously concluded that it was one of the first three icons painted by the apostle Saint Luke during the lifetime of the Holy Virgin. Many believe the *Megalochari* received its wonder-working power directly from the Holy Virgin herself who blessed it with the words, 'The grace of him who was borne by me, be through me with it.'

"In the mid-10th century Saracen pirates invaded Tinos, burned and leveled the church, and the holy icon vanished. Nine centuries later, in July 1822, a nun named Pelagia from a monastery northeast of the town had three recurring, consecutive Sunday visions of the Holy Virgin instructing her to convince her superiors to order digging at a specific place where they would find the missing holy icon and must build a church to the Holy Virgin.

"Her superiors believed the nun, but the place in her vision was a cultivated field and the owner was away in Constantinople, so excavations did not start until September. Within a matter of days the ruins of the ancient temple were discovered, but as more days wore on without finding the *Megalochari* the islanders lost heart and work stopped. Soon after, a great cholera epidemic struck the island, killing hundreds. The townspeople were frightened, believing they'd brought the epidemic on themselves by not following the Holy Virgin's instructions. They prayed for forgiveness, resumed excavations, and began rebuilding a church on the unearthed ruins.

"On January 30, 1823, a laborer discovered the Holy Icon of the *Megalochari* by splitting it in two with his shovel. On one half was the Virgin Mary and on the other half the Archangel Gabriel. It had been buried for almost 850 years, yet when found was virtually undamaged. A miracle in and of itself.

"Sister Pelagia was sainted in 1970."

Andreas reached for a biscuit, sneaking a peek at his watch as he did. He'd asked for the whole lecture. There was nothing he could do but listen.

"There was another immediate miracle recorded by historians of the time. From the moment the holy icon was discovered no more cases of the epidemic were reported and those suffering with the disease recovered."

Andreas took a sip of coffee.

"The people of Tinos decided to build a much larger church than the one they'd started. Although they would finish the smaller one, work immediately began on what would become our magnificent Church of Panagia Evangelistria. The construction of the church and much of the eastern part of the complex you see today was completed in less than eight years, virtually all of it during Greece's War of Independence with Turkey. That was another miraculous achievement, considering Tinos was a poor island and everything was done while it operated a wartime port, sent its young off to fight alongside other Greeks, and struggled to feed thousands of refugees fleeing here from other islands.

"They transported marbles and columns, mainly from ancient temples on the nearby holy island of Delos but also from Tinos' ancient temple of Poseidon. Marble was mined from our finest quarries and the most famous artisans and technicians of the time worked side by side with unskilled laborers. Passing ships loaded with timber and other building materials generously donated part of their cargo for the construction. And when all seemed lost, the Holy Virgin would provide."

"By a miracle, I presume," said Tassos.

Eleni smiled. "Yes, uncle, 'a miracle.' At one point during the first years of construction the church faced serious financial difficulties and there seemed no choice but to halt work. A large English frigate, anchored at the time off the town's beach, was suddenly engulfed in an unexpected storm driving it toward certain destruction on the rocks. The English vice-consul standing on the frigate's deck saw our church under construction above the town and prayed for salvation from the storm, promising a substantial donation should he be delivered from harm.

"An eyewitness said the storm raged all across the sea but around the frigate there was absolute calm, as if protected by a divine hand. Faithful to his promise, the vice-consul went to the church, gave thanks to the *Megalochari* and one hundred Spanish pieces of eight to the church treasury. His generosity allowed construction to continue."

"That's the sort of money-making miracle Greece could use right now," said a smiling Andreas.

Eleni's tone turned sharp. "I'm afraid the Foundation has done just about all that it can for our country."

Andreas forced a smile. "Uhh, no need to take that personally. It was meant to be funny. A witty observation on our times some might say."

Eleni cleared her throat. "Sorry, I misunderstood. I thought you might be leading into the purpose for this meeting. I'm a bit sensitive on the subject of 'financial miracles for Greece,' it seems they're always tied to some pitch for the Foundation to help 'save our country.'"

"For yet another time," said Tassos.

Eleni nodded. "Yes, the Foundation's treasury has supported the Greek state in famines, floods, earthquakes, and all manner of other things."

"As I recall," said Tassos, "The Foundation offered all of its treasures in support of Greece's defense against the Italian invasion in World War II."

"Yes, the Italians commenced war against Greece by sinking the Greek destroyer *Elli* in a submarine attack in Tinos' harbor on August 15, 1940, a day dedicated to celebrating the *Megalochari*. The Foundation responded by dedicating all of its resources toward Italy's defeat.

"But the Foundation has always been there for our country. Right from the beginning we helped establish its national fleet. We were born out of the same times and our histories are interwoven. The very discovery of the *Megalochari* was taken as a divine sign that Greece's fight for independence was just." She shook her head, "But what our country faces today is well beyond our resources."

"And just what are those resources?" said Andreas.

Eleni turned to Tassos. "Is that what this meeting is all about?"

"Whoa," said Andreas. "Greece's financial problems have nothing to do with why we're here. I want to know what the Foundation has because we're worried someone wants to steal it."

Eleni stared at Andreas. "You can't be serious."

"As a matter of fact he is," said Tassos.

"I can't believe anyone would try to steal the *Megalochari*. Yes, during the day it is on display for all to worship and embrace. It must be. That is its purpose. But when not, it is locked in a safe. It is never out of sight or unprotected. Not since it was stolen."

"Stolen?" said Andreas.

Eleni nodded. "Once. One hundred and seventy years ago, on December 15, 1842 to be precise. An ex-convict passing through Tinos saw the holy icon draped in jewels and gold. Around midnight, after everyone was asleep, he used a rope to drop into the church and stole the holy icon, its gold and jewel offerings, and whatever other precious articles he could find." Eleni crossed herself.

"The next morning the theft was discovered and the town went wild. Patrols scoured the island and rallied Tinians to find the thief. Every available ship circled the island to cut off the thief's escape.

"He'd made it to the northwestern tip of the island, a quarter-mile from the neighboring island of Andros, and tried to convince some sailors to take him there. But they couldn't agree on a price. A patrol found him around noon drinking at a spring. They searched him and found silver articles he could not explain, so they brought him to the governor of Tinos for questioning. The thief confessed and showed them where he'd hidden the holy icon and everything else he'd stolen."

Tassos smiled. "I assume they obtained his cooperation through modern methods of police interrogation."

"Probably," smiled Andreas. "Yours."

"He was sent to prison and died there, insane. Since that robbery, as I said, when not on display the *Megalochari* is locked in a safe."

"I don't mean to sound disrespectful, but in the hundred and seventy years since that robbery bad guys have gotten a lot more sophisticated," said Andreas.

Eleni shrugged. "We've had no more problems of that sort."

"So far. What else does your church have to steal besides the icon?" said Andreas.

She looked at her uncle. "I feel uncomfortable talking about that sort of thing without the permission of my boss. After all the Foundation is a private institution."

"What is there you can tell me?"

"You still haven't told me 'what's on your mind,' and since I can't tell you what 'else' might attract a thief without first obtaining my boss's permission, what if I tell you how the Foundation works? Maybe that will help you with your unstated questions."

Andreas smiled. "Sounds like a place to start."

"The founders of the Church of Panagia Evangelistria were forward thinkers who established a separate legal entity making Panagia Evangelistria neither a monastery nor a parish church. Its independent status as part of our Evangelistria Foundation was established by an act of the Greek state in 1835 and confirmed by royal decree in 1851. The Foundation's operations are run by that ten-member commission I mentioned before, and its administration and management are under the supervision and control of the Greek state, not the Greek Church. Employees are appointed by the commission and paid out of the Foundation's treasury. The Greek Church does not intervene in the administration of Panagia Evangelistria and the clergy hired to exercise religious duties in Panagia Evangelistria are employed and paid for by the Foundation, not by the state as with other Greek clergy.

"The Foundation derives its income mainly from donations, the performance of ritual celebrations and rites, legacies from deceased donors, the sale of offerings, and rents from properties."

"Are you saying the Greek Church has no say in what the Foundation does with its money?" said Andreas.

"Essentially, yes."

"That must make the Greek Church really happy."

"Same answer, 'essentially yes.' The Foundation's aims include religious, and we support pious clergymen and their families in need when there is no one else to help, and many of the clergy we helped have risen to positions of influence in the Greek Church. The Foundation also makes significant voluntarily contributions to the clergy's pension fund and insurance, supports missionary activities outside of Greece, maintains and supports all of Tinos' church organizations and parishes, and assists churches all over Greece affected by calamities. And our non-religious aims are in keeping with the good works of the Greek Church."

Andreas caught himself nodding at the thought of how adept the Foundation was at keeping the Greek Church happy.

"We have supported our country in times of need, but also provided aid to those beyond our borders affected by natural disasters and war. On Tinos we have built or subsidized practically every school and related facility, granted college scholarships to poor but promising students no matter where in the world they chose to study, offered financial aid to the poor, sick, old, and incapable of working, created an old people's home, helped finance the hospital, offered dowries to indigent girls, and supported the poor nuns of Saint Pelagia's Kechrovouni Monastery.

"Most people outside of Tinos don't realize all that we do for our island. In order for the Foundation to do its good works we rely upon the continuing generosity of our visitors and pilgrims, so the Foundation does what it must to make their stays pleasant. The Foundation has been behind most major public works projects on Tinos. In 1926 we funded the creation of an aqueduct system to replace the island's reliance on wells, and thirty-five years later financed a new water distribution system. We're responsible for the large avenues connecting Panagia Evangelistria to other parts of town, and in one way or another financed virtually every significant road-building project on the island. Major funding for Tinos' man-made port and modern quay came from the Foundation, as did much of the funding for the power plant and high-tension distribution network bringing electricity to most of the island. Plus, we constructed hostels for pilgrims and help pay for many public services, such as fire fighting. The list of what the Foundation does for Tinos is endless."

"Is there any part of life on Tinos not touched by the Foundation?" said Andreas.

"You mean that matters?" She smiled.

"*Touché.*"

"The Foundation tries to be low-key. Its purposes are good works. And everyone connected with the Foundation knows that everything we have we owe to the Holy Virgin."

"You mean the *Megalochari*," said Andreas. "I don't mean to be disrespectful, but without the holy icon Panagia Evangelistria would be just another church, impressive yes, but no longer a major draw for pilgrims and their offerings."

Eleni started to say something, but Andreas put up his hand to stop her. "Honest, I respect what the Foundation does, but it's all based on one very real and *por-*

*table* holy icon." Andreas cleared his throat. "And that makes your church the target for what we have reason to believe is some very serious harm planned by some very bad guys."

Eleni raised her voice, "What are you talking about?"

Andreas looked at Tassos. "Can we trust her?"

"Stop being cute, Chief Inspector."

"I stopped being cute years ago. I just want to know if you feel obligated to tell your boss or the commission what I'm prepared to tell you?"

"Depends."

"'Depends' doesn't work for me. I need an absolute 'no,' at least until we get a better handle on what's going on."

"How can I agree to keep a secret like that from my boss if it's as important as you say?"

"Trust me, it is important. But if you tell your boss, he'll tell my boss, and that will end any chance your uncle and I will find out what's supposed to happen before it does. All I can tell you is that whatever is planned is serious enough to get two men incinerated."

"Are you saying the murder of those two *tsigani* brothers was related to a plot against our church?"

"I certainly wouldn't bet against it."

Eleni looked at Tassos. "What should I do, uncle?"

"I'll tell you what I always say when someone asks me that question. But this time I actually believe it. 'I think it's best for you and everyone who might get hurt that you tell us what you know before it's too late for us to help.'"

Eleni bit at her lower lip. "Do you really think there's something to this?"

"Enough for us to be here," said Tassos.

Eleni ran her fingers through her hair. "Okay, Chief Inspector, I promise not to tell anyone, including my boss, until you say it's okay."

Andreas looked at Tassos. Tassos nodded.

Andreas said, "We understand that recently an unusually high number of *metanastes* have come here looking for work and are willing to do so for whatever wage gets them the job."

"There are a lot of new faces working on the island these days but I have no idea what they're paid. At the Foundation we employ mostly Tinians in our office but there are many *metanastes* working on our construction projects. After all, it seems they're the only ones willing to do hard labor these days."

Andreas smiled. "For the time being. So, how are offerings to the church holding up in these times of crisis?"

"Not sure why that's relevant, but I can tell you that in hard times many seek out the *Megalochari* who otherwise might not."

"It's okay if you don't want to tell me numbers. After all, it doesn't take a genius to count the people crowding daily into Panagia Evangelistria, multiply that by an estimated average value per offering, and conclude that there's serious wealth passing to the church every day. And since much of what's being offered is in the form of precious metals and gems, there has to be a place to store it all. Not every offering can stay draped around the *Megalochari*. The pile would reach the roof. And then there are all those offerings of oil and candles to contend with."

Andreas shook his head. "Remember that transient foreign thief you talked about who took a shot at stealing the icon?" Andreas tapped his right index finger on the table. "At this very moment you have an island filled with transient bad guys who I can assure you are a lot worse than that first *Megalochari* thief ever was. And I can also promise you that whatever escape plan they have in mind won't have them hanging around Tinos waiting to make a deal with local sailors."

"What do you want from me?" said Eleni.

"I need to know what's valuable enough in your church to get two human beings who claimed to know about a plan to rob Panagia Evangelistria murdered in a way that made a very public point." Andreas decided not to mention the third dead brother. The woman was already alarmed enough.

"What point?" said Eleni.

"Wish I knew. Then I wouldn't be bothering you as much as I am for help."

"The *Megalochari* is, of course, our most priceless treasure but it is also worthless to anyone trying to sell it."

"Not so," said Tassos also gesturing no with his head. "There are mega-rich collectors out there holding priceless missing treasures in secret collections. They'd pay a fortune for the holy icon."

"Plus any number of rich nuts out there, religious and otherwise, who'd love to have the power of the *Megalochari* all to themselves," said Andreas. "And let's not forget ransom. Can you imagine what the Foundation would pay to get the holy icon back?"

"I can assure you all of that has been considered and appropriate safeguards are in place." Eleni sounded defensive.

"And in case you're wrong?" said Andreas.

Eleni stared away. "There is also the Foundation's art collection of icons, relics, paintings, sculpture…so many priceless things that I cannot possibly put a value on them." She turned back to Andreas. "And, yes, places where the offerings and treasures are stored. Some are kept until they're sold to help fund the Foundation's purposes and others are saved for the true treasures they are."

"In other words," said Andreas, "the Foundation has a lot to steal."

Eleni nodded.

"Can you think of any other potential targets on the island?" said Tassos.

"Many. There are some very wealthy families on Tinos."

"Let's just stick to the churches," said Andreas.

"The Catholic Church's presence here is more significant than almost anywhere else in Greece. Its Cathedral of Saint Nicholas sits down by the harbor, just below Panagia Evangelistria, and half of the more than one hundred-twenty formal churches on Tinos are Catholic, plus a third of the hundreds of others. There is also a Jesuit monastery."

"But I assume none of those other churches, Catholic or Orthodox, has anywhere near your church's wealth," said Andreas.

Eleni nodded. "There are miracle-working icons in other churches, but none as sacred and revered as the *Megalochari.*"

"Have you noticed anyone or anything unusual recently?" said Tassos.

"Not that I can think of. But the island's in the midst of preparing for the Feast of the Assumption of the Virgin on August 15th. It's Tinos' busiest day of the year by far, all in honor of the *Megalochari.* There's so much happening around this time that even the unusual seems usual."

"Would that be a likely day for a robbery?" said Andreas.

Eleni gestured no. "I can't imagine a worse one. Tinos is a madhouse on August 15th. The population swells to such unmanageable levels that Tinians have virtually ceded that celebration to visitors and treat July 23rd, the anniversary of Saint Pelagia's third vision of the icon, as their time to celebrate the *Megalochari.*"

"What happens on the 15th?" said Andreas.

"The holy icon is paraded from Panagia Evangelistria down Megalochari Avenue to a marble rotunda at the base of the hill where a service is conducted. Then it's carried back up the hill to the church along the same route. It's a procession filled with religious dignitaries, government officials, military, and police surrounding the holy icon. Frankly, if you're looking for a festival on which to pull off a robbery, July 23rd would be a far better choice." She smiled.

"Why July 23rd?" said Andreas.

"Both involve dignitaries and the same amount of police, but when the procession reaches the harbor on the 23rd it turns left and continues to the edge of town where the holy icon is transferred to nuns from Saint Pelagia's convent. They take the *Megalochari* back to their convent in a taxi and keep it there until eight that evening when it's walked back to Panagia Evangelistria in a two and a half hour procession.

"There would be a lot more chances to pull off a robbery then, but that festival day has come and gone and the Megalochari is still here." Eleni forced a smile and looked at her watch. "Oh my, I've got to run. I'm late for a meeting with my boss." She stood up.

Andreas stood and handed Eleni his card. "Thank you. You've been very helpful and I hope we'll have the chance to talk again."

As Tassos rose he said, "If you think of anything else, no matter how crazy or insignificant it may seem, please let me know."

"I will, uncle." Eleni kissed Tassos on both cheeks. She reached out to shake Andreas' hand. "And, Chief Inspector, good luck."

"Good luck? With what?"

"Your wedding. Have you forgotten?" She laughed. "That's not a very good sign."

Andreas shook Eleni's hand. *Ain't that the truth.*

# TEN

IT WAS FAR too early for lunch when Eleni left Tassos and Andreas sitting at the table, but her father and brother insisted they stay "a bit longer" and try what was "special on the menu for lunch," amounting to enormous portions of *sklavotyra*—round cheese balls surrounded by fresh figs, sun dried tomatoes, and capers—deep fried meatball-shape *keftedes* made of tomatoes, and an omelet of local sausage and cheese.

Tassos said it would be rude not to accept. Andreas said it would just be fattening.

"So, what do you think of my niece?"

"I'm getting married."

"I thought you were over that *macho* every-woman-can-be-mine Greek bullshit."

"I am. I'm just not over busting your balls." Andreas smacked Tassos lightly on the side of his arm. "She's very impressive. Smart, but a bit anxious. I wonder if she'll tell her boss about our conversation?"

Tassos gestured no. "Not a chance. She knows we're trying to help. But I can't blame her for being nervous. There's a lot at risk. Just a few years ago the Foundation put sixteen million euros into renovations and a new museum addition. We're talking big business here."

"How in the world did the Tinians manage to keep the Foundation and all that wealth out of the hands of the Greek Church?"

"They're very resourceful people. It's the only island that successfully resisted Turkish rule. The Venetians were in charge during most of those Ottoman times, keeping Tinos a Christian oasis amid Turkish domination of the Aegean. When the Turks took over about a hundred years before our War of Independence it was in a negotiated way giving Tinians rare economic and religious privileges. Turkish fleets had to stay twelve miles away, Tinians could wear traditional dress and build and run their own schools and churches. Four elected Tinians governed the island and the only permanent Turkish residents there were the governor and the judge. Tinos was the economic center of the Cyclades and had its largest population. It was called 'Little Paris.' Things only fell apart for Tinos at the end when political infighting and corruption allowed the Turks to assert themselves in the final decade or so before the revolution."

"And then came a nineteen-hundred year-old piece of wood to the rescue." Andreas shook his head.

"Back then it was only seventeen-hundred years old, but if we're talking rescue, I'll take whatever help is out there to save Greece today," said Tassos.

Andreas smiled. "Do you think the *Megalochari* is what they're after?"

"Hard to say. Like you said, the holy icon is portable, making it relatively easy to steal. But all that church's gold, jewels, paintings…" Tassos rolled his hand off into the air, "would be a lot less difficult to sell than one of the world's most revered religious treasures. And then there is all that valuable stuff in churches all over Tinos that would be far easier to rob than Panagia Evangelistria."

"Maybe the plan is to rob them all?" said Andreas.

Tassos gestured no. "Pirates tried that for centuries. Tinians are quite accomplished at hiding their treasures."

"It just doesn't makes sense to me why anyone would bring so many bad guys together on a relatively small island just to rob a single church, no matter how rich it is. There has to be more to it than that. And why is everything coming to a head so close to August 15th?"

"Maybe it's just a coincidence? I have to agree with Eleni that it seems a lousy day to pick for a robbery."

"Yeah, it's 'lousy' if you're going after the *Megalochari*. But what if the target is something else? Say, like *everything else*. With everyone focused on the procession it might be the perfect day for hoisting the rest of the church's treasures."

Tassos shrugged. "I think perhaps we should take a different approach and stop trying to figure out what the bad guys could steal."

"A 'different approach' for you generally means head-busting," said Andreas.

"I don't think we have to go that far, but I do think it's time we pay a visit to some of Tinos' more recent émigrés and try to find out what brought on their sudden attraction to life on this island."

"Like I said, head-busting."

TASSOS AND ANDREAS had been driving around for almost a half hour looking for a dovecote. When you mentioned Tinos to a native Greek the second most likely thing to come to mind were the island's nearly one thousand intricately designed, two-story stone dovecotes. They were almost as famous as the Church of Panagia

Evangelistria. Decorated in elaborate geometric patterns and natural shapes like cypresses and the sun, dovecotes were mainly built on slopes near water and cultivated areas in the eastern and central parts of the island where the wind offered easy takeoffs and landings to attract the doves. Venetian occupiers had introduced them to Tinos in the 18th Century to satisfy their taste for pigeon meat and provide a high quality source for fertilizer.

But Tassos and Andreas weren't sightseeing. They were looking for one dovecote in particular. Eleni's father told them that a Tinian contractor specializing in restoring dovecotes had a lot of new *metanastes* working for him. He remembered seeing some that morning on a farm on the far side of a village "about twenty minutes from here if you know the way."

"That must be it." Tassos pointed to an open field off to the left fenced in by centuries-old stonewalls. Beyond the field sat a traditional white Cycladic farmhouse and next to it on the left a freestanding, two-story white and natural stone dovecote. The bottom story was for storage and gathering bird droppings, the top for the doves. Three men in work pants and tee shirts stood smoking in front of the dovecote.

"Must be break time," said Andreas.

Tassos looked at his watch. "More likely boss-is-away time."

"Well, let's see if we can get their attention." Andreas made a left onto the gravel and dirt path leading up to the farmhouse. He turned on the flashing roof lights as the cruiser approached the men.

"What are you doing that for?" said Tassos.

"To see how they react. And to let them know this

is a formal visit. May as well start getting the word out that there's a new sheriff in town."

"You and those damn American westerns." Tassos opened the door before the car stopped and stepped out the instant it did, keeping the door between him and the men. "Okay, guys, over here." He pointed to a spot in front of the car.

The men looked at each other as if waiting for one of them to make the first move.

"Like I said, 'over here.' And that means *now*."

One man started forward and the other two followed.

Andreas stepped out and leaned against the driver's side of the car. "You, in the green tee shirt. Drop the hammer."

The man kept coming and Andreas put his hand on his holster. A dark-skinned, wiry man in a white tee shirt turned to the one in green and said something in a language Andreas did not understand. The man dropped the hammer.

"Those two don't understand Greek," said the man in the white tee shirt.

"That could be dangerous," said Andreas not taking his hand off his holster.

"Papers please," said Tassos.

The man in white said something to the other two, before reaching into his pocket and pulling out a passport and working permit. The other two men did the same.

"Is there a problem officer?"

"I'll let you know," said Tassos.

"Call them in," said Andreas. "Let's see what we have on them."

Tassos reached into the car for the transmitter. Andreas slowly walked to the front of the car and leaned back against the hood. He was about six feet from where the men stopped. He stared at them for about a minute without saying a word.

"Where are you from?" said Andreas.

"They're from Romania, I am from Pakistan."

"I meant in Greece."

"Athens."

"How long have you been here?"

"Since the end of June."

"And the other two?"

"I don't know, about three weeks I guess."

"Before those two *tsigani* were murdered?"

The man shrugged.

"How come you speak Romanian?"

"I'm good with languages. It's how I got this job. I do the translating and they do most of the work." He smiled.

"No outstanding warrants," said Tassos. "But some very interesting arrest records. For all three."

"How'd you manage to get working papers?" said Andreas.

The man didn't respond.

"Let me guess," said Andreas. "No convictions and friends in very low places."

Andreas got off the hood and stepped to within a foot of the man's face. He was a head shorter than Andreas. Andreas patted him on the shoulder. "You and GADA's Chief of Special Crimes are about to become a 24/7 item."

"Why are you hassling me?"

"Why are you on Tinos?" said Andreas.

"To work."

"Please don't tell me you found religion," said Tassos.

"Sort of."

"*Stop messing with us*," shouted Andreas.

The two Romanians looked at each other.

"You better tell your buddies to relax."

The Pakistani said something to the others. "We came here because we heard we'd find work. And that if we kept out of trouble the pay would always be good."

"Who told you there was work?" said Tassos.

"Someone I met in Athens."

"Got a name?" said Tassos.

The man gestured no. "He said he was a 'priest.'"

Andreas nodded. "A priest." Andreas cleared his throat. "Was he dressed like a priest?"

"No."

"Did you meet him in a church?"

"No. I met him on Sophocleos Street, just off Pireos."

He'd just named perhaps the worst section of street in central Athens, a veritable no man's land of 24/7 vice and crime. "He acted like one of those missionary types seeking converts but he wasn't talking religion."

"Then how did you know he was a priest?" said Andreas.

"I didn't say I knew he was a priest, I said that's what he called himself."

"And you left Athens to come here based on that?"

"No, I checked with friends who were working here. They said it was legit."

"I'm sure you have names for your friends," said Tassos.

The man looked around, as if for a place to run.

"You won't make it," said Andreas. "The names." He knew they'd be phony.

The man mumbled out four names. Tassos wrote them down.

"And where can I find those friends of yours?" said Andreas.

"I don't know."

"Like I said, 'stop messing with us.' Where do they hang out when they're not working?"

He looked at his feet, then up at Andreas. "Promise me you won't tell them I told you."

Andreas smiled. "Why, of course."

He gave the name of a bar that he said was not far from the port. "We meet there after work."

"You mean at three in the afternoon?" said Tassos.

"No, after they're done at work. They don't work construction. They work at hotels and tavernas in town. I meet them around eleven at night."

"And what do you do between now and then?" said Andreas.

"Sleep, get something to eat."

"How can you afford to hang out in a bar every night?" said Tassos.

"I don't understand?"

"What do you do for money? You sure as hell can't afford it on what you make doing this sort of work."

"I make good money. Like I said, that's why I came here. All I had to do was find an 'honest job,' and no matter what my employer pays, as long as I 'behave' I get enough extra cash each week to bring my earnings to nine hundred euros a month." He nodded back at the Romanians. "They have the same deal."

Andreas hoped his jaw hadn't dropped. A new cop only made eight hundred a month and, after ten years on the force, twelve hundred.

"Who's paying all that money?" said Andreas.

The man shook his head. "Don't know. All I know

is I'm in charge of paying the brothers on my crew and every Friday a package arrives at my place with envelopes for each of them. I just turn over the envelopes."

"I bet you do," said Tassos.

"Better believe it. A few who tried stealing from their brothers are no longer on the island. That sort of thing isn't tolerated."

That's the second time he used the word "brothers," thought Andreas.

"What happened to them?" said Tassos.

The man shrugged. "I never asked. But everyone got the message."

"From whom?" said Andreas.

"Like I said, I don't know."

"Does mister 'I don't know' have a name?" said Tassos.

"I never heard one."

"What have you heard?" said Andreas.

The man looked back down at his feet. "Some *tsigani* were talking on a job I had when I first came here, before I hooked up with these guys, and they didn't know I understood their language."

"Are you now going to conveniently tell me they're the ones who were murdered?" said Andreas.

The man looked up. His eyes were twitching. He gestured no. "But they were from the same clan, and they were talking about someone who'd come to their camp the night before to meet with their clan leader."

"And?" said Andreas.

His voice was weak. "They talked about the visitor as 'the money man behind everything.'"

He glanced back at the two Romanians, leaned in toward Andreas, and whispered, "They called him the 'Shepherd.'"

"I HAVE TO call Lila and tell her I won't be making it back to Mykonos tonight." Andreas smacked the steering wheel with the heel of his right hand. "When I tell her I have to spend the night in a bar she's going to kill me."

"Wait to call until we're back in town. We're almost there," said Tassos.

"Are you worried about me driving while talking on my mobile?"

"No, I'm worried about the potential nuclear fallout streaming through your phone."

Andreas glanced at the sea. "I wish I had a handle on what's going on. Those three guys at the dovecote weren't churchgoers, but nor were their arrest records for violent crime."

"Yeah, they're more the sort I wouldn't trust around my *ya-ya's* silver than killers."

"Your grandmother's still alive? She must be a hundred-fifty."

Tassos placed his open palm in Andreas' face, a slightly less endearing gesture than the middle finger. "I'm sure they'd steal anything they were told to take."

"Then why are they so well-behaved?"

"The easiest answer is that they're waiting to be told what to do," said Tassos.

"But why make everything so goddamned complicated? Someone who calls himself a 'priest' recruits the Pakistani out of the closest place we have in Athens to hell, and once the guy's here he keeps his 'brothers' in line by delivering them envelopes of cash without skimming a single euro."

"That last part probably qualifies as a true miracle," said Tassos.

"And who the hell is this 'shepherd'?" said Andreas.

"All very good questions, which is precisely why to-night will be a late one."

Andreas pulled up in front of the police station.

Tassos opened his door. "I'll find us a place to stay in town. Say 'Hi' to Lila. And tell her that for sure *I'll* be there on Sunday."

This time it was Andreas who flashed an open palm.

# ELEVEN

EVERY TOWN HAS places where its dirty work gets done. The more elegant communities may try to keep them out of sight, the less so may not care, but they all have them. It's where one goes to find the materials and labor necessary to keep a town running and to dispose of what is no longer desired.

It's also where you're most likely to find the grittiest *metanastes* bars. Tinos was no exception. The bar the Pakistani described was off a road winding up from the port, tucked behind a trucking company warehouse yard filled with broken pallets and an electrical supply depot filled with giant, empty, wooden cable spools.

Tassos and Andreas were sitting in a car parked across from the bar and alongside a chain link fence enclosing the depot. The bar looked as if in another life it might have been a two-bay gas station.

"We're going to fit right in there," said Andreas.

"Yeah, sort of makes me wonder why we bothered to switch to an unmarked car. It would take a blind man not to spot us," said Tassos.

"Not even sure he'd miss us."

"Maybe they'll think we're just two lonely guys out looking for companionship?" Tassos smiled.

"Only a madman with terrific long term health insurance goes into a strange *metanastes* bar to hit on their women."

"Kill joy. But this place might be different. It looks pretty mixed, ethnically."

"I still doubt that two Greek cops asking for identity cards will fit their welcome profile."

"Look on the bright side. At least Lila still loves you."

"Not so sure about that either. When I told her I wouldn't be making it back to Mykonos tonight all she said was, 'Fine, see you Sunday.'"

"That was it?"

"No, there was the distinct 'click' of the call being terminated."

"Ouch."

"The good news is that it prepared me for the sort of welcome we'll likely get in there."

Three men walked past their car, staring in at them as they did, and went inside the bar.

"Well, for sure now everyone in the bar knows we're out here." Andreas looked at his watch. "It's almost midnight, might as well go in."

Tassos was the first to reach the front door. Two men in a hurry brushed past him coming out of the bar. It was the Romanians from that afternoon.

Andreas put his hand on the chest of the taller of the two. Both men stopped. "What's the hurry?"

The man looked frightened. "No understand."

"Where's your friend, the interpreter?"

"No understand."

Andreas dropped his hand from the man's chest and waved him on. "A waste of time talking to them."

"Even if we could understand them," said Tassos.

Inside, the place was pretty much as it had seemed from the outside. The front door opened into a tiny room with a badly stained marble-top bar to the right.

In front of the bar were three empty metal bar stools, and behind it a cash register, a top sliding beer cooler, a loudly humming refrigerator, and a decade old television angled for whoever worked behind the bar, not the customers. A fat, clean-shaven, middle-age man in jeans and a crisply ironed work shirt sat alone at the only table. There was no one else in the front room.

Past the bar was a larger room filled with beat-up taverna chairs tossed together around a dozen cheap, round-top plastic tables. More light seemed to be coming into that room from the moon through the windowed garage doors on the left than from two dim ceiling fixtures along the wall to the right.

The word that came to mind was *dive*. But there were people at every table. And all of them were staring at the two new arrivals.

Andreas stopped next to the fat man's table. "What's the matter, you anti-social?"

He looked up. "I prefer not to mix with my customers." He spoke perfect Greek.

"You own this place?"

"Yes."

"Nice place," said Andreas.

"It's a shit hole," said the man. "But it makes more than it ever did as a garage."

A wiry, middle-age woman, with more salt than pepper hair and dressed in black except for dirty blue bedroom slippers, shuffled out of the big room carrying a tray filled with empty beer bottles. She squeezed by Tassos and went behind the bar.

"Are you two going to order anything?" said the guy at the table.

"Two beers," said Tassos. "Mind if we sit with you?"

The man raised two fingers to the woman and pointed at Tassos and Andreas.

"Like I said, 'I prefer not to mix with my customers.'"

Andreas pulled up a chair and sat down. "We're not customers, we're cops."

"No wonder those two guys ran out of here so fast."

"Where were they sitting?"

He pointed at a table with two women.

"Are they regulars?"

"The women are, the guys just started coming in a couple of weeks ago."

"What's your name?" said Tassos.

"Petros."

"You're Greek?" said Tassos.

"Born and raised on the island. Just like my great, great, great, great-grandparents and all my family since then."

The woman put two beers on the table and walked away. No glasses were offered.

"You get quite a mixed bag of customers in here," said Tassos.

"Everyone but the Greeks."

"Business looks good," said Andreas.

Petros shrugged. "Not complaining."

"Those two who left. Do they hang out with anybody in particular?" said Andreas.

"Some Pakistani." Petros looked around. "I don't see him." He looked at his watch. "He's usually here by now."

Guess he figured we'd show up tonight and decided to pass, thought Andreas. "Did those murdered *tsigani* brothers ever come here?"

Petros gestured no. "So, that's why you're here. Lucky me you're not interested in any of my live customers."

"*Tsigani* come here?" said Tassos.

"Not many."

"Where do they go?" said Tassos.

The man shrugged. "No idea. But you might ask those two." He nodded toward the same two women. "They were in here the night after the two dead ones were identified, chattering away about how they'd 'partied together with the brothers.' In case you haven't guessed, they're working girls."

"Thanks." Andreas stood up and picked his beer off the table. He looked at Tassos. "I'll be right back."

"Knock yourself out, Romeo," smiled Tassos.

The women were at a table in the center of the room. One was decidedly taller than the other, but both were blond, blue-eyed and chubby. Probably Polish, and definitely not smiling at Andreas.

"Hi ladies, mind if I sit down?" Andreas sat without waiting for an answer. "So, come here often?" He flashed a smile.

The women said nothing.

"Permit me to introduce myself. My name is Andreas Kaldis, GADA's Chief of Special Crimes. But you probably already know that. I've been telling that to a lot of people these days. In fact, I told something like that to a friend of your two friends who just ran out of here."

The tall woman said something to the other in Polish.

"Uhh, uhh," said Andreas. "Ladies, you're in Greece and courtesy requires that you speak Greek. If you don't I'm going to have to take you to a place where someone will speak to you in Polish. But it may take a day or two to find a police officer that does. Don't worry, the state will provide you with a place to stay until then." He smiled.

The tall woman said something else in Polish.

Andreas smiled. "That you can say. I know 'fuck you' in Polish. So, do we have an understanding?"

The women looked at each other. "Yes."

"Good. Now tell me what happened just before your two friends hurried out of here."

The short woman said, "Three men came in and went around telling everyone two cops were sitting in a car out by the fence. That's when the two guys said something to each other and left."

"What did they say?"

"I don't know. They didn't speak Polish and I don't understand Romanian," said the short woman.

"Then how did you understand the three men who said there were cops outside?"

"What do you mean?"

"Did they speak in Polish?"

"No, Greek."

Andreas smiled and turned to the tall one. "So, you're the one who speaks Romanian."

She stared at the tabletop.

"Remember what I said before about arranging housing for you until I find a colleague who speaks Polish. Would you like me to do that for you now?"

She looked up. "How did you know I spoke Romanian?"

"Because your two friends who left don't speak Greek. Someone had to translate for them. Now, what did they say?" Andreas did not smile.

The woman swallowed. "That the two cops outside had to be the same ones who were trying to question them that afternoon about the murdered *tsigani* brothers. They said the Pakistani they worked with 'must have told the cops about the bar.'"

"What else did they say?"

"Something about not wanting to be here if you and your partner were looking for some farmer the Pakistani told them about. Then they got up and left. Didn't even pay for our beers."

As if on cue the woman in the slippers was at the table and pointing at the ladies' nearly empty bottles. Andreas nodded, "Yeah, another round. 'Farmer?' What the hell were they talking about?"

"I don't know," said the tall woman.

"Me either," said the other.

Andreas took a sip of his beer. "So, tell me about the Carausii brothers."

"What do you want to know?" said the short one.

"Oh, for starters how about who killed them and why?"

"No idea."

"I'm shocked," said Andreas. "So, let's take a different approach. When and where did you first meet them?"

"About a month ago through *tsigani* friends at another bar." The short one gave Andreas the name of the bar and said it was close to the brothers' *tsigani* camp. "They were nice boys. Close to our age, too."

"Yeah, not like the other ones," said the tall one.

Andreas took that to mean their johns. "So, the four of you partied together?" He used the street word for their business.

"Yeah, a couple of times," said the tall one. "Like I said, they weren't like the others."

"Did they pay?"

The tall girl looked down. "Yes."

"But not as much as the others," said the short one.

"What did you talk about?"

The women took turns talking about things completely irrelevant to Andreas but obviously very relevant to them. Things like how none of the four felt accepted by the larger world, how lucky they were to still be alive doing what they had to do to survive, and their doubts at any future beyond today.

"And just when things seemed to be getting better for them, look what happened. We're all cursed," said the tall one.

"What do you mean 'better'?" said Andreas.

The short one answered. "They said something about getting their big break. That some 'major guys' in their old Athens neighborhood would owe them 'big time.'"

"For what?"

"Information."

"About what?"

"Someone on this island was of great interest to people back in Menidi."

"Ever hear a name or a description?"

"Only once, but nothing I understood. They made some sort of toast to a foreign sounding name. I thought it was Romanian. A lot of *tsigani* speak Romanian."

The tall one said, "I don't remember them saying a name in Romanian."

"Never?" said Andreas.

She shrugged. "Not that I remember. And they stopped seeing us right after telling us about their 'big break.'"

"Why did they stop seeing you?" said Andreas.

"They found new girls," said the short one. "Greek

girls. Tall, skinny, model types but with big tits. The kind men fantasize about."

"We can't compete with that type," said the tall one.

"No offense intended, but I'm surprised those girls would be interested in *tsigani*," said Andreas.

"We thought the same thing, especially since the girls looked the expensive type, way out of the brothers' price range," said the tall one.

"Were they pros?"

"Is there a difference between doing it for cash or for an expensive dinner and clothes?" said the short one.

Andreas smiled. "Where'd they meet?"

"No idea. But one night we showed up at that *tsigani* bar to meet them and a friend told us they'd just left with two girls. We saw them there the next night with the girls, but they didn't talk to us. And then they were dead."

"Do you have names for the girls?"

Tall one gestured no. "As if they would be real if we did."

Andreas nodded. He asked them all sorts of other questions through two more rounds of beers but no answers yielded more information than they'd already told him.

"Thanks, ladies, and if you think of anything else, please let me know." He handed the tall one his card. "Like any more about that 'farmer' your Romanian friends were talking about." He smiled because he'd used the Polish word for farmer.

"What do you mean?" said the tall woman.

"You told me that the Romanians said I was asking about some 'farmer.'" This time Andreas used the

Greek word for farmer. The same one the tall woman had used.

She shook her head. "No, if that's what that Greek word means in Polish I didn't mean that. What I meant was a word for something different." She looked at the short girl and said a word in Polish.

The short girl said, "Sheep farmer."

"Shepherd?" said Andreas.

"Yes," said the tall girl. "That's what the Romanians meant when they said you were looking for a *cioban*."

The short girl's eyes widened. "Wait a minute, that's the name the *tsigani* brothers were toasting the last night they were with us. Don't you remember, they said, 'To the *cioban*,' because something they knew about him was about to make them 'very rich.' You and I talked about it later. We even toasted to him."

The tall girl picked up her beer and took a swig. "Yeah, I do. So what. Instead they're dead. Life sucks."

Andreas had nothing to add.

"Did you get anything from the fat guy while I was talking to the ladies?"

They were sitting in the car next to the fence and Andreas had just finished telling Tassos what he'd learned from the two women.

"A lot of local gossip about everything but what I wanted to know. From what I could tell he probably owns all this land." Tassos waved his hand above his head. "Lives off the rents and spends his nights sitting at that table watching the cash register and his sister doing all the work."

"Thought she might be his wife," said Andreas.

"That would be the traditional way a Greek love

story turns out, but this time it's the spinster sister. Her boyfriend jilted her twenty-plus years ago and she's been wearing black ever since. In mourning for her lost love. Petros said that place is all that keeps her going."

"Terrific. I'm so happy for them both. Let's get back to the hotel."

"What about that *tsigani* bar? Don't you think we should check it out? Find out what we can about the two new women in the dead brothers' lives."

Andreas looked at his watch. "It's nearly three, and I've got to be on a 7AM boat to Mykonos or Lila will kill me. I'll get Yianni over here first thing in the morning to help you chase that down. And while you're at it, maybe you could find out how those two Romanian guys knew the Pakistani had told us about the 'shepherd'?"

"My guess is that after we left they threatened to beat the hell out of him if he didn't tell them what he'd whispered to you. Not smart to whisper when the people you don't want to hear already can't understand you. It makes them think what you said was very important. And about them."

"What the hell, we're never going to wrap this up before the wedding anyway." Andreas started the engine.

"Spiros will be pissed."

"Tough, let him close the case. I have no intention of turning up as the next dead body by screwing up all of Lila's wedding plans."

"Don't worry." Tassos smiled. "Lila's smart enough to make sure you'd never be found."

Andreas looked at Tassos and slowly said in Polish, "Fuck you."

# TWELVE

ANDREAS MADE THE seven AM ferry. It arrived thirty minutes later at Mykonos' new port. Andreas saw Lila waiting for him on the pier. She was wearing the Greek island woman's official August uniform: sundress, sandals, and sunglasses.

Andreas was one of the first down the ramp and off the boat. He waved and when Lila waved back he yelled, "See, I made it. I'm a man of my word."

Lila waited until he was almost up to her. "Yes, fear is a terrific motivator." She smiled and kissed him.

He put his arm around her back and gave a quick squeeze to her butt. "Missed you."

"You, too."

"Where's Tassaki?"

"Your mother and mine are watching him." Lila smiled. "Frankly, I think he'll be spoiled rotten by the time we get back. Get in, I'll drive."

Instead of turning right out of the port toward the main road that led to the middle of the island and on to her parents' home, Lila turned left.

"Where are we going?" said Andreas.

"It's a surprise."

"Great, I like surprises." He squeezed her thigh.

The road ran up a hill alongside the sea and down again into Aghios Stefanos, a tiny beachside village reminiscent of earlier times. As the jeep passed by the shorefront Andreas said, "Are we going there?" He pointed to a taverna dead ahead.

Lila smiled and said, "Nope."

The jeep wound up another hill, made a few switch back turns, and headed down into Houlakia, a shoreline area famous for round, salt-and-pepper color stones the size of soccer balls. Andreas liked it best for its remote, rugged proximity to the sea.

"I know where you're headed," Andreas said. "To my friend Elena's. That's wonderful, I haven't seen her in ages."

As Lila drove past the entrance to Elena's hotel she said, "Nope, wrong again. You'll just have to wait until the wedding to see her."

They were now at the base of Mykonos' northwest coastline hills, directly across from Tinos. Their heights were home to arguably the most spectacular views of sunset on the island, and once barren hillsides now resembled photographs he'd seen of Los Angeles' Hollywood Hills, *sans* green.

Lila turned right and drove as straight up the hill as the roads allowed, jumping from asphalt to gravel to dirt and back again without slowing down.

"I sure as hell hope you know where you're going."

"Me, too," said Lila. "I haven't been up here in years, but a friend who lives somewhere around here told me the road goes through."

"Through to where?"

Lila smiled. Thirty seconds later Andreas had his answer when the jeep popped over the top of a rise. Directly in front of them was Mykonos' only lighthouse, the *Armenistis*.

"Great choice," said Andreas.

"The ride's not over yet."

Originally built in 1891, *Armenistis* was now fully automated, which meant there no longer was a need to maintain the access road for a lighthouse keeper, and what did remain of that road was now as bad as any on Mykonos. Even the ruts had ruts. Lila plowed straight ahead without slowing down. At fifty feet from the lighthouse the road split in two, with the part to the left edging along a cliff until seemingly disappearing over it into the sea. Lila went right, up toward the front of the lighthouse.

"Good choice," said Andreas.

At what looked the last conceivable place to stop Lila kept going. She squeezed along an overgrown path between the lighthouse wall to the left and a sheer drop to the right.

"Having a good time?" said Lila.

"If you're trying to make the wedding seem less frightening you're doing a damn good job."

Beyond the wall the road abruptly ended, but with just enough room to make a sharp turn to the left. Lila made the turn and stopped. They were on a peak behind the lighthouse overlooking the sea.

"Now I see how they get those cars on the very tops of mountains for television commercials. You drive them." Andreas looked out his passenger side window. "Is it safe to open my door or will it be one hell of a big first step."

"Are we talking about marriage again?" Lila pinched his belly. "There's a picnic basket and blanket in the back seat. Grab them and let's enjoy our breakfast with a view."

He paused.

"Don't worry about turning around," said Lila. "This connects over there with the road that split off where I turned up to the lighthouse." She pointed to the end of a wall in front of the jeep.

"I see you've been here before."

She smiled. "Many times. And leave your phone in the car. This is our time."

Lila led him up the few steps to a terrace at the base of the lighthouse. She took the blanket and hung it over a low wall edging the terrace. They sat dangling their feet off the wall, quietly holding hands and staring out to sea.

The winds had not yet picked up, leaving the sea all one deep blue. No white puffs of waves, or any of the silver-gold sheen that comes to the water at sunset. The only splashes of different color were the reds, whites, and yellows of toy-like passing ships, the distant ones more distinguished by their wakes than their forms. At this height the Aegean seemed a canvas, not real, with muted brown islands drawn on in perfect symmetry: Delos, Rhenia, Syros, Tinos and the faint shadows of far off others.

"I thought you could use a transition." She put her arm around his neck.

"From murder to marriage?" Andreas smiled and kissed her cheek. "Tinos looks so different."

"In what way?"

"Every way. From up here it's just a timeless, distant shape. No good, no bad, no people. Nothing of any concern."

"Good, let's keep it that way for the next forty-eight hours."

Andreas smiled.

Lila swung her feet back onto the terrace and opened the picnic basket. "Croissant?"

"What else do you have?" Andreas swung around.

"All sorts of things. Orange juice, coffee—"

"Uhh, uhh, that's not what I want." He put his right arm around her back and pulled her close. He kissed her ear, her cheek, her lips, and moved his left hand to her breast.

Lila pushed back. "Are you crazy? Someone will see us. There are houses all around here. Most of them with telescopes hoping to catch tourists getting carried away with just what you have in mind."

Andreas smiled. "We're not tourists." He dropped his hand to just below the bottom of her dress and began lightly stroking her thigh with his fingers. "Besides, this is a sunset place and all anyone in those houses can see is our backs."

She didn't move and he moved his hand higher. "And this is the last alone time we're going to have until way after midnight. Unless, of course, you want to announce to your family when we walk into their house that their future son-in-law would like some private playtime with their daughter before becoming sociable with a wider audience."

Lila leaned in and kissed him. "Okay, sweet talker. But not here." She stood up. "Come."

She picked up the blanket and led him around the building to its far northeast corner, where the angle of the lighthouse cut off the view from everywhere but the sea.

"Dare I ask how you know about this spot?" said Andreas.

Lila stuck out her tongue. "I was married once, remember." She spread out the blanket. "If anyone comes by here walking their dog I will kill you."

"Don't worry, I have a gun in the jeep. They'll never live to tell a soul."

Lila was standing in the middle of the blanket. She kicked off her sandals and motioned for Andreas to come to her. He pulled off his shoes as she pulled her sundress up over her head. She wore no bra and her panties were barely visible. Andreas started to fumble with his pants but she took his hand and pulled him toward her. He kissed her cheeks, her neck, her shoulders. He reached again to undo his pants, but Lila stopped him to do it for him. He yanked his shirt off over his head.

Lila ran her fingernails along his bare chest and down his belly to the insides of his thighs. Instinctively, Andreas spread his legs wider. Lila smiled and dropped down to bring her lips onto him. He ran his fingers through her hair. As Lila moved she groaned but ultimately it was Andreas who had to pull away. She struggled to get her mouth back around him, Andreas held her away and moved to press her onto her back, but she had him lie on his instead.

Andreas watched from below as Lila lifted and dropped her hips above him. Slowly and deliberately she moved, never taking her eyes off of his and refusing to let him do anything but lie there and stroke her body. He ran his thumbs and forefingers around her nipples as her thighs drew up and off of him, then back down again. He pressed his hand against her belly when he sensed her coming. He felt his own rush of heat and knew he could hold off no longer. He thrust up with his hips as she pressed down, but she moved at a pace he could not match. He relaxed and let her ride him into orgasm. She wouldn't stop moving and he wouldn't stop coming as she muffled his mouth with her hand smiling, "Shhhh, my love."

She leaned down to kiss him and Andreas held her. They did not move until Lila rolled off to lay beside him on the blanket.

"You're amazing," said Andreas.

Lila said. "You owe me for that."

"What are you talking about?"

"If you have to ask why…"

"I was more than willing to be on top."

"The concrete is too hard."

Andreas leaned up on his elbows. "Are you telling me that in the midst of all that passion you were actually thinking about concrete?"

She looked at him. "You better believe it. You get carried away. On a mattress it's terrific. On concrete it's black and blue marks." She rolled over on her side and stroked his belly. She smiled. "Don't worry, I'll give you plenty of chances to make this up to me." She was running her hand down his belly when a tan Labrador came bounding onto their blanket.

Lila screamed. Andreas jumped up and shooed the dog away. Lila grabbed for her dress and pulled it in front of her as a man in a Panama hat and white linen coat came around the corner.

"Excuse me," he said. "I was looking for my dog."

"Not here," said a naked Andreas blocking the man's view of Lila.

"So sorry," said the man tipping his hat and flashing a smile. "May the rest of your life be as lovely as your morning."

Andrew watched the man walk away before turning back to Lila. He expected she'd murder him any second. Lila was sitting up on the blanket holding the dress up to her face. She seemed to be shaking in a fit of tears.

"I'm sorry, it was all my fault. I never should have made you do this." He wasn't sure what else to say. He sat next to her, reached up, and pulled the dress down from her face.

Lila was laughing uncontrollably. "'May the rest of your life be as lovely as your morning.' The man's a prophet!"

Andreas smiled. Lila kissed him as she laughed and Andreas started to laugh. Then it was all laughter, on and off the blanket and each other. Concrete be damned, this was going to be *their* lovely morning.

ANDREAS HEARD HIS phone before they reached the jeep but by the time he got to it the ringing had stopped.

He looked at the number. "It's Tassos. I better call him before we start driving. Reception's spotty out here."

Lila smiled as she opened the jeep's door. "You don't have to make excuses. I've things to do, too. I'm getting married tomorrow." She reached inside for her phone, blew Andreas a kiss, and walked back toward the lighthouse.

Tassos picked up on the first ring. "Where the hell have you been?"

"It's a long story."

"Well, it better be a damn good one," said Tassos.

"So much so that it's going to take the best you've got to put me in a bad mood."

"The Pakistani is dead. Throat cut and dropped at

the front gate of the Tinos dump. Perfectly placed so no one could miss him."

Andreas throat tightened. "When did it happen?"

"The body was discovered about two hours ago by a municipal worker who opened the place. Not sure yet when he was killed but the best guess is sometime last night after we got back to the hotel."

"Motherfuckers."

"They found your card on him."

"Yeah, I gave it to him."

Andreas heard Tassos clear his throat. "It was jammed into his mouth. With 'revenge or death' written across your name."

Andreas felt his heart skip a beat.

"This is serious," said Tassos.

*"You don't have to tell me that."* Andreas looked to see if Lila heard him raise his voice. "Someone's decided to make this personal."

"And we don't have the slightest idea who this Shepherd is."

"Or if whoever that might be is the one behind the killings," said Andreas.

"All we have on the Shepherd is that it's paying *metanastes* and *tsigani* to work and behave," said Tassos.

"So far." Andreas paused. "Where's Yianni?"

"Not back yet. When his boat docked, I sent him off with a local cop who speaks Romanian. They found the Pakistani's two Romanian buddies working at that dovecote as if nothing had happened. Doubt they're involved or know any more than we do, but Yianni is bringing them back to town for questioning."

"As soon as Yianni's back have him call me. I want him out to the murdered brothers' *tsigani* camp turning screws on that clan leader and any other son-of-a-bitch we can think of who might be tied into the bastards behind this. If that clan leader won't cooperate, we'll shut down their goddamned camp and ship every single *tsigani* in it off the island on the next boat. I've had enough of this shit."

Tassos paused. "There's something I'd like you to seriously consider before answering."

"What's that?"

"Your wedding is tomorrow. I'm sure the bad guys know it, too. I think you should have a simple, private wedding ceremony at Lila's parents' home. Call off the one at the monastery. It's too public. The party we can handle. It's going to be at their home anyway and we can control who gets close. But a wedding in the middle of Ano Mera on a Sunday evening…no way to control that, and we have to assume these guys are capable of anything."

"Are you talking car bombs?"

"Who knows? Anything is possible if they feel threatened by you."

Andreas walked to the edge of the cliff. "If that's what Shepherd has in mind there could be rocket propelled grenades dropping into the middle of the party. Or during the ceremony for that matter."

Andreas was looking in the direction of the sea but his mind was nowhere near it.

"My instinctive answer is, 'There's no way I'll let scum control my private life.' But my more considered thought is, 'This isn't just about me, Lila should have a say in the decision.'"

Andreas turned to look for her. She was sitting on the wall talking on her phone.

"But I'm not going to ask her. This is not the first, nor will it be the last time my life is threatened. We both know that sooner or later the press will find out that the church ceremony was cancelled because of 'terrorist threats.' Our wedding will be the headline story in every tabloid wanting to scream 'no one is safe from terrorists.'

"We've all heard the stories about cops' wives being approached in supermarkets and told that if their husbands testified against captured terrorists their children would be killed or maimed. How can we expect those cops to stand up to that sort of threat if I cancel the church ceremony and prove to all of Greece that even I, GADA's Chief of Special Crimes, fear that this sort of scum can reach out and harm my family? That I'm afraid I can't even protect my own wedding.

"But forget about the message that sends to our countrymen. It will plant a seed of fear in Lila that I cannot bring myself to do. Besides, I know Lila will say I should do whatever I think best. And going forward with the ceremony as planned is what I think is best. Telling her any of what we're worried about would only frighten her, not change things."

"Great speech," said Tassos. "But your canary in the mine just died. We're now at a whole new level of urgent activity. They've practically told you, 'you're next.'"

"You're not making this any easier," said Andreas.

"I'm not trying to, asshole."

Andreas paused. "Okay, I agree we can't ignore the threat. I know it's real. I'll call Spiros and suggest that with all the government ministers attending the wedding we treat the ceremony as a potential terrorist target. He'll love showing his fellow ministers how he's pulling out all the stops to protect their safety."

"Not to mention his own," said Tassos.

"As opposed to some insignificant cop's sorry little ass."

"Great," said Tassos. "But if you don't mind I'd like to have some of my cops from Syros hang around the wedding."

"Thanks. I appreciate it."

Andreas could hear Tassos fluttering his lips. "What is it?"

"I sure as hell hope you're right about going ahead with the ceremony at the monastery."

Andreas saw Lila walking toward him. "Got to run. I'll call you from Lila's house. And just to be safe, don't hope, let's *pray* that I'm right."

# THIRTEEN

ABOUT A WEEK before the August 15th festivities begin on Tinos, thousands of *tsigani* start arriving. Whether or not there were enough hotels to accept all of them was never the point, for *tsigani* preferred to live in tent camps. And the hotels liked it that way. The town was surrounded by *tsigani* camps, each vying to be as close to the *Megalochari* as possible for *tsigani* revered the Virgin Mary as their mother, and did so with a passion transcending all else, including traditional *tsigani* ways. The word most often used by Tinians in describing *tsigani* behavior during that period was "respectful."

That was not the word one would expect a certain swarthy, broad-shouldered *tsigani* clan leader to use in describing detective Yianni Kouros. Kouros was standing with the leader and two other *tsigani* at the edge of a highway bordering a tent camp set up on an abandoned building lot above the port town.

"What part of what I just asked you don't you understand?" said Kouros.

"We don't have papers for every child in the camp," said the leader.

"Then how do I know you're not kidnappers?" said Kouros.

"We're *rom*. We don't have papers for all of our children. You know that."

"Like I said, 'Then how do I know you're not kidnappers?' This is serious. If I don't have papers on every minor in this camp in my hands in fifteen minutes, I'm arresting all of you."

The shorter of the two other *tsigani* laughed. "Yeah, sure you are. So what is it you want? A little spending money, a taste, a special favor perhaps?" He nodded toward a girl leaning against the redbrick skeleton of the abandoned building.

"No, asshole, I want you leaning over a barrel in Kordydallos pulling the train for your cell block."

The man stepped toward Kouros.

"Another step and your journey to butt-hole heaven will start with my foot up your ass."

"You talk big," said the other man. He was a head taller than Kouros.

"Come to think of it," said Kouros to the tall man, "he's probably more used to having you up his ass. Or is it the other way around?"

The tall man lunged at Kouros, but lost his balance when Kouros stepped to the side and delivered a sweeping kick to the back of his knee.

"Try that again asshole and you'll be walking with a stick for years."

The short guy reached behind his back.

Kouros smiled at him. "For your sake I hope that whatever you come up with in that hand, little man, is tasty. Because you're going to end up eating it."

The leader said something in a language Kouros did not understand. The two others shouted at him in the same language. He shouted louder. The short guy brought an empty hand around from his back, and tall guy limped over next to him.

The leader said, "What is all this about?"

Kouros nodded toward tall guy. "About a year for him for assaulting a police officer." He pointed at short guy. "And about six months in a beauty parlor for that one. As a public service. He's one ugly bastard."

"*Stop*!" said the leader. "I don't know why you're trying to start something with us. We are peaceful. We have come here to honor our Blessed Virgin." He and the other two crossed themselves.

Kouros shook his head. "Not this year, pilgrims. You're off the island on the next boat to Athens. All except for tall guy here. He's got a court appointment."

"Why?"

"You don't take very good care of your children."

"What are you talking about?"

"The Carausii brothers."

"They weren't children."

"See, that's just the kind of attitude I'm talking about. They were God's children, even if none of you gave a damn about them."

The leader said nothing.

"Like I said, you have no respect for children. So, get your people packed up. The boat leaves in two hours."

"What if we refuse to go," said the leader.

Kouros smiled. "Trust me on this, you won't want to do that."

The leader said something to the two others. They argued for a few seconds, but they left, leaving the leader alone with Kouros.

"I heard that police from Athens were on the island asking about the two brothers."

"Did you now? And from whom did you hear that?"

"A lot of people. Your Athens cop friends didn't make a secret of what they were looking for. No more than you did asking questions this morning. Word gets around fast."

"Well, then give me some words I want to hear," said Kouros.

The clan leader shrugged. "The brothers' murders were a tragedy."

"Yeah, I can tell you're all choked up."

"You are a very difficult man."

"This is my nice side. Stop messing with me. *Why were they murdered*?"

"No idea."

"Fine, start packing."

"I'm not afraid of you."

"I'm not asking you to be."

"Then we will not leave."

"Do you have any gasoline?" said Kouros.

"Gasoline?"

"Yes, or should I have it brought up from town?"

"What are you talking about?"

"We're going to have to burn your trucks, tents, and everything else in the camp. Public health hazard."

"You can't do that!"

"File a complaint with the E.U." Kouros looked at his watch. "Better get busy. One hour and fifty minutes until the boat leaves or the barbeque starts."

The leader mumbled a *tsigani* curse Kouros recognized.

Kouros smiled, reached into his pocket and pulled out a lighter. "And I don't smoke." He flicked the lighter and held the flame up to the clan leader's face. "Your choice," and repeated the curse.

"Two women, Greeks. They were the last ones anyone saw with the brothers."

"The ones from the bar?"

"Yes."

"Who were they?" said Kouros.

"No idea, women like that read too much. They think the *rom* life is romantic. Our boys take advantage of them. Can you blame them?" The leader smiled.

"What do you know about the women?"

He shrugged. "The boys said they liked sex."

"I see the brothers liked talking about their women."

"When the women aren't *rom* we all do. It's a tradition. But the brothers were here only the first morning after they met the women. They never came back to camp after that."

"What else did the brothers say about them?"

"Nothing that mattered."

"What does that mean?"

"Most girls like that want booze and drugs before sex. These two weren't into drugs. They wanted to get high on something else. The brothers said it was weird at first, but after they got used to it they said they liked it."

"What was 'it'?"

"Gas. The women called it 'laughing gas.'"

Kouros swallowed hard. "Where'd they get the gas?"

"They didn't say."

"Where are the women now?"

"No idea. No one has seen them since the brothers disappeared."

"Any ideas on who might have wanted the Carausii boys dead?"

"If I did, I'd have told the other cops who asked me."

Kouros paused. *I sure as hell hope Chief knows what he's doing having me say this.* "I want you to tell Shepherd that my boss wants to meet."

The clan leader's head jerked slightly to the left.

"I'm sorry, did I say something that surprised you?" said Kouros.

"I don't know what you're talking about."

"Just tell Shepherd that GADA's Chief of Special Crimes wants to talk about three dead Carausii brothers, a dead guy in Syntagma, and a Pakistani who passed away unexpectedly this morning. I'm sure Shepherd knows how to find him, but if not, here's my card."

The clan leader took the card without looking at it. "What do you want me to do with this? I have no idea who you're talking about."

Kouros shook his head. "Then I'm very sorry for you, because the rest of the message to Shepherd is, 'If you don't agree to meet, it will be a very lonely August 15th for you.' There won't be a member of Shepherd's flock left on Tinos. And the first to go will be guess who?" Kouros pointed a finger at clan leader's forehead.

"By the way, if you don't pass along the message what do you think is going to happen to you when Shepherd finds out that everyone disappeared because you didn't do what my boss asked you to do?"

Clan leader put Kouros' card in his pocket.

"Good choice," said Kouros.

The clan leader's face seemed paler. "Your boss may regret that I made it."


"*NITROUS OXIDE!*" ANDREAS said the words so loudly Kouros might have heard them on Tinos without his phone.

"Those two women definitely set up the brothers," said Kouros.

"They might even be the killers," said Andreas. "Once the gas knocked them out, all the women had to do was get them into the van, drive it to the spot, and torch it."

"One could have driven the van while the other followed to pick up her partner."

"But somehow I just don't think it's going to be that easy," said Andreas. "Either way, we've got to find those two women."

"They've disappeared, no one has seen them or has any idea who they are."

"Not surprised. I think you should go out to that *tsigani* bar—"

"I already did, Chief. Like I said, no one has any idea who or where they are or can give a description better than big blond hair and even bigger tits."

"What I was going to say, Yianni, was 'I think you should go out to that *tsigani* bar' and locate every building in the area with a field of vision that includes the bar and anywhere customers might park. Then check out the buildings to see if any has a surveillance camera that might have caught something. It's about time we get lucky."

"Will do. But what are you going to do if the Shepherd calls?"

"Be very surprised," said Andreas. "I can't imagine he will, but I wanted to shake things up, see if he makes a mistake."

"In my book, five murders already qualify as pretty well shaken."

"You're starting to sound like Tassos."

"Hey, I did what you asked and my guess is he's going to pass along the message. I just think that with all the distractions of the wedding you're too easy a target for the bad guys."

"Don't worry about me. Just chase down those cameras and make sure you're over here tomorrow in time for the wedding."

"Wouldn't miss it for the world. Bye."

Andreas was alone in their bedroom. He put the phone in his pant pocket.

Those bastards are terrorists. "Goddamn them. Goddamn *us*." He'd said the words out loud but not loud enough for anyone to hear.

As far as Andreas was concerned, Greece really blew it in 2004. It had the best minds from the CIA, MI6, Mossad, and everywhere else in the world focused on preparing Greece for the Olympic games, sharing their latest ideas and information on how to protect against terrorism. It was Greece's perfect chance to learn, to build on what the world's best counter-terrorism experts were giving it. But what did Greece do? Nothing. Let it all go to waste. Now the terrorists were back and Greece had no idea where to begin dealing with them, much less finding them. And no one else in the world seemed to care anymore. At least not as much as they once did. They all had their own problems.

Maybe I made a mistake calling out Shepherd so close to the wedding? Andreas shook his head and swallowed. No reason to chase that thought. If Shepherd takes the bait and comes after me, there's nothing more I can do about it than I am. Andreas bit at his lower lip.

He looked out the window. The sea was calm. Tomorrow should be a beautiful day. He crossed himself.

"No, no. I want something larger. That is too small."

The salesgirl said, "I'm sorry, madam, I misunderstood. You said you wanted a silver bowl for a wedding gift, so I showed you our most popular size for that occasion. What size are you looking for?" This was the shop of the most famous jeweler in Greece, an international legend and a man of impeccable reputation.

The woman in the huge sunglasses, a tent of a long sleeve dress, and an enormous floppy hat pointed to a display of hammered silver bowls and pitchers, a hallmark of his craft. "I'll take that one, the big one." It was a foot and a half in diameter and about six inches deep.

"Certainly, madam. Here, let me tell you the price."

"It doesn't matter. My employer said I am to buy 'the biggest.'"

"Yes, madam. Is there a card you wish to put inside?"

The woman nodded.

The salesgirl put out her hand to take the card.

"I'll put it inside myself. I'm supposed to arrange it in a particular way." She shrugged. "Those are my instructions."

The salesgirl smiled. "As you wish." She took out a large red box, symbolic of the store, arranged the bowl amid tissue paper, and pointed the customer to the bowl. "Please."

The woman said, "Could I trouble you for a filter coffee?"

"No trouble at all. How do you like it?"

"Medium sweet, no milk. Thank you."

The salesgirl left. By the time she returned the box was closed. She carefully placed the coffee on a table by the customer, finished wrapping the gift with ribbons, put it into a large red shopping bag, and sealed the bag shut.

"How will you be paying?"

There was no attempt to bargain. The woman

reached into a large beach bag she carried on her shoulder and handed over cash in the exact amount owed. The salesgirl noticed the woman was wearing white cotton gloves of the sort used to handle silver and had not touched her coffee.

"Thank you," said the salesgirl. "Will there be anything else?"

"Could you possibly have this delivered to the church? My employer doesn't want to carry it there herself." She spread her arms and shrugged her shoulders again. "What can I say, those are my instructions?"

The salesgirl smiled. "I understand. We all have our bosses. Where is the wedding?"

"In Ano Mera at—"

"The Vardi-Kaldis wedding?"

"Yes."

"No problem, our owner is invited and he's bringing presents from several of our clients with him. Consider it done."

The woman smiled. "Thank you. You have no idea how happy you've just made my employer."

# FOURTEEN

EVERY FAITH CONSIDERS marriage a primary rite. Most also accept it as the excuse for one hell of a party. The Greek Orthodox Church was no exception, especially on Mykonos. On the night before a local boy married a local girl, the groom spent the night partying with his guy friends, and his bride with her girlfriends. It was sort of a "kids' last night out," for after the wedding locals no longer called them "boy" and "girl," but "man" and "woman." Lila and Andreas, though, were not locals, and no one was likely to call them kids, so they skipped that ritual and stayed home Saturday night. Not that either got much sleep.

Andreas was on the balcony outside their bedroom staring at the sea. Sunlight was breaking over the horizon bringing color back to the sky.

Lila came up to him from behind and pressed her face against his bare back. "Nervous?"

"About becoming your husband until death do us part, forever and ever, until the sun stops rising in the morning, until—"

"So, you are."

"A bit." Andreas smiled.

"Me too." Her tone sounded serious. "But it'll be worth it for the party."

Andreas turned around and hugged her. "Do you know how much I love you?"

"Yes, but feel free to tell me again."

"Words fail me."

Lila laughed.

"So, where do I have to be today and when?"

Lila cocked her head. "Why, do you have plans?"

"Nothing more important than whatever you want me to do."

"Nice try, Kaldis. What's on your mind?"

He didn't want to tell Lila about the threat. He also didn't want to lie. So he decided to break his rule against discussing his cases with her. But just a little bit. "The Tinos murders."

"What about them?"

"Until now the case only involved *metanastes* and *tsigani* bad guys killing each other. That's the perfect way to keep Greeks from caring much about it. We love pointing fingers, blaming others for our troubles. We blame immigrants for crime, drugs, and change to our way of life. We ignore that few in this country want to pay taxes, corruption is everywhere, and only the honest seem to get screwed. Our system is 'every man for himself,' so why are we surprised when new arrivals want to get their piece of the action, too? But, for some, violence is the only way they know, they're not sophisticated or connected enough yet to do it with a pen, and that makes the lot of them perfect scapegoats for whatever goes wrong here."

Lila stared at him. "You're on a rather cynical rant for so early in the morning. Even for a cop."

"I know, but it's as if someone were taking great care to make sure that only *tsigani* and *metanastes* were involved. Then out of the blue two Greek women pop up as potential killers. It just doesn't fit. Or, more likely, I'm missing something."

Lila snuggled her head against his chest. "As long as you don't miss the wedding. Only twelve hours to go."

Andreas kissed her on the forehead. "I think you've mentioned something like that to me before."

"Hopefully the message has sunk in." Lila leaned back and smiled. "But, I think for this morning you should go off and play with your buddies. You're way too serious for our wedding day."

TASSOS AND ANDREAS were sitting in a scruffy, virtually deserted *kafeneion* by the edge of Ano Mera's town square, thirty feet and a few steps up from the entrance to the monastery of Tourliani. Most of the town's early rising locals seemed to have headed to the harbor for their Sunday morning coffee and gossip. Ano Mera was the other town on Mykonos, with roots tracing back to 4500 BC. It sat at the island's rural heart, five miles from the far better known harbor town bearing the island's name.

Tradition had it that two monks from the nearby island of Paros, while escaping pirates, found asylum in a small Ano Mera church and decided to establish a monastery there. During its construction in 1542, an icon of the Virgin Mary was found on a beach on the west side of the island. According to legend, each time the icon was placed at another site, at night it miraculously found its way back to the monastery and now resided within its walls as the revered icon of *Panagia Tourliani*, the protector of the island.

"You know, if someone were interested in stealing a priceless icon it would be a lot easier going after this one than the *Megalochari*." Tassos nodded in the direction of the monastery.

"Or practically any other icon in Greece. But the *Megalochari* is the big prize."

"So, how do you want to handle security?"

Andreas bit at his lower lip. "Shut everything down as much as we can." He pointed to the town square only a few feet away from where they sat. One-story buildings, virtually all tavernas, surrounded a flagstone square containing a broad walkway encircling a slightly elevated central oval set off from the rest of the square by a foot-high stonewall. Within the oval children played and the town celebrated civic events and festivals.

"That walkway connects to the municipal parking lot at the far end. So does the path running along the front of the monastery and behind the tavernas on this side of the square. Vehicles aren't supposed to use them, so let's make sure we keep them out."

"Yeah, but locals drive where they want."

"Not tonight," said Andreas.

"What about people who want to get inside the church?"

Andreas shrugged. "No ticket, no laundry. If they're not on the list they don't get in."

"I see, you're planning on doing everything you can to piss off the locals," said Tassos.

"I'm not running for mayor, I'm trying to keep my family alive. Which reminds me. I want a metal detector. Put it over there," Andreas gestured with his hand toward an archway containing a brass-trimmed red door. It was the only door on the monastery's four-story front wall. "And make sure to put it on the outside of the archway, before anyone can get into the courtyard and anywhere near the church."

"How the hell are we going to find a metal detector, get it here, and up and running in time for the wedding?"

Andreas looked at his watch. "When is Yianni arriving?"

"On the noon boat."

"Good, tell him that as soon as he lands to see the director of airport operations and borrow a metal detector."

"The airport can't do that, it needs the detector to screen departing flights."

Andreas shook his head. "We'll borrow one that they use for charter flights heading out of Greece. They fly out of a different gate than domestic flights."

"I get it, let's just delay and piss-off the tourists, not the Greeks," smiled Tassos.

"No, wiseass, charters use two detectors, domestic only one." Andreas waved toward the monastery. "And let's make it obvious security is tight. I want to discourage as many bad intentions as I can, or at least force an uncalculated risk that might give us an edge."

"Things could be set to happen when you come out of the church service."

Andreas patted Tassos' forearm. "I'm trusting you to make sure there aren't any snipers out there. We don't want another Syntagma."

Tassos pointed to the sky. "If we want to get really paranoid, there could be a drone, one of those unmanned aerial vehicles, drifting around up there just waiting to take out the whole village."

Andreas smiled. "Let's just hope whatever might be planned is of human rather than divine proportions, and that nobody's perfect, which should make the bad guys as worried as we are that something might go wrong." Andreas stood up. "Come on, let's take a look inside the monastery."

"I already checked it out, and three of my Syros cops are stationed in the courtyard under orders not to allow anyone in without personal clearance from the abbot. Even then, no one gets to go anywhere in the monastery without one of my guys for company."

"Sounds good. Thanks." Andreas looked at his watch. "I guess I better get back to Lila's. Our families are expecting me. Last chance to bust my you know what before the wedding." He grinned.

Tassos nodded toward the monastery's front door. "Come on, let's take a quick look inside anyway. You won't get a chance to appreciate the beauty of the place later. That's what happens when it's your own wedding."

Or funeral.

THE WHITEWASHED RECTANGULAR monastery of Tourliani, with its blood-red dome, soaring intricately carved marble bell tower, and fortress-like perimeter walls cutting it off from the rest of the village was the architectural highlight of Ano Mera.

Andreas and Tassos stood in the stone and marble courtyard between the archway and the church. Stairs and doorways off that cloistered space led to the warren of rooms so common to monasteries. There seemed an endless number of places to hide.

Andreas waved his right hand at the doorways. "You've checked them all?"

"Every single room, nook, and cranny. The abbot assured me we saw places even the Germans didn't find during World War II, and I don't have to tell you how hard they looked. Whoever and whatever is in here belongs here."

Andreas drew in and let out a breath. I hope so, he thought.

Tassos pointed at the church. "Let's go take a look inside."

Andreas followed Tassos the few steps to the church's central doorway, but stopped just outside.

It was a Byzantine church at the center of the mon-

astery, built upon eight slabs of marble. Three front
doors opened onto three aisles draped with silver in-
cense holders and crystal chandeliers. Each aisle led to
the massive, elaborately carved, 18th Century baroque
*iconostasis* separating the main part of the church from
the altar area. The *iconostasis* was covered in icons and
gold, and painted with red, green, and gold leaf flowers.
Carvings of the apostles ran along its top and above it
all loomed the elaborately painted dome of the church—
with its four small windows.

Tassos pointed up at the windows in the dome. "We
checked, and the only thing that could get an angle on
anyone inside is a bird. And if one craps on you that's
good luck."

"Thanks, I could use it," said Andreas.

"Why are you standing outside?"

Andreas grinned. "For sort of the same reason you
want a bird to target me. It's bad luck to go inside your
church on your wedding day without your bride."

"Never heard that one before."

"Probably because I just made it up." Andreas
laughed. "But doesn't it seem an unlucky thing to do?"

Tassos laughed. "No argument here. If that's your
instinct, go with it. Mine is to light a candle."

Andreas nodded. "Make it a big one."

THEY WERE ALMOST back to Lila's parents' house when
Andreas' phone rang.

Andreas looked at his phone. "It's Yianni." Andreas put
his phone on speaker. "I'm here with Tassos. What's up?"

"I found three cameras that were operating during
the period of time we're interested in. I've been looking
at tapes non-stop since four this morning."

Andreas looked at his watch. It was almost ten. "You must be bored to death by now."

"Not really, amazing the things that go on outside bars at night. Especially in parked cars."

Andreas looked at Tassos. "I'm sure you're not calling just to chat about how easily you get turned on."

"I'll take that to mean you want me to get to the point. I'll make it simple. About fifteen minutes ago, my time, the two Carausii brothers exited the bar with two women."

"Could you make out their faces?"

"And just about everything else. The guys could hardly wait to get them to their motorbikes."

"Spare me the details. Do you think we can get an ID?"

"I've sent the tape off to Athens to see if any of our vice guys recognize the girls as pros or can find someone on the streets who knows them."

"I want a copy, too," said Andreas.

Kouros laughed. "On your wedding day? It might tarnish your view of 'love ever after.'"

"Just bring it, wise-ass." Andreas looked at Tassos. "I'll look at them tomorrow."

"Will do. See you in a few hours. Bye."

Tassos smacked his hands together. "Things are looking up. We finally got a break. Today's our lucky day."

Andreas smiled. "I sure as hell hope so."

# FIFTEEN

ANDREAS MADE IT back with Tassos from the monastery in time to spend most of his Sunday morning playing with Tassaki and reminiscing with Lila's mother and father, his mother, sister, brother-in-law, two nephews, and niece. It seemed the best stories were those that made Lila blush and Andreas threaten to start shooting if another word were said. Maggie, Kouros, more friends, and family started showing up around two in the afternoon. It was fast approaching show time.

Traditionally, when two locals married, several hours before the service the bride, her family, and friends gathered at her parents' home, and the groom did the same at his parents' place. Amid singing, drinking, and nuts symbolizing fertility, everyone pitched in to make sure the groom was readied and the bride prepared. The groom and his entourage, accompanied by musicians, always arrived at the church first, to cool his heels waiting outside for his bride to arrive.

But Andreas was from Athens and staying at Lila's family home, so the only traditions for him to observe were to keep out of Lila's way and make sure that he made it to the church ahead of her. Two hours before the ceremony Andreas told his mother and sister that he was leaving for the church and that they should come with Lila's family.

His mother laughed, calling him a "nervous bride-groom."

Tassos and Kouros left with him.

It was a fifteen-minute drive to Ano Mera, most of it over one-time donkey trails and the last few on the main highway between Ano Mera and Mykonos town. At a road next to a walled-in field running from the highway up to the rear wall of the monastery Tassos slowed to make a turn. Andreas noticed that the access gates to the field were closed and two marked police cars sat in the field.

Tassos jerked his head in the direction of the police cars. "I told them no one gets into that field, and they're to stay put until the ceremony is over and everyone's gone."

Andreas nodded.

Tassos parked at the upper edge of the monastery wall, taking care to block the entrance to the narrow lane running along the front of the monastery.

"That shouldn't be a problem for Lila," said Tassos. "She's coming in from the other side. Does she know what to expect?"

"I told her Spiros went crazy on security, that he insisted on a metal detector and military."

"Did she believe you?" said Kouros.

"I think so. After all, Greek government ministers aren't very popular these days and she knows what an ass-kisser Spiros can be." Andreas waved in the direction of the entrance to the monastery. "Let's see how things are going over there."

The three walked past the monastery's fenced-in garden. Its gates were locked and two uniformed cops stood inside.

"So far so good," said Andreas.

The wedding was called for six-thirty. Guests had been drinking for hours, either at Lila's home or in one of the dozen tavernas surrounding the town square. Cops had been standing in the sun for most of the early afternoon with nothing much more interesting to do than look at each other and hustle an occasional passing girl. They were all young, and Andreas knew they had to be wondering what bad luck had them here, instead of at home with their families or hanging out with friends.

Kouros nodded toward the archway in the monastery's front wall. "I'll check on how that guy's coming along with setting up the metal detector."

"Those kids across from the entrance, are they yours?" said Andreas.

"Yes, they're a crew of homegrown Syros islanders," said Tassos.

Andreas walked over to a half-dozen uniformed cops. "Welcome to my wedding."

The cops straightened up and looked at Andreas.

"I appreciate what you're doing for me. Thank you."

A mixture of nods and "you're welcome, sir" came back.

"Let me tell you what we're dealing with here today. In about an hour this area will be filled with government ministers, members of parliament, business and civic leaders, and, most important to me, my family. To some, those are called 'targets of opportunity.' I don't have to tell you what our country faces. Political assassins, bomb throwing revolutionaries, criminal kidnappers, and terrorists willing to die for their causes. In other words we face the same challenges as the rest of the world."

Andreas cleared his throat. "But we are *not* like others. *We are Greeks*, and we will not allow them to shut down our lives, threaten our family traditions, and attack us in our churches during our most vulnerable moments. No, we will not permit that. *Ever*."

Andreas looked each cop in the eyes and repeated separately, "Do you understand what I'm saying?" Each nodded yes.

"Thank you," said Andreas and he shook hands with each cop.

While Andreas was shaking hands, Tassos walked over to Kouros and listened to him arguing with the metal detector technician. When Andreas joined them Tassos said, "Good thing our prime minister didn't hear you. He might think you're running for his job."

Andreas smiled. "No comment."

Andreas looked at the metal detector positioned outside the archway. It was right where Andreas wanted it to be but Kouros didn't seem pleased. To non-Greeks, Kouros and the technician sounded as if they were about to kill each other. To Greeks it was just business as usual.

"What's wrong?" Andreas said to Tassos.

"Don't worry," said Tassos. "Yianni will straighten him out. The guy wants to leave so he can watch a soccer match."

Andreas nodded. "Oh, that's why I heard Yianni say, 'Would you like your nuts to be my soccer balls?'"

Tassos smiled. "Yes, the boy does have a certain way with words. So, what do we do now?"

Andreas looked at his watch. "Is there anyone inside the monastery?"

"Other than the florist, no. No one's allowed inside

until the metal detector is up and running. Besides, most of the guests will wait outside with you until Lila arrives."

That was Andreas' biggest concern. It was where he, and everyone else, was most vulnerable to attack. Inside, the monastery was a fortress, successfully withstanding generations of marauders of all kinds. It still had the slot above the archway for raining boiling oil and molten metal down on old time bad guys.

But standing around outside the church for an hour or so waiting for his bride to arrive—and tradition always had the bride arriving late—made Andreas and everyone with him easy prey.

The worst thing about the situation was that there was absolutely nothing Andreas could do about it. It was one of the most symbolic moments of the wedding: the groom standing outside the church waiting for the father and mother of the bride to turn their daughter over to him so that the two could enter the church and move on into their new life together as one. That exchange always took place outside the archway. If Andreas suggested a change, even something as innocent as his waiting for her in the courtyard just beyond the archway, it would send a red flag to Lila that something was seriously wrong.

"I'd like to start drinking," said Andreas.

"Me too," nodded Tassos. "But not today."

Andreas shrugged. "Getting married sober was not how I pictured this day."

Tassos laughed. "Coffee?"

Andreas nodded.

Tassos put his arm around Andreas' back and led him up the few steps to the first taverna. Everyone

moved aside to make room for the groom, smacking
him on the back and teasing him as they did. That was
the predictable way for people to treat the groom on
his wedding day. Andreas hoped all else remained that
way. Predictable.

IT WAS NOW six-thirty and Andreas had successfully re-
sisted most of what seemed a thousand proffered drinks.
He had a slight buzz, but nothing he couldn't handle.
Or so he hoped.

The metal detector was up and running, military
were positioned on the far side of the square restricting
access to any building with a line of sight at the monastery, and a mix of cops and soldiers prevented vehicles
from entering an established perimeter around the area.
Everyone entering the monastery had to be on the guest
list, show proper ID, and pass through the metal detector. No exceptions. Andreas had done all that could be
done, or so he hoped.

"Are you ready?" asked Tassos.

Andreas nodded. "As ready as I'll ever be."

"Good, your family just arrived and I think we
should head down to the monastery entrance."

"I'll be right back." Andreas stood and walked toward a door marked WC.

"Nervous!" said a matronly lady at a nearby table.

Andreas smiled. "For sure."

The lady and the others at her table laughed.

The bathroom was illuminated by a single, bare
light bulb over an unframed mirror above a tiny sink.
Andreas pulled a few paper towels from a dispenser,
moistened them, and pressed the wet towels against his
face. He stood quietly holding them in place for a min-

ute before throwing them in a bin. Andreas looked up
and stared at the mirror. People always said he looked
like his father.

"Well, Dad, the day is here. Wish you could be with
us." Andreas cleared his throat, combed his hair, and
adjusted his tie. He took another look in the mirror and
turned to leave. As he opened the door the light bulb
began to flicker and would not stop. Andreas paused
and looked back. "Love you too, Dad."

ANDREAS AND HIS family were standing in a line along
the front wall of the monastery greeting arriving guests.
When Andreas heard blaring car horns he knew Lila
had arrived. He motioned for Tassos to come over to
him and whispered in his ear. "No matter what I'd like
to think, I know I'm going to be out of it from now until
after the ceremony. I'm relying on you."

Tassos smiled. "Don't worry. Just enjoy your wedding." He patted Andreas on the shoulder.

Kouros was in front of the metal detector checking identity cards against the guest list. The florist had
done a terrific job of covering the detector in flowers,
but it still had a serious purpose and a sounding alarm
meant a mandatory, no exceptions, physical search. "Be
courteous, but firm," Kouros told the cops assigned to
do the screening. "If the detector goes off, no one talks
his or her way out of a body search."

Andreas heard the three musicians before he saw
them. One was playing a *santouri* dulcimer hung from
his neck, striking away at its strings with two small,
wooden, cotton-tipped hammers. The two other musicians played accordions. It was the simple, old-style
Mykonian way of arriving for a wedding, and about

the only thing at the moment that seemed simple to Andreas.

That, and his decision on what to wear to his wedding: a midnight blue suit, white shirt, and silver-blue tie. But what to wear was simple only because Lila had picked everything out for him. When Lila told him who designed her dress, "just in case anyone asks," Andreas promptly forgot, but always smiled when the subject came up. He never had the courage to ask her to repeat the name.

But Andreas had been to enough weddings to know that as much as women might like to say otherwise, weddings were significant fashion events for them. Athenians came dressed to impress, and locals to show they could do better.

I sure hope no one asks me who designed Lila's dress, he thought.

Andreas caught a glimpse of Lila's father behind the musicians, then a bit of her mother. As soon as the musicians reached Andreas they stepped aside and there was Lila, linked arm-in-arm between her parents, her dark hair pinned back in flowers.

Andreas felt a smack against his chest. It was the florist jamming the bridal bouquet of white roses into his hands. "You forgot this."

Andreas gave a nervous smile. "Thank you," and wondered what else he might have forgotten. He gave a quick glance at his brother-in-law whom he'd chosen to be his *koumbarous*, an honor akin to, but far more significant than, best man.

The *koumbarous* smiled, and gave Andreas the thumbs-up sign.

Lila and her parents stopped directly in front of Andreas. First her mother, then her father kissed Lila on each cheek before turning to face Andreas. He embraced them both, everyone smiling. Andreas handed Lila the bouquet and they lightly kissed before turning and stepping toward the archway.

"You look terrific," said Andreas.

Lila smiled. "The color is ivory, it's a Lanvin gown, Manolo Blahnik shoes, and Susan van der Linde headpiece and veil—just in case Yianni or Tassos ask. If anyone else does, don't worry. I've got you covered."

Andreas laughed and squeezed Lila's hand. At that instant an alarm went off freezing him in his tracks.

"Sorry about that," shrugged an obviously embarrassed Kouros. He waved for them to move on through the metal detector. "You can frisk each other later."

THE LINE WAS moving very slowly. The old man looked at his watch. I knew I should have gone inside before the bride arrived. He put down the four red shopping bags bearing the symbol of his store and waited patiently. The line began to move. He picked up the packages, took a few steps forward, put them down again, and waited to repeat the process. As he approached the archway, he watched two men examining identity cards and checking them against a list of names.

"Hello, Inspector Stamatos," said the old man.

Tassos looked up. "Why Mister Ilias, how nice to see you, sir. How are you?"

The old man shook his head. "Tired. It was a lot easier carrying wedding gifts from my shop to new brides when I was younger."

Tassos smiled. "I remember when you carried a few to my wedding. That was a very long time ago, my friend." Tassos looked at the shopping bags. "What's in them?"

"Candle sticks, silver bowls, picture frames, the usual."

Tassos nodded. "Sorry, but you'll have to go through the metal detector. We can't make any exceptions."

The old man smiled. "I understand. There are a lot of very important people here this evening. But what about the gifts?"

"No gifts are allowed inside the monastery. You'll have to take them back to your car and leave them there."

The old man's smile faded.

Tassos paused for a moment, leaned over, and whispered. "A few family members also forgot they weren't supposed to bring gifts to the church. Don't worry, I won't make you carry them all the way back to your car. Let me have them. I'll put them with the family's, in the corner of the courtyard next to the church."

The old man nodded thank you and stepped inside, followed by Tassos carrying four carefully wrapped packages.

# SIXTEEN

AN ORGANIZED FAITH must offer more than words in exchange for the lifetime commitment of one's soul. Symbols, advocates, and inspiration are required. Andreas and Lila stood before a priest, under the dome of the church, in the presence of the revered icon of *Panagia Tourliani* prepared to do as centuries of Greek Orthodox brides and grooms had done before on that very spot according to the same traditions.

Andreas stood to Lila's right, facing the altar and the priest. Andreas' *koumbarous* was to his right, and to Lila's left stood her *koumbara*, her bride's maid. The church was filled with friends and family and more stood in the courtyard. For the next hour all eyes would be on the soon to be bride and groom; that is, all but those of Tassos, Kouros, and every cop under their command. They would catch the service on video. This was crunch time for preventing an attack.

Tassos studied the scene around Andreas and Lila. No unexpected faces, objects, or packages, and the silver tray on the small table by the priest held only the usual: a bible, almonds, wine cup and decanter, and two *stefana* bridal crowns of starched white leather, orange blossoms and ivy joined together by a single silver ribbon. Tassos had checked out the wine and almonds personally. No surprises there. Now to make sure there were none elsewhere. Tassos looked at the couple and smiled. "Good luck, kids," he whispered to himself and left.

In the Greek Orthodox faith the priest read from the wedding service as he performed the expected traditional rites, such as touching the wedding bands, and later the *stefana*, three times to the forehead of the bride and of the groom. But everyone attending a Greek wedding had some traditional part to play.

The *koumbarous* and *koumbara* were charged with switching wedding bands three times from the couple's left ring fingers—where worn when engaged—to their right where worn when married, and with holding the *stefana* above the couple's heads waiting for the moment to switch them three times between bride and groom.

The bride had the most whimsical, and some said instructive, tradition. Near the end of the service the priest read, "The wife shall fear her husband." At that point the bride brought to life the expression, "It's time to put your foot down," by stepping on her man's foot to the cheers of onlookers.

The guests played their parts after the couple drank three times from the common cup and began their ceremonial first steps together as husband and wife. The bride, groom, *koumbaroi*, and priest circled the small table three times amid a barrage of rice and, in Mykonos tradition, powerful whacks to the groom's back by his buddies.

Yes, those were all expected traditions at a Mykonian wedding. What was not were two men in Greek army uniforms bearing Heckler & Koch G3 assault rifles standing directly across from the archway.

TASSOS HAD CIRCLED the perimeter on foot three times. He looked at his watch. The wedding should be ending soon. Then it would be twenty minutes of Lila and Andreas greeting their guests in the courtyard, and another ten of the *koumbaroi* gently shooing stragglers out of the courtyard so all could get on to the reception.

Tassos drew in a deep breath and let out a sigh. It was not one of relief. So far so good, he thought. But only for the moment, there still was a lot of time for all hell to break loose. He'd moved the gifts from the courtyard to his car. No reason to waste time moving them later. Now he was back by the archway, staring across at two armed soldiers standing on the steps leading up to the square.

The two had moved to that position from the far end of the square only a few minutes before. One of the soldiers had suggested that move to Tassos when Tassos made his first circle of the perimeter. The soldier said that the far end of the square was virtually deserted, and with all possible sniper positions shut down, and six other soldiers keeping an eye on the square, it made more sense for the two of them to be in position by the archway where they could react instantly if necessary.

Cops already were at the archway, but what the soldier said made sense, if only for the deterrent effect of their ready for armed combat appearance. Tassos thought about the suggestion on his second tour of the perimeter and asked their commander for his opinion on the move when he made his third round. The commander agreed, and that's how two men with automatic weapons at the ready stood waiting for Andreas and his wife to appear in the archway.

ANDREAS KNEW THIS was his wedding. He just wasn't sure that at all times he was actually present, and not hovering about somewhere watching from afar. His eyes fixed on the holy icon. How many stories she must have heard over the centuries from so many seeking guidance and intervention, how many souls she must have calmed. And how many more her sister icon on Tinos. He glanced at his mother. She was holding Tassaki up so that he could see. She caught his glance and cocked her head slightly up toward the dome. Andreas smiled. Yes, Mom, Dad's with us. He fought back a tear. Some may have thought it a tear of pain, for at that moment Lila drove her foot onto his.

Andreas' first thought was to thank God Lila had used her sole and not the heel. Otherwise, she would have anchored them both to the marble. His second thought was more long term—whether this was how she planned on bringing his wandering thoughts back to the here and now.

As the two of them followed the priest in their walk three times around the small table, Andreas kept catching back slaps from guys built like bulls. "I should have worn a ballistic vest," he said to Lila.

She smiled. "And steel-toe shoes."

THE BRIDE AND groom were standing in the courtyard greeting the last of the *tsunami* of well-wishers that had engulfed them in hugs, kisses, and handshakes. Andreas squeezed Lila's hand. "Well, Missus Kaldis, are you ready to step out and meet your public?"

"Public?"

"*Paparazzi*. They're waiting outside." He pointed toward the archway. "We told them to behave until after the ceremony, then we'd give them photo ops. Only way to control them."

Lila shrugged. "Where's Tassaki?"

"Your parents took him back to the house. It's just you, big Tassos, and me. We're taking Tassos' car."

"Why?"

"So you get to play with the siren and lights on our wedding day," said Andreas.

Lila shook her head. "What's the real reason?"

"Trying to avoid a lot of unnecessary attention. There's a crowd of curious people waiting for us on the other side of this wall. They're expecting us to go to the right, to where your car is waiting. Tassos' car is off to the left. Ready?"

Lila didn't answer, just moved toward the archway and up onto the steps leading out of the courtyard. She waited at the top for Andreas to catch up, and together they stepped through the archway.

There was an immediate roar of "*kalo riziko*," "*na zesete*," "*vion anthosparton*" wishing their marriage "good roots," "long life," and "full of flowers." Louder still was a rush of photographers yelling, "This way, please." No one seemed to notice the two soldiers slowly raising their rifles, shielded from the couple by the crowd of photographers.

The first rifle shot was almost lost in the shouts, but Andreas had no trouble making out the second, the third, or the fourth. Photographers scrambled for cover, Tassos drew his gun as he dropped to a crouch. Andreas swept Lila into his arms, shielding her from the direction of the sound of the shots, and leaped through the archway. Inside, he pushed Lila toward cover, pulled out the semi-automatic hidden in his pants, and was back in the archway aiming to return fire.

The soldiers were still firing, one after another in

sequence, but not a single cop was firing back. The cops stood by the wall, guns drawn, watching the two soldiers empty their magazines into the sky as they shouted, "*na zesete, na zesete, na zesete.*"

"What the hell's going on?" said Andreas.

Tassos shook his head. "Care to bet those assholes are from Crete. That's what they do at a wedding on Crete, and on virtually every other occasion, fire guns into the air."

"Yeah, but not on Mykonos. They scared the hell out of me," said Andreas.

Tassos ran his hand over his face. "Me, too. And the *paparazzi* are still running. Wouldn't want to be doing their laundry tomorrow."

"Are you *malakas* done yet?" screamed Kouros.

One soldier gave him the open palm middle finger equivalent. The other yelled, "*kalo riziko,*" and saluted Andreas.

Andreas shook his head. "This is too goddamned weird to believe."

"If their commander knew they were going to do this I'll have his balls," said Tassos.

Andreas put away his gun. "Let's just get out of here." He turned to go back into the monastery for Lila. She was standing in the archway.

"Sirens, lights, *and gunfire*? Any more surprises in store?" Lila said.

"Not that I know of," said Andreas forcing a smile.

"And don't tell me this is all Spiros' doing out of concern for his fellow ministers. I want you to tell me what's going on."

Andreas swallowed. "Tomorrow morning, I'll tell you everything."

"No, I want you to tell me now. I'm not a fool, there's enough security here for a visit from the President of the United States."

"Not really, but I get your point. I promise I'll tell you everything tomorrow, but it will take too long to explain now and this was all precautionary. There is nothing more to worry about. Honest." Between a white lie and ruining her wedding, the decision was easy. He'd face the consequences tomorrow.

Lila stared at him for what seemed an eternity before saying, "Okay, first thing tomorrow morning."

As Greek weddings go, that should be about the time the last guest left for home.

WHEN THEY REACHED Tassos' car the gifts were on the back seat. Tassos moved them to the front and motioned for Andreas and Lila to get in the back. "What do you want me to do with these?" he said nodding toward the gifts.

Lila said, "If you wouldn't mind, could you please give them to Marietta and tell her to put them in our bedroom?" She looked at Andreas. "I've no doubt they'll be a welcome distraction from what I expect you'll be telling me 'first thing tomorrow morning.'"

Andreas swallowed, gunfire tonight, an explosion tomorrow, and fireworks at the party in between. Quite a welcome to married life.

IT'S HARD TO imagine how many cars Greeks can park along a road barely wide enough to be called two lanes. And when it's a crumbling mountain lane, with a hill on one side and a cliff on the other, the feat can seem downright miraculous But there they were, squeezed off to the very edges of the road, Hummers, BMW X-5s, Porsche Cayennes , Mercedes G-550s, Jeep Rubicons, and a host of more practical island vehicles such as Suzuki Jimnys, Fiat Pandas, and Smarts, leaving barely enough room in the center of the road for Tassos' car to squeeze by.

"What the hell's going to happen if someone's coming the other way?" said Tassos.

"It's why God invented reverse," said Andreas.

"But it's too late for you to back out," Lila squeezed his hand.

Andreas laughed and kissed her. "Isn't it a bit early for us to show up at the reception? I thought we weren't supposed to be there until dinner was ready to be served?"

"That's to give the bride time to stop at her new home and change clothes. But the reception is at our home and I'm not changing."

They were nearing the house and Lila looked out the side window. "Then again, perhaps you'd like to spend that time explaining precisely why those trigger-happy military types from the monastery are up there, too." She pointed to soldiers deployed along the hillside overlooking the house. "And police everywhere else." She made an arc with her finger spanning the car. "Let me guess, it's 'all precautionary.'"

Andreas cleared his throat. "You're absolutely right, we should go straight to the party."

Lila nodded. "I thought you liked what I'm wearing."

No one was allowed onto the grounds of the house without an invitation checked against the wedding list and confirmed by an ID. The only exceptions were uninvited guests brought along and vouched for by invited family members and close friends, but that was expected at a Greek wedding because there always was more than enough food, drink, and room for one more. Presents brought by guests were discreetly moved to an armored bank truck capable of withstanding an explosion.

From the time Andreas and Lila stepped inside the house, it took thirty minutes of posing for photographs, snuggling Tassaki, and accepting apologetic good wishes from guests unable to attend the church ceremony before the couple made it to the rear of the house. They stood in the doorway holding hands. Long tables set up family style sat on three of the four broad terraces stepping down toward the sea. A temporary dance floor was erected on the fourth terrace and music was playing, but no one was dancing. As soon as the band realized the newlyweds were at the doorway, the music changed to a tune that let everyone know the couple had arrived. A roar of applause and shouts erupted drowning out the music as the couple made their way from terrace to terrace, hugging and kissing their guests until reaching the dance floor.

With a nod from Lila the band started playing the *ballos*, the traditional six-step dance of the Cycladic islands, one of the most beautiful to watch, and the first done at any true Mykonian wedding. The party was officially underway once the bride and her husband began to dance, and they were joined in sequence by their parents, *koumbaroi*, immediate family, and guests until a full line of partiers were dancing in the *syrto* style that symbolized the essence of Greek life to much of the world. Later came the *kalamatiano*, ar-

guably Greece's most popular dance and one played at
every Greek wedding.

Tonight was a time to let loose and worry about nothing more than passing out before the last guest departed.
True to tradition, when it came time for the cake cutting
and fireworks display, neither Andreas nor any of his
buddies was sober. Even Maggie had a hard time walking a straight line as she dragged Tassos away a little
after dawn. No one had any idea where Kouros ended
up. In other words, the party was a tremendous success.

Andreas and Lila made it to their bedroom just before nine in the morning. Assuming Andreas could even
remember his promise to tell Lila everything "tomorrow," he was in no condition to talk and she was in
no condition to listen. They barely had the strength to
throw off their clothes, push the presents Marietta had
piled on their bed to the floor, and crawl into bed. Besides, to Greeks "tomorrow" was a relative term.

# SEVENTEEN

"ARE YOU AWAKE?" The voice was delicate and sweet. "Darling, are you up?"

"You sound like an angel come to take me to heaven, but if this is how it feels to be there, I think I'll wait for the next bus," said Andreas.

Lila laughed. "It's almost three in the afternoon."

"Wake me tomorrow." He was on his stomach with a pillow pulled over his head.

"It *is* tomorrow," said Lila.

Whoops, bad choice of words, thought Andreas. "Okay, when the dark haze clears I'll tell you what I promised."

"Good, I'll get us some coffee."

Andreas tried drifting off toward sleep but couldn't quite make it. He heard Lila tell the maid to bring coffee; then she started humming to herself. It made him smile. He liked it when Lila was happy. It made him happy. He felt her move off the bed and plop back on. She's trying to keep me awake. He heard the crinkling of paper.

"These are beautiful, darling. A pair of sterling silver candle sticks in the shape of the charioteer of Delphi. Ilias does such fascinating things." She read the card aloud.

I'm not going to move. I'm not going to give in. Andreas smiled into the mattress.

Lila opened two more packages, giving a running commentary as she did. She picked up a fourth gift. "I know you're enjoying this as much as I am, even if you're not saying a word."

Andreas turned his head away from her and laughed into his pillow.

"Okay, my husband, now I'm undoing the ribbons on the last of the gifts from Ilias' shop. The box is huge. I'm taking off the lid," she dropped the lid on Andreas' butt. "And now I'm pushing aside the tissue paper and—"

Total silence.

Andreas sensed something was wrong. "What is it?"

Lila dropped the box and ran out of the room, screaming, "*Tassaki! Where's Tassaki?*"

Andreas was right behind her. "What's wrong?"

"Tassaki!"

Andreas caught up to her in the living room. Tassaki was calmly playing with his cousins. Lila started to reach for him, but stopped. She put her hand to her mouth and spun around to face Andreas. "The box." She drew a deep breath and pointed toward the bedroom. "It's in the box."

Andreas wasn't sure what to do, so he went back to the bedroom. The box was on its side lying on the bed. He carefully peered in without touching it. The tissue paper was hiding most of what he could see, but he could make out one thing: baby toes. Attached to a foot.

Andreas cleared his throat. It wasn't a real baby's foot. It was a doll. He turned over the box and gingerly pushed back the paper. Inside was a large silver bowl, and inside that a naked baby doll—with a real bullet hole through its heart and a photograph of their son from a magazine article covering its face. Attached to the baby's belly just below the bullet hole was Andreas' card with two words written across it in red: FINAL WARNING.

Andreas calmly picked up the box and carried it outside to the armored truck. He realized for the first time that he was wearing only underpants when he walked by his brother-in-law who laughed and asked if that meant Lila had already kicked him out.

As soon as the box was safely inside the armored truck Andreas borrowed a cell phone from one of the cops watching the house and called Kouros. There was no answer. He tried Tassos.

The phone rang six times. "Hello." The voice sounded as drowsy as Andreas' had until five minutes before.

"Tassos, it's Andreas, we have a big problem."

"What's wrong?" The tone now was crisp and professional.

"Get over here ASAP. Inside one of the gift boxes from Ilias' shop was a threat to kill Tassaki if we don't walk away from the Tinos investigation."

Tassos didn't respond for a few seconds. "It's my fault. I never should have made an exception for the old man's packages."

"I'm sure he's not part of any of this. Besides, I don't think what's inside is lethal. If it were it would have gone off the moment Lila opened the box." Andreas crossed himself. "But I want an explosives expert over here now, and anybody else you can think of who might know about booby-trapped packages. There could be anthrax or God knows what other sort of biological or chemical agent inside."

"I'll have someone there within an hour. But I want

to find out how something like that ended up in a gift box intended for you."

"Good. Just get over here as soon as you can. Any idea where Yianni is? He's not answering his phone."

"On our couch. Out cold. As of three hours ago."

"Wake him up and bring him with you. Bye."

Andreas drew in and let out a deep breath. He handed the phone back to the cop. "Thanks. Now, I want you to go inside the house and not move from my son's side until I tell you it's okay. No matter what anyone else tells you, don't move unless I say it's okay. Understand?"

The cop nodded and both men started back toward the house. Andreas saw Lila standing in the doorway, arms crossed in front of her robe.

Lila's face was stone. "Tomorrow is now."

ANDREAS' EXPLANATION CONTINUED for a good hour after an interruption by the arrival of two military demolition experts from the Greek air force's mountaintop radar installation on the far northeast end of Mykonos. There was another, brief interruption when Tassos and Kouros showed up, but they chose to stay with the bomb squad where, according to Kouros, "things might be safer."

Andreas and Lila were sitting in the library by a window that allowed Andreas to keep an eye on what was going on outside. He could tell from the way the experts were looking at their watches and leaning against the armored truck that they must be waiting for him. No problem, Tassos and Yianni would keep them there until he came out.

"So, that's all of it, right up until this very moment. Any questions?"

When Andreas had begun his explanation Lila had

a lot of questions, but they'd tailed off and for the last fifteen minutes she'd said not a word.

Lila shook her head. "I can't believe this. It sounds like one of those terrible conspiracy films I can't bear to watch."

Andreas nodded. "I know what you mean. I wish it were made up, but it's not."

"If someone put this in a book no one would believe it."

Andreas stood up. "I've got to go outside and see what the bomb boys have to say."

"I'm coming with you."

Andreas gestured no. "Not until I know it's safe."

"But—"

"No buts. As soon as I know it's safe, I'll include you. Until then, wait here."

"Okay, but I'll be watching through the window."

Andreas kissed her on the forehead. "I would expect nothing less."

As soon as Andreas stepped out the front door, Tassos waved for him to come to the back of the truck.

"So, what do we have?" said Andreas.

"The experts say, 'A non-explosive, non-corrosive, not a threat package,'" said Tassos.

"Are they sure?"

Tassos pointed to a thin man leaning against the front of the truck chatting with a chubby guy smoking a cigarette. "Ask him, he's in charge."

The thin man spoke without being asked. "It was simple, almost as if whoever put this thing together made it easy for us to run our tests. It's just a common, everyday baby doll with no potential chemical or biological risks."

"Find any prints or DNA possibilities?" said Andreas.

The thin man gestured no. "Rarely do on professional jobs. Even amateurs are learning how to be careful from all those TV crime scene shows."

"The salesgirl at the jewelry shop said the woman who bought the gift wore the sort of white cotton gloves people use not to tarnish silver," said Tassos.

Andreas looked at Tassos and Kouros. "Let's go inside. We have things to talk about."

Andreas thanked the two experts, and the three cops walked toward the house.

"Sir," said the chubby man.

Andreas turned. "Yes."

"Do you want the doll?"

Andreas paused, then motioned for Yianni to take it. "Yes, thank you. It will be inspiration for what's to come."

LILA, ANDREAS, TASSOS, and Kouros sat in the library.

"So, how did the package get here?" said Andreas.

Tassos said, "A middle-age woman purchased the bowl. Said it was a gift from her boss who wanted it delivered to the wedding. No names and she paid in cash. The salesgirl didn't know the woman and never saw what she put in the box, thought it was just a card. I'm sure the woman's long gone by now."

"What was her nationality?" said Andreas.

"The salesgirl wasn't sure. They spoke in Greek, but the woman had a strange accent."

"What kind of accent?"

"None she recognized. She said that at times the woman sounded like a native Greek, at other times from somewhere else."

"Maybe she was faking the accent?" said Kouros.

"Could be," said Tassos.

"I thought that shop had surveillance cameras?" said Kouros.

"Only one. And the woman made sure to keep her back to it at all times," said Tassos.

"So, what do we know?" said Andreas.

"Five dead. Three *tsigani*, two non-Greeks. Two of them after talking to us," said Tassos.

"Two were killed instantly, two rendered unconscious first," said Andreas.

"Make that three in the 'unconscious' category," said Tassos.

"Three?"

"The Syros coroner called me this morning with results on the Pakistani's autopsy. He was drugged and out of it when his throat was cut."

"Why didn't you tell me this before?" Andreas' tone was sharp.

Tassos paused. "I know you're tense, but at the time of his call I was not in much better condition than the corpse."

Andreas drew in and let out a breath. "Sorry. I am tense."

"We all are," said Kouros.

Lila shook her head. "Not me. Tense is not the word I would use to describe my feelings at the moment."

Andreas looked at the floor, "If you're going to tell me to give up on the investigation—"

"Are you insane? I'm way beyond tense. I'm in the redline zone of angry mother. *I want you to find the goddamned bastards behind this.*"

Andreas laughed. "Sorry, that was a nervous laugh." Andreas leaned over and kissed Lila on the cheek.

"What was the drug?" said Kouros.

"One of those date rape drugs that puts the target in no condition to resist. The tasteless, invisible kind found all over the islands this time of the year."

"Sounds like another dead end," said Kouros.

"What else do we have?" said Andreas.

"Two of your business cards. One on the Pakistani, one on the doll," said Kouros.

"Make that three," said Andreas. "You're forgetting the one they found in the pocket of the third dead Carausii brother, Punka."

Tassos said, "With that record, you ought to think twice about giving out your business card to anyone you want to keep breathing."

"Can't imagine what might happen to someone who gets a Christmas card from you," said Kouros.

"Okay, guys, enough with the jokes. We've got—" Andreas slammed his hands together. "That's it."

"What's 'it'?" said Tassos.

"I gave four cards to people I talked to about this case. Anyone care to bet if one of them ended up on that doll?"

"You gave one to Punka that ended up in his pocket and one to the Pakistani that that ended up in his mouth. Who else did you give them too?" said Kouros.

Andreas said, "One to the two women in that *meta-nastes* bar, and—"

Tassos interrupted, "One to my niece. I can vouch for Eleni."

"I'm not suggesting she's involved. I just want to know what she did with my card."

"It's probably still in her purse," said Tassos.

"Good, then that leaves us with the two women from the bar. But ask Eleni anyway. Yianni, I want you to locate those two other women and find out what they did with my card."

"I don't know what they look like."

Andreas looked at Tassos.

Tassos shrugged. "I never really got a good look at them. I was busy with the owner. You're the only one who talked to them."

"Sounds to me as if you're about to take a trip to Tinos," said Lila.

"Not until after you and Tassaki are out of here."

"Where do you have in mind for us to go?"

"To where we planned."

"Capri? But that was for our honeymoon."

Andreas shrugged. "I'm open to other suggestions. But I want you out of Greece for now."

Lila frowned. "Okay, but I'm taking Marietta with me."

"Fine, I'll get there as soon as I can. But first I have a shepherd to catch."

"A what?" said Lila.

"Shepherd. That's what they're calling whoever's behind bringing all the new workers I told you about to Tinos," said Andreas.

"And don't forget the priest," said Tassos.

"A priest?" said Lila.

"Not a real priest. At least as far as we know. The murdered Pakistani referred to the men he worked with as 'brothers' and said he was recruited to Tinos by someone who called himself a 'priest,'" said Tassos.

"The two Romanians working with the Pakistani

told us the same thing. But they said it wasn't the same priest as recruited the Pakistani," said Kouros.

Lila started rocking back and forth on her chair.

"What's on your mind?" said Andreas.

"Nothing," said Lila.

"Please don't say 'nothing' because when you're rocking like that there's always something on your mind."

"It's silly."

"Just say whatever it is. At this point even 'silly' is an improvement over where we are," said Andreas.

"*Filiki Eteria.*"

"Society of Friends?" said Andreas.

"Like I said, it was a silly thought."

"Are you talking about the secret society that instigated Greece's War of Independence in 1821?" said Kouros.

Lila nodded. "Yes."

"But Tinos is all about foreigners, not Greeks," said Tassos.

"So was the Society in many ways. Three native Greeks founded it but they recruited large numbers of Greeks and non-Greeks from what today we call Eastern Europe and Russia. Even the Russian Tsar was believed to be a member. By the time our War began the Society's secret membership numbered in the thousands."

"How's all that tie into what's happening on Tinos?" said Kouros.

"The Society was organized like a pyramid, with an 'Invisible Authority' at the top coordinating everything below. No one was allowed to ask who founded the Society, question a command, or make an independent decision. New members were recruited without knowledge of its true revolutionary purposes. They were attracted by glamorous rumors of a celebrity membership and an avowed but vaguely stated general purpose of 'doing good' for the nation."

"Are you suggesting the *metanastes* and *tsigani* recruited to Tinos have no idea of what's actually going on?" said Tassos.

"All I'm saying is that's how *Filiki Eteria* operated. Its recruits were motivated by the Society's perceived glamour and altruistic goals. If you want a parallel to Tinos, I guess you could say today's recruits are motivated by the money."

"Sorry, but that doesn't seem like much of a parallel to me," said Kouros.

Lila nodded. "I agree, but what got me to thinking of *Filiki Eteria* was its pyramid organization. It was based on four levels. Those at the lowest two levels had no idea of the Society's true purpose. The third level was responsible for recruiting, and the top level was in charge of implementing what had Greeks fighting for independence under the battle cry 'Freedom or Death.'"

Lila paused. "Those at the bottom two levels were called the 'Recommended' and 'Brothers.' The recruiters were called 'Priests' and those at the Society's top level were called 'Shepherds.'"

Lila looked at Andreas and shrugged. "Like I said, 'Silly.'"

Andreas picked up a pencil and began tapping it on the desk. "Jesus, what the hell is going on?"

"How should I know? I'm just an art historian. You're the detectives."

# EIGHTEEN

THE NEXT MORNING Andreas kissed Lila and Tassaki goodbye at the Mykonos airport. Lila's father had arranged for a private jet to fly them directly to Naples, and a friend of Tassos on the Naples police force promised to escort them from the airport to the private motor launch of the Capri Palace Hotel.

Kouros took a flight back to Athens, and Andreas and Tassos caught the Fast Ferry *Theologos* to Tinos. The boat was halfway there when Andreas' phone rang. He didn't look to see who was calling. He knew it would be Lila.

"Miss me already, my love?"

"This is no time to be funny!"

Andreas held the phone away from his ear so Tassos could hear. "I agree completely, Minister."

"I want to know why the Tinos matter that was supposed to be closed *before* your wedding is still listed as open. Just how much longer do you think it will be until foreign headlines start screaming that Greece has declared war on non-Greeks? We're up to five dead in what is obviously a major *tsigani* clan war."

"Are you including in that '*tsigani* clan war' the murdered Eastern European hit man in Syntagma and the Pakistani?"

"Of course. This mess has boiled over into *tsigani* battling foreign criminal elements no different than they are. Frankly, as long as Greeks aren't involved I don't give a damn. Let's just call it the tribal warfare that it is, and keep the Greece-hating foreign press pricks off our backs!"

Andreas knew it would be a waste of time to argue. Spiros was hell bent on fitting a square peg into a round hole. "Sorry. The wedding had me busier than I anticipated and things just got backed up."

"Allow me to repeat what the Prime Minister personally told me this morning, 'There is nothing more important than closing this case.' *Nothing.*"

Andreas held his hand over the phone and whispered to Tassos, "I sure hope he's pushing this hard only because he really is scared shitless of the press stirring things up again."

"Did you hear me, Andreas?"

"Loud and clear."

"Then what are you doing about it?"

"I've already canceled my honeymoon."

"You what?"

"Well, actually I postponed it. I knew you wanted the matter closed by the wedding and when it wasn't I felt an obligation to stay and make certain it's resolved ASAP."

"Lila must be furious!"

Andreas winked at Tassos. He knew Lila's potential anger at her new husband was not what alarmed Spiros. The distinguished minister was worried about himself. Lila's position in Athens society far outranked his own, and incurring Lila's wrath was not prudent for one who relied on ass-kissing and favors to move on up the social and political ladder.

"Well, she's not exactly happy but I promised her I'd have it wrapped up by the end of *Tis Panagias*."

"August 15th is this weekend," said Spiros.

"I know, but I'm sure by the time the holiday is over you'll no longer have to worry about closing the case."

"Is that a promise?"

"Promise."

"Good. And my best to Lila." Spiros hung up.

Andreas stared at the phone. "Because from the way things look now, dear minister, you and I will be too busy looking for a new line of work."

Tassos smiled and gave the thumbs-up sign. "Nicely handled. But what are Yianni and I going to do?"

"You, I'm not worried about. You'd find some way to keep your job even if the Turks took over. As for Yianni, he'll probably follow the rest of his generation and take the advice of that American cowboy who said, 'Go west, young man.'"

"It wasn't a cowboy. It was a newspaper man named Greeley."

"Whatever." Andreas put the phone in his pocket. "But for now, I just want to go outside for some fresh air."

They went out onto the starboard upper deck. The boat was about a mile or so from the harbor and close enough to shore that whether they looked right or left all they saw over a slice of bright blue water was land and Mount Tsiknias looming off to the northeast. It was Tinos' highest mountain, but not its most famous. That title belonged to Xobourgo, a soaring granite height, faced with sheer cliffs on three sides, that sat due north of the port. From pre-historic times the island's inhabitants flocked to Xobourgo for protection from all sorts of invaders, and when control over Tinos fell to Venice in 1204 it became the island's fortified heart for five hundred years of Venetian rule.

"What's that?" said Andreas. He pointed at a conical, dirt and stone brown mound laced with ancient looking stonewalls. The mound looked more than twice as high as the ferry and came up to the very edge of the water as if standing on the rocks. "It looks like an alien spaceship."

A crewmember smoking a cigarette nearby said, "Everyone asks the same question. It's the *Vriokastro*."

"The what?" said Andreas.

"A prehistoric acropolis going back to Mycenaean times, maybe even earlier," said Tassos.

"That's almost four thousand years ago," said the crewman.

"Give or take a thousand," smiled Tassos.

"And before you ask," said the crewman, "it's two-hundred thirty feet high and covers twenty-two acres."

"How come no one's built on it? Looks to be prime real estate to me." Andreas pointed to the right. "And they're building next to it."

"It's a protected, national historic site," said Tassos.

"As if that matters any more these days," said the crewman. "Next week we'll be selling it to the Chinese." He flicked his cigarette into the sea. "Got to go, guys. We're almost in port. Enjoy your time on Tinos, the island of miracles."

From his mouth to God's ears, thought Andreas.

KOUROS GOT A lucky break. Or rather, Maggie earned it for him. She'd put the photographs from the surveillance tapes of the two Greek prostitutes who'd last been seen with the *tsigani* brothers out on Greece's "Do you know this person" law enforcement hotline and came up *bingo*! One of them had just been arrested and was sitting in Kordydallos prison.

"What's she doing in there?" said Kouros. "Isn't Kordydallos a bit much for hookers?"

Maggie said, "She crossed the wrong customer when she pocketed his watch as a bonus for her services."

"That still doesn't seem to qualify her for Kordydallos time."

"It was a five-hundred thousand euro Patek Philippe," said Maggie. "And yes, I said the same thing, '*five-hundred thousand euros for a watch!*'"

"I guess I don't have to ask whether the victim was connected enough to have her put away there."

"The customer was a very rich Saudi."

"Then she's lucky she ended up in jail. It usually ends a lot worse for hookers who screw around with those guys. So to speak."

Maggie handed Kouros an envelope. "Here's her file, mister comedian. I've told Kordydallos to hold her no matter who shows up to get her out. But you better get right over there, just in case."

Kouros smiled. "On my way, chief."

KORDYDALLOS PRISON COMPLEX wasn't very pretty to look at: a walled, multiple square-city-block, gray amalgam of not more than four-story warehouse-like structures crowded around a tiny central patch of green. Although an uneasy place at best, it was most well known to the public for two separate, recent great escapes in a rented helicopter—each time by the same notorious kidnapper/bank robber.

Women were housed separately from the rest of the

general inmate population. But that didn't make life any easier inside for a woman as attractive as Maria Fioropoulou, and from her file she wasn't one used to the sort of violence she'd find there. Her record was strictly busts for high-end prostitution, starting five years ago when she was sixteen.

Kouros was leaning against a virtually colorless wall in a second floor interrogation room. Maria was standing in front of a square metal table anchored to the floor. She was wearing handcuffs and staring at the floor. Kouros motioned for the officer who'd brought her into the room to remove them.

"I don't think they'll be necessary." Kouros studied her. There were bruises and scratch marks on her face, arms, and legs. "Do you?"

She nodded "no" without lifting her eyes from the floor.

As the handcuffs were removed Kouros walked to a chair across the table from where she stood. He pointed to an empty chair next to her. "Please."

She sat down. Her eyes looked everywhere but at Kouros. "Where's my lawyer?"

Kouros waited until the officer left the room before sitting down. "You won't need him, this is an unofficial meeting."

"Nothing with police is 'unofficial.'"

Kouros nodded. "A wise way to look at things. But just listen to what I have to say. There's no reason for you to talk if you don't want to." He stared at her, but she still wouldn't make eye contact.

"You've made a very powerful enemy. But, of course, I don't have to tell you that. I'm sure you already know it. Isn't fate a bummer? Bet you didn't even know how valuable that watch was when you lifted it. Had it only been a Rolex your boyfriend might not even have missed it."

She didn't say a word.

"Yeah, you're just having one hell of a run of bad luck. I mean you never should have ended up in Kordydallos for just turning tricks. But you did. And if you hadn't I might never have found you."

She glanced at his face.

He was smiling. "Like they say, some days you eat the bear and other days the bear eats you. Guess today is just my lucky day."

"What are you talking about?" She was looking at the tabletop.

"Maria, I know you think you're in trouble now. But you have no idea the trouble you're really in." He paused. "Or, perhaps you do?"

"Like you said, I have 'no idea' what you're talking about."

"You and a friend of yours are about to stand trial for murder."

"*What*?" she shrieked, and looked straight at Kouros.

"The two Carausii brothers. You remember them don't you, from Tinos."

She looked puzzled. "What about them?"

"Don't tell me you don't know what happened to them? That would make you the only person in Greece who doesn't."

"I don't read much. Or watch television."

"Did you hear about the two *tsigani* incinerated on Tinos?"

"I don't pay much attention to that sort of thing. It seems to happen all the time."

"Not really."

"Are you trying to tie me to two murdered men?"

"Not trying, my love. I have you on tape." He picked up an envelope from the table, took out a photograph and handed it to her. "It doesn't really do you justice."

She stared at the photograph.

"How did you meet them?"

"I want a lawyer."

"Sure, but I can assure you that with the charges we'll be filing once your lawyer gets involved, you'll have plenty of time to make a lot more new friends in here. On the other hand, if you cooperate I can promise to put you somewhere a lot less…how do I say it…exciting."

Maria stood up. Kouros jumped to his feet, but she held up her hands. "I think better on my feet." She turned and walked toward the door, shook her head, and turned around to face Kouros.

"My girlfriend got a call from a friend. The friend said she and another girl had a sweet deal lined up involving two *tsigani* on Tinos and they wanted us to do it instead of them."

"What sort of deal?"

"To entertain the *tsigani* for a couple of days."

"How much did the deal pay?"

"Four thousand euros for each girl. Two thousand up front, two thousand after."

"That's a lot of money for just 'entertaining' two guys. There had to be something special involved."

"The job required them to leave immediately for Tinos and the *tsigani* weren't expecting them. They'd have to be seduced. But that wouldn't be a problem. Even if they were gay we could have worked something out."

Kouros scratched his cheek. "Like I said, 'there had to be something special involved.'"

Maria walked back to her chair. "The final payment depended on us getting the *tsigani* hooked on gas."

"Didn't that seem kinky to you?"

"Laughing gas? Kinky? If you think that, you have no idea what kinky means." She sat down.

Kouros hoped he hadn't blushed. "How'd you get them to do the gas?"

"It wasn't hard. We told them it gives you better sex than drugs."

"Where did you get the gas?"

"It was already inside the place the girls told us to stay."

"That was it? You got high with them and walked away? And for that each of you got four thousand euros? Don't try hustling me unless you're in a hurry to get back upstairs."

Maria bit at her lip. "On the last night we only faked taking gas. We held our breath. Got them to keep doing it until they passed out."

"Why did you do that?"

"The other girls told us to. They said the instructions were that if we didn't we wouldn't get paid."

"What were you to do after they passed out?"

"Nothing. Just make sure they were out cold and leave them there."

"Where?"

"At the house where we found the gas. The girls said the place came with the deal."

"Where was it?"

"No idea. It was some white house out in the middle of nowhere. I had an address for it written on a piece of paper and gave it to a taxi driver in the port. He took us there."

"How'd you get around?"

"Another taxi driver took us to the bar where we picked up the brothers. I had the address for the bar on the same piece of paper. After that, the brothers took us everywhere on their motorbikes."

"Got a name for any of the taxi drivers?"

"No."

"Where's your girl friend now?"

"No idea."

Liar, thought Kouros. "Where did you go after the brothers passed out?"

"We took their motorbikes and went to the port. We had tickets on the first boat in the morning to Athens."

"Why did you take both of the bikes unless you knew the brothers wouldn't be needing one to get out of 'the middle of nowhere'?"

"The instructions were to take them both if we wanted to get paid."

And remove evidence linking the victims to the house. "How did you get the rest of the money?"

"It was left in an envelope at the purser's office on the boat. We just had to give him the name on the envelope."

"What was the name?"

"Alexander Ypsilantis."

Kouros didn't have to ask who that was. "How did you get the upfront payment?"

"We didn't. The other girls kept it. The deal was we got to keep the back end money."

"Which brings up the obvious question, Maria. Why did the other girls decide to pass on the opportunity of making another two thousand euros each?"

"They had a better deal. Some Arabs were taking them on a Mediterranean cruise for a week, all expenses paid. Those guys pay really big."

"When was that?"

"The day we left for Tinos."

"Where are they now?"

"Don't know, haven't heard from them."

"That just might make you the lucky one. All you got was arrested."

Maria shrugged.

"Got a name on who hired your girlfriends for the Tinos job?"

She gestured no.

"Was it a male or a female?"

"No idea."

"Did whoever hired them know you'd be going instead of them?"

"No, the girls told us the deal would be off if that got out."

"Why?"

"The person who hired them did not want Greek girls involved."

"Your friends weren't Greek?"

She gestured no. "Ukrainian."

"Names please."

She gave them.

"Anything else?"

She swallowed hard. "Yes, you promised not to send me back upstairs."

Kouros nodded. "A deal is a deal. I'll get you transferred."

Maria's eyes welled up with tears. "Thank you."

# NINETEEN

"I TELL YOU, CHIEF, if she wasn't telling the truth she deserves an Academy Award. I don't think she had a clue about what was going on, or even who Ypsilantis was."

"At least it explains why Greeks suddenly ended up in the middle of this mess. The hookers who took the Carausii brothers away from the Polish girls were supposed be *metanastes*," said Andreas. "And it's making Lila's theory on *Filiki Eteria* look pretty good. Either that, or someone has a freaky, coincidental sense of humor."

Alexander Ypsilantis was the leader of *Filiki Eteria* at the start of Greece's War of Independence in 1821.

"It also means another dead end," said Kouros.

"Maybe. But get over here on the next boat. I want you running down those taxi drivers. Maybe you'll get lucky again."

"Let's hope so."

"And tell Maggie to see what she can come up with on the two Ukrainian hookers who were supposed to be on Tinos instead of the Greeks. See you this afternoon. Bye."

Andreas put his cell phone down on the table and picked up his coffee. "Did you hear?"

Tassos nodded. "I wouldn't bet on finding those two Ukrainian girls before August 15th. If they're still breathing it's probably under a lot of different guys.

You'd think they'd know better than to go off on a ship with strange johns. Foreign ones no less."

They were sitting in a taverna at the foot of Megalochari Avenue, across from where pilgrims began their long crawl up the hill to the Church of Panagia Evangelistria.

"Any luck with your local cop buddies finding those two Polish women I spoke to in the *metanastes* bar?" said Andreas.

"No word yet. They know where the girls live, but if they're not at home it's anyone's guess where they are. We might have to try catching up with them at the bar."

Andreas pushed back from the table. "Let's take a walk up the hill. Maybe we'll find some inspiration there."

"I haven't spoken to Eleni about your card."

"We can do it now," said Andreas.

"I thought you might be thinking that."

"Such a good detective. Let's go."

Megalochari Avenue was wide enough to accommodate two-way traffic, one line of parked cars, and a narrow lane partitioned off from the rest of the roadway by orange and white traffic cones for those choosing to crawl. Shops at the base of the hill sold whatever one might need for completing a pilgrimage; candles running from a few inches to several feet in length, metallic shapes called *tama* symbolizing the purpose of the pilgrimage, and everything else up to and including knee pads.

The thirty-five degree grade up the one-half mile hill was steep enough to have Tassos pausing at each of the half-dozen intersecting streets.

"Perhaps you'd like to crawl a bit?" said Andreas.

"You think that's easier in this heat? It must be a hundred degrees. Look at those poor women. I don't see a man out there trying it today. We're all wimps when it comes to that sort of thing."

"I see Maggie's trained you well."

"Just you wait, mister newlywed."

Andreas' phone rang. He looked at the number and answered. "You will live a thousand years. We were just talking about you." He looked at Tassos. "It's Maggie." He held up the phone so Tassos could hear. "So, what do you have for us?"

"I assume you two were saying only extraordinarily nice things."

"Of course."

"Good, then I'll tell you the truth. All we have on the Ukrainian women are arrest records for prostitution and shoplifting. No one has seen either of them in weeks."

"That checks out with what the Greek hooker in Kordydallos told Yianni."

"That's all I have for now. Hardly feel as if I earned my pay today. Say hello to my love. Bye."

Andreas put the phone back in his pocket. "She loves you."

"Good, let's get up to the church already. The sun is killing me."

The upper part of the avenue was more park-like than the lower and ended at a broad flagstone plaza in front of the church. In a tree-shaded spot at the point where the carpeted lane ended, a massive bronze sculpture of a shrouded, faceless supplicant crawled life-like along a marble base toward the church, right arm outstretched ahead and reaching toward heaven.

Off to the right, another avenue emptied into the

plaza from the harbor, and across from each avenue a
set of steps led up through a low white-capped stonewall onto a terrace spanning the front of the church. The
terrace was as long as a soccer field, about half as wide,
and covered in intricate mosaic geometric shapes and
patterns created entirely out of black and white pebbles.
A small sign on the wall separating the terrace from the
church inside read simply SAINT PELAGIA SQUARE.

The two cops crossed the plaza and took the steps to
the right. A carpet resumed at the top of the steps. This
one was crimson and twice as wide as the one running
up the hill from the harbor. They followed it across the
terrace and up another five steps through an intricately
carved marble archway appointed with massive black
wooden doors bearing carved golden images of the Virgin Mary and Archangel Gabriel.

A broad, marble staircase started just beyond the
doorway and ran up to the first level of the church.
Andreas noticed that this staircase had three separate
crimson runners and at the top fed into an upper, fully
carpeted staircase leading to the *Megalochari* on the
second floor. He wondered whether the sudden switch
from one lane to three was in order to accommodate
additional worshipers only wishing to crawl the final
steps of their pilgrimage.

At the top of the first staircase was the white marble courtyard of Panagia Evangelistria. Another staircase off to the left also led to the second floor. Andreas
stared up at the facade. It was three-stories of elegant
cream and white arches highlighted by discreet blazes
of crimson. Arched porticos filled the first two levels
and arched windows the third, all crowned by a *tiara* of
more rolling arches surrounding intricate marble carv-

ings. A simple marble cross was atop it all. To Andreas
it looked like a giant wedding cake.

Tassos and Andreas took the staircase to the right up
to the second floor, turned left, and stopped just inside
the middle of three doors to the right. They were now
inside the tripartite, basilica-form Church of Panagia
Evangelistria. Brilliantly colored icons and tapestries
surrounded by gold and silver adorned every wall, and
an elaborately carved, icon-clad marble pulpit seemed
to float above the floor, but it was the silver and gold
creations hanging everywhere that captured Andreas'
attention. Enormous chandeliers of crystal, silver, and
gold hung amid rows of hundreds of similarly appointed
icon lamps adorned with hanging gold and silver tama
offerings of ships, homes, men, women, children, an-
imals, parts of the body, and whatever else the pious
brought into their prayers to the *Megalochari*.

Off to the left behind a low, thin brass-tube fence
flanked by massive, sand-filled brass candle stands
stood an altar-like structure of carved white marble.
The altar held four, fluted Corinthian columns, one on
each corner, which in turn supported an ornately de-
tailed four-sided entablature topped by a dome reminiscent of the one above Saint Peter's Basilica in Rome,
at the other Vatican.

The holy icon, enclosed within a silver case faced
with glass and elaborately trimmed in gold, sat between
the columns on a stand surrounded by fresh flowers
and offerings of gold and gem encrusted cameos. The
case was rectangular on three sides and arched at the
top. The *Megalochari* rested inside the case, its back
and sides enclosed within a golden frame, its front covered in relief gold plate encrusted with rings, medal-

lions, brooches, earrings, precious stones, and pearls. The whole case was no more than three feet high, by two feet wide, by one-half foot deep—a simple thing to carry for anyone used to manual labor.

Andreas stepped out onto the black and white checkerboard part of the marble floor and walked over to the icon. Guidebooks described it as portraying the Virgin Mary to the right, kneeling in a room with her head bent in prayer before a small, low stand. A book on the stand was open to the words she pronounced when the Archangel Gabriel announced to her that she would be the mother of Jesus. Facing the Holy Virgin and to the left, stood the illuminated figure of Archangel Gabriel holding the symbolic lily of purity in his left hand as, in the top center of the icon, the Holy Spirit descended from heaven in the form of a dove.

At least that's what you would see if the icon were not almost two thousand years old and covered in gold and precious gems. Andreas could barely make out where the faces of the Holy Virgin and Archangel Gabriel should be. No matter, he knew what was there and that was all that mattered. If he cared to see what it once looked like, a replica hung in the chapel immediately below where he stood, honoring the actual spot at which the holy icon was discovered. Andreas said a prayer, crossed himself, and kissed the glass protecting the *Megalochari*.

"I'm not going to ask what you prayed for," said Tassos.

"Good." Andreas pointed to a nearby tall rectangular shape draped in a crimson velvet cover. It was embroidered at eye level with an image of the Holy Virgin. "Want to bet that's where they keep the *Megalochari* at night?"

Andreas walked the few steps to the shape and ran his fingers along the right edge of the velvet. He felt two hinges, slid his hand across its face and felt a handle.

"Very good detective work, Chief Inspector, you found our security system." It was Eleni coming in through a side door behind him.

"Hi, my love." Tassos stepped forward and kissed her on both cheeks.

"Thank you for agreeing to see us on such short notice," said Andreas.

"Well, when uncle calls to say he's *walking* up Megalochari Avenue to see me I know that it must be important."

"Hey, I exercise everyday."

"Yeah, right," said Andreas.

"Come, let me take you to my office. We can talk there."

Eleni's office was in a separate wing of the complex, across a marble courtyard from the church and even farther away from the wing housing many of the Foundation's most valuable museum collections.

"Quite an operation you have here," said Andreas.

"Yes, we're very proud of what the Foundation has been able to achieve through the Blessed Virgin. Please, sit down." She pointed to two chairs in front of her desk and waited for Tassos and Andreas to sit. "So, what can I do for you?"

"Do you remember that card Andreas gave you at your father's restaurant?"

"Yes."

"Where is it?"

She laughed and looked at Andreas. "You want it back? Was it something I said or is our government in such deep financial trouble that you're only allowed to loan them out, short term?"

Andreas smiled. "No, we were just wondering what you might have done with it."

She shrugged. "What I do with all the business cards I receive. I gave it to my secretary to enter into my computerized address book."

"What happened to the actual card?"

"I assume she threw it away, the same as she does with all the others."

"Could you please ask her what she did with mine?"

"What is this all about?" said Eleni.

"Please, just ask," said Andreas.

She looked at Tassos, "I'll want an explanation, uncle." Eleni picked up the phone and asked her secretary to come into the office. The secretary's answers were simple and direct. She'd typed in the information and tossed Andreas' card in the wastebasket. They had no paper shredder.

After the secretary left Eleni said, "Okay, you got your answers. Now, please tell me why all the mystery over your business card?"

"One of my cards turned up in a place it shouldn't have and we wanted to know how it got there," said Andreas.

"Well, at least it wasn't the one you gave me."

"Who picks up your trash?" said Andreas.

"You're kidding."

"No, he's not," said Tassos.

"We have women who clean up every night. They take out the trash and put it in a dumpster for collection and disposal by the town."

"Are the women foreign?" said Andreas.

"Yes."

"Do you know the woman who collects your trash?" said Andreas.

"It could be one of several."

This was looking more and more to be a waste of time, but Andreas took down the women's names. He'd get Kouros to speak to them later.

"Does this have to do with that Pakistani man who was found murdered at the dump last week?" she said.

"Why do you ask?" said Andreas.

"We're not used to murders on Tinos. So, when right after you started asking questions about two killings another murder happened, it's not that hard to make a connection."

"Yes," said Tassos. "They're related. It also appears there might be some connection to *Filiki Eteria*."

"How can that be? The Society hasn't been active for close to two hundred years?"

Andreas cleared his throat. "Well, seeing that your uncle has decided to share our innermost secrets with you, let me tell you a bit more."

"Still don't trust me?"

Andreas smiled. "Sorry, force of habit. Remember when we told you that an unusually high number of tough guy *metanastes* and *tsigani* had come to Tinos looking for work?"

Eleni nodded.

"Well, it appears someone's been recruiting them to Tinos with promises of supplementing whatever they're paid for their work as long as they behave themselves."

"Sounds like God's work to me," said Eleni. "Redemption is always available to the willing. But what's the tie in to the Society?"

"The one in charge apparently is called the 'shepherd,' and has 'priests' recruiting 'brothers,'" said Andreas.

Eleni nodded, "Same classifications as used by the Society."

"How did you know that?" said Tassos.

"I actually studied in school, uncle. Besides, Tinos' history is tied into it. There are families here who trace their ancestors back to Society membership. Some were even war heroes."

"Any whackos among the descendants," said Tassos.

"This is Tinos, uncle, everyone here has at least one 'whacko' in the family."

"Let me guess who qualifies for that title in yours," said Andreas.

Tassos flashed a quick open palm at Andreas. "Seriously, can you think of anyone in any of those families deranged or violent enough to be involved in this?"

"Getting bad people to mend their ways?"

"No," said Andreas. "Murdering whoever gets in the way of whatever very bad things are planned to happen to your church at any moment."

"Did any one ever tell you that you do have a certain edge, Chief Inspector?"

"Yes, I've heard that before, but it's called being direct and I don't have time now to change." He smiled. "But, please, call me Andreas."

Eleni nodded. "I'll accept that as a gesture of your potential willingness to change. But the answer is still no, Andreas. There are many, shall I say, idiosyncratic types on our island. We have always attracted the artists and the unusual. I would not know where to begin. Do you have any particular family in mind?"

Tassos said, "What about the ones who own that *metanastes* bar?"

"I'm sorry, I don't know what you're talking about."

Tassos gave Petros' name.

"Oh, yes, they would definitely qualify as," she paused, "eccentric. And their family also descends from one of the most heroic names in our War of Independence."

"Were they members of the Society?" said Andreas.

"Absolutely. Leaders."

"Could they be involved in this?" said Andreas.

"If you've met the family I don't see how you could think that. Petros is exactly what you see, his sister is practically catatonic all the time, and Trelos is on another planet 24/7."

"Trelos? That means 'crazy.' Who'd call their kid Trelos?" said Andreas.

"It's what everybody calls the younger son. His real name is Pandeleis. He's not all there. You might have seen him dancing through the town or along a highway with his iPod. He must walk the entire island at least once a day listening to his music."

"Should keep him in shape," said Andreas.

"What's he look like?" said Tassos.

"He's about five-feet six-inches tall, one hundred forty pounds, has long, curly brown hair and usually dresses all in black. Trust me, if you spend any time on the island, sooner or later Trelos will dance on by you."

Tassos nodded. "Yeah, I've seen him. Just never knew his name."

"He keeps to himself, make that his own world."

"How long has he been on Tinos?" said Andreas.

"Since he was born. He's probably in his mid-forties. His brother and sister take care of him."

Tassos shrugged. "Well, it was a shot."

"Sorry I couldn't be of more help but there are hundreds of families on Tinos with an ancestor somehow tied into the Society. Any more questions?"

"Only one," said Andreas. "If you were going to steal the most valuable thing on this island, how would you go about doing it?"

# TWENTY

KOUROS WAS ON Tinos early enough in the afternoon to have spoken to what seemed every taxi driver on the island before finding one who said he recognized the Greek hookers.

The driver was about fifty and stood next to his cab staring at the picture of the two coming out of the bar. "Better believe I recognize them. I still think of them every time I do it with my wife."

"How did you meet them?"

"They called my dispatcher looking for a taxi to take them to a bar."

"What bar?"

"Some piece of shit *tsigani* hangout."

"Have an address?"

"It's not the kind of place that has an address."

"How did you find it?"

"They had a piece of paper with directions on it."

"Anything else on the paper?"

"Yeah, directions to where I picked them up."

"How'd you know where to find them?"

"They read the directions to my dispatcher. It was simple. I took a left off the highway just past the first cutoff to Volax and kept going until I saw a house. Never knew one was there. People build in the damnedest places these days."

"Any idea who owns the place?"

"Not a clue, but there was a 'for rent' sign on the front door. Looked like one of those places Germans build in the hope of retiring there some day. Probably rent it out whenever they can to cover expenses."

"Was there a phone number on the sign?"

"Don't remember, but there must have been."

Kouros muttered, "damn" under his breath. "What are those directions again?"

The driver smiled. "Hop in, I'll give you a good rate."

The ride to the house took twenty minutes, during which Kouros heard in exhausting detail every word the driver had said to the women between picking them up at the house and dropping them off at the bar. Despite Herculean efforts on the driver's part to convince them they would have a much better time partying with him and his friends than going to that bar, the women did not say a single word to him the entire trip. They talked between themselves as if he weren't even there. Kouros almost felt sorry enough for the guy to tell him not to take it personally, it wasn't about him; the women were on a mission.

The house was just where the driver said it would be, and virtually invisible from any road but the one they were on. There was a car parked by the front door and Kouros had the driver honk so as not to alarm whoever was inside. It turned out to belong to the owners. Not Germans, but a French couple. The driver had guessed right about the rental part though. They'd rented out the house for the week the two Greek hookers stayed there.

A woman had phoned them in France and said that she saw the sign on their house while trekking along a trail that ran by it. She wanted to rent it for a week, starting immediately. The rent was paid in advance through a cash deposit made directly into a bank account the couple maintained on Tinos. They didn't know the woman but said she spoke French with a decided Greek accent. Her name was a strange sounding one, and the husband couldn't remember it. The wife said she thought she'd marked it down somewhere and found it in her calendar. She showed the name to Kouros: Manto Mavrogenous.

It was a name known to every Greek. She was their country's legendary female hero of the War of Independence; her father was a member of *Filiki Eteria* and her fiancé the brother of *Filiki Eteria*'s leader, Alexander Ypsilantis. Manto Mavrogenous was aristocratic, highly educated, wealthy, beautiful, and dedicated to freedom for Greece. She had risked not just her life but her entire fortune for that cause. She also was among the first of Greece's war heroes to pay homage to the *Megalochari* and, though her family's roots were on Mykonos, for a while she'd made her home on Tinos.

This time on the taxi ride in from the house it was Kouros who said not a word to the driver.

"THIS IS GETTING freakier by the minute," said Tassos. "Now we've got male and female war heroes giving us grief."

Kouros pointed across the taverna table at a bottle of water. "By the way, neither of them was born in Greece," said Kouros.

"And Mavrogenous' life didn't have a fairy tale ending," said Tassos. "Her home was destroyed by fire, her remaining fortune stolen, and her engagement broken off. She was never able to get the Greek government to reimburse her for all she'd contributed to the war effort and died penniless and in oblivion at fifty-four on Tinos' neighboring island of Paros." Tassos pointed due south in the direction of that Cycladic island.

Andreas put down his fork and handed Kouros the bottle. "Not sure what any of that means."

Kouros took the bottle. "And just what part of all this are you sure of?"

"Good point."

Tassos said, "I'll get someone at the bank to see if there's a way of finding out who put the money in the French couple's account, but my guess is the odds of getting any where with that are between slim and none."

"Looks like we're back to trying to catch up with those two Polish girls," said Andreas.

"After what happened to the Pakistani they might have taken off," said Kouros.

"That would have been the smart move," said Tassos. "But if they did, they didn't take anything with them. The Tinos' cops checked their place and everything seemed to be there, including their clothes."

"I'll take that as a sign that we have a shot at finding them tonight…" Andreas threw an open palm gesture at the ground, "or that Shepherd already has."


AS FAR AS the cops sweltering in the rented van could tell, the heat of the day hadn't realized how close it was to midnight and the Cycladic winds that generally made mid-August bearable had taken the night off. They were parked down the road from the turnoff to Petros' *metanastes* bar in a spot that gave them a view of its entrance. They watched a man in a blue tee shirt park his beat-up motorbike as close to the front door of the bar as he could get it. He was wearing standard *metanastes* dress:

tee shirt, jeans, and work boots. The man went into the bar and the cops put down their binoculars.

A fat man was sitting at a table just inside the doorway and an old-looking woman in a housecoat and slippers was doing something behind the bar. He walked past them and stood in the doorway to another room. His eyes moved from table to table. He turned and went back to sit on one of the stools in front of the bar.

"You looking for someone?" said Petros.

The man in the blue tee shirt gestured no.

"Do you want something?"

The man pointed at a beer bottle.

"You don't talk much do you?"

The man gestured no.

"Get him a beer," said Petros to the woman. "But make sure he pays first."

The man placed two euros and a cell phone on the bar.

The woman put a bottle in front of him and shuffled off into the other room. Petros went back to doing whatever he was doing. The man took a sip of his beer, put it down, and sat as still as a stray cat hoping for dinner to pass by.

Thirty minutes passed and the man had taken no more than three sips of his beer. He'd glanced at everyone coming through the door but hadn't moved from his stool.

Two blond Polish women, one tall and one short, walked through the door, passed the man at the bar, and went into the other room.

The two said hello to some men at other tables before sitting down at a table in the middle of the room. The man in the blue tee shirt pressed a button on his

phone before putting it into his pocket, picked up his
beer in his left hand, and walked toward the women.
He reached behind his back with his right hand as he
stopped at their table. The women didn't seem to notice
him until that moment but immediately gave him their
best smiles. The smiles vanished the instant he brought
his right hand around from behind his back.

"My badge, ladies. Detective Yianni Kouros at your
service." Kouros sat down and put his beer on the table.
"Don't mind me, I'm just your baby sitter. My friends
will be here any minute."

Thirty seconds later, Andreas came through the front
door headed straight toward Kouros. Tassos was right
behind him.

Petros stood up. "What's this?"

Tassos pointed at Petros' chest. "Sit down and shut
up."

Petros paused for a second and sat.

"Smart move. Now send a round of beers over to that
table." He pointed to Kouros. "Understand?"

Petros nodded.

"Good." Tassos patted Petros on the shoulder and
went to join Kouros and Andreas. They sat where each
could cover the other's back.

"Sorry about the drama, ladies," said Andreas. "But
since we couldn't seem to find you to make an appointment, and didn't want any of your friends in here who
might recognize us calling you to suggest you'd be better off not showing up tonight, we thought we'd give
you the chance to meet detective Kouros."

Kouros nodded. "Ladies."

"Yeah, but your grand entrance just screwed us,"
said the tall woman.

"Such language," said Tassos.

"Now everyone on Tinos will be saying we're working with cops."

"Does that have you worried?" said Andreas.

"The Pakistani is dead!"

"One of many," said Tassos.

"I told you we should have left the island," said the short one.

The tall one said something to her in Polish.

"Uhh, uhh, ladies. Remember the ground rules. Only Greek," said Andreas.

"Or what? That you'll arrest us? That would be safer than being loose on this island," said the short one. "Why do you think we haven't been back to our place? It's too dangerous."

"But you still come here," said Tassos.

"We have to work," said the short one.

The tall one said something again in Polish. Kouros shot out his hand and gripped it firmly over her mouth. "Perhaps you didn't hear the man. 'Only Greek.' *Prosze.*" After he'd said "please" in Polish, Kouros took away his hand.

Andreas nodded. "Ladies, you're right. You do have a very serious problem. Whoever killed your Pakistani friend and your two *tsigani* friends must be very nervous over what you might be telling us at this very moment. But, it's too late to change all that. The only way things can get better for you now is if you help us find whoever killed your friends."

Andreas paused, but neither woman said a word. "And I'm the one cop in Greece who can actually help you when he says that he can. You do know that I'm

GADA's Chief of Special Crimes? I gave you my card, didn't I?"

The tall one said, "Yes."

"Do you still have it?"

"No way. We left it on the table," said the short one. "If we took it with us anyone who saw you give it to us might think we intended to call you, and God knows what rumors that would start."

Andreas stared at the short girl. She had street smarts. And she was right. He turned his head and looked around the room. All eyes were on their table except for when his were on theirs. That was to be expected. This was where you came to learn your community's gossip. The Greeks had their *kafeneions* for morning coffee, the *metanastes* their after work places for beers. Andreas wished he could hear what they were saying at their tables.

He watched the sister in her slippers shuffle toward them with a tray of beers. One by one she put a bottle down in front of each of them, taking care as she did. He waited until she'd left.

"Do you remember when you told me about the two Carausii brothers talking about their 'big break' and that guy they called 'the shepherd'?"

"'*Cioban*,' yes."

"Did they ever talk about that in here?"

"No, they never came in here," said the tall one.

Andreas looked around the room as he said, "Did either of you ever talk to someone in here about the brothers or their big break?"

"Before they died?" said the short one.

"Yes."

"No, we kept all that to ourselves."

Andreas focused his eyes first on one, then on the other of the girls. "Did you ever talk in here between yourselves about what they told you?"

"Of course," said the tall one.

"Why wouldn't we?" said the short one. "It was the only interesting thing going on in our lives."

The woman returned with a tray of glasses and began putting them down separately in front of each person at the table.

Andreas reached over to a nearby table and dragged an empty chair up next to him. "*Kiria*. Please, come join us." He'd used the respectful title for a woman and stood to pull the chair out for her.

The woman kept putting down the glasses as if she'd not heard him. He reached over and touched her arm. "Please, sit."

She mumbled something and shuffled off toward the bar.

"*I said sit.*" Andreas said it so loudly that two men getting up from a nearby table immediately sat down. But the woman kept walking toward the doorway.

"Yianni, bring her back."

Kouros lurched out of his chair after her as she went through the doorway into the bar, but Petros stepped into the doorway with his arms spread out above his head, hands on the frame, blocking Kouros' way.

"Please move, sir. We want to speak to the lady."

"She's my sister. Nobody talks to her."

"Move or be moved."

Petros swung his right hand down from the door-frame at Kouros' face. Kouros didn't duck. He leaned in and drove his forehead into Petros' chest, knocking the fat man off-balance, as he grabbed Petros' testicles in his right hand and squeezed the screaming man back into his chair in the bar.

"Stay," said Kouros. He spun around to find the woman but she wasn't there. He ran out the front door. She wasn't there either. He heard a motorbike starting up behind the building and raced to the back just in time to catch a glimpse of a taillight disappearing behind a neighboring building.

"Damnit." Kouros turned and looked at the wall. "How the hell did she get out there so fast?" The back of the building was solid. She could only have come out the front door. He went back inside to where Andreas was sitting.

"Sorry, Chief. She got away."

"How the hell did she do that?" said Tassos.

"That's just what I was wondering. There's no back door."

"Ladies, if you'll excuse us." Andreas stood. "By the way, if I were you I'd continue keeping myself scarce. At least for the time being."

Andreas walked into the bar, followed by Tassos and Kouros. He put his hands on Petros' table and leaned in until he was nose-to-nose with him. "Where did she go?"

"No idea."

"Yianni, take him outside. Around to the back."

This time Kouros didn't ask Petros to move. He grabbed him in a wristlock, twisted hard and dragged him from the table out the door.

Tassos had been watching the main room, just in case someone might get the idea of being a hero. "Ladies and gentlemen, thank you for your patience and understanding. On behalf of the management I'm happy to say that

all drinks this evening are on the house. Enjoy yourselves." He left the bar to the sound of clinking bottles
and shouts of foreign language equivalents for *yamas*.

Behind the building Kouros had Petros' face pinned
against the bar's concrete wall.

Andreas leaned in and whispered in Petros' ear.
"Like I said, 'where did she go?'"

"Fuck you."

"You threatened to kill my son and now have the
balls to say 'fuck you' to me?" Andreas drove his right
and left fists into Petros' kidneys.

Above Petros' scream Andreas said, "You have no
friends, no one is going to come out here to help you.
It's just going to be you and me and big pain until you
tell me what I want to know."

"I don't know what you're talking about. I never
threatened anyone."

"You threatened me, asshole," said Kouros bringing
Petros' face off the cement just far enough to bang it
back against the wall.

"But you were going after my sister. She's not right.
I had to protect her."

"If I were you, I'd start worrying about who's going
to protect you from me," said Andreas.

"Please, I don't have any idea what you're talking
about. Fine, if you want Meerna's address I'll give it
to you. Everyone knows it anyway." He blurted out an
address. "But I don't know where she is now. Honest."

"Pretty smart," said Andreas. "Getting her to eaves-
drop on your customers. I wouldn't have picked up on it
if she hadn't taken such time and care in putting down
first the bottles and later the glasses. A hell of an improvement in service from the last time we were here.

What's the matter, you don't speak your customers' languages, and so you make your sister do your dirty work?"

"She never talks to anyone. Barely to me. I don't know what she does or doesn't understand. All she does is listen. It's her life. She has nothing else but this place and me."

"What about Trelos? Does your sister talk to him?" said Andreas.

"I don't like you calling my brother that name. His name is Pandeleis."

"Just answer my question."

"He talks even less than she does, and the voices he listens to aren't even live. It's whatever comes through his iPod. But they're my only brother and sister, and with our parents dead, it's up to me to protect and take care of them. Even though they only say a goddamned word to me when they need something. Welcome to my life."

Andreas motioned for Kouros to let him loose. "So, why did you stop us from questioning your sister?"

Petros turned around, leaned back against the wall, and rubbed at his left wrist and elbow. "I didn't know what you wanted her for. All I saw was that look of fear in her eyes, and I had to do something."

"What look of fear?" said Andreas.

"She hasn't been right for decades. Tried to kill herself twice. Once by hanging and it screwed up her voice when she does talk. She's supposed to be on medication but doesn't always take it. Stress does her in. I try to keep her life simple. Why do you think I operate this shit hole? For sure as hell we don't need the money. It's to give her something to do that keeps her worry free. You scared her. That's not good."

"What did you do with my card?"

"What card?"

"Are we going to go back to kissing the wall again?" said Andreas.

"No, I don't know what you're talking about."

"Last time I was here I gave my card to the two Polish girls. They left it on the table. I want to know what happened to it."

Petros smirked. "You believed those two hookers when they said they left the card on the table?"

"They didn't run away when I tried to talk to them. Or attempt to assault a police officer. So, the answer to your question is 'yes.' Now what happened to the card?"

"No, idea. Meerna probably threw it away when she cleared the table."

"Where can I find your brother?" said Andreas.

"He lives with my sister. It makes things easier for everybody that way."

Andreas stared at Petros. "Don't try leaving Tinos without my permission. If you do I'll put you away for assaulting a police officer. And don't even think of interfering again with my talking with your sister, or your brother, because if you do…" Andreas patted Petros on the cheek. "I don't really have to tell you, do I?"

Petros gestured no.

"Do I?"

"No."

"Good."

Kouros said, "I just want to know how your sister managed to get out the front door and onto her bike so quickly?"

"She's only slow in her mind. She shuffles along because that's how she likes to walk, but when she was younger she came close to winning Greece's national cycling championship. She still has the legs to move her when she wants to."

"I have only one question," said Tassos. "Who's the Shepherd?"

Petros shrugged. "I know a lot of shepherds and if you're looking for a lamb for August 15th I can give you a couple of good names, but you better hurry before the *tsigani* make away with all their best ones."

Andreas rubbed at his forehead. Great, now tell me something I don't know.

# TWENTY-ONE

THE TINY HOUSE was about a mile and a half east of the port, across the road from the northeast corner of the *Vriokastro* prehistoric settlement, and a few hundred yards from the sea. The closest building to the house was a church a hundred yards to the north. It was after three in the morning when a van with its lights out stopped fifty yards up the road from the house.

"Remember, be careful and expect anything," said Andreas.

The three cops got out of the van, spread out, and carefully made their way up to the house. Kouros went around to the back, Tassos and Andreas waited until he was out of sight before moving up to the front door. One stood on each side of the door, guns drawn.

Andreas nodded and Tassos banged his fist on the door. "*Open up, police.*" Both cops pressed their backs against the wall and waited.

Nothing.

Tassos banged his fist on the door again, and repeated the order.

Still no reply.

Tassos was banging away at the door for a third time when he heard a voice, "Hold your horses," and the sound of an opening lock.

"It's Yianni," said Andreas.

The door opened and Kouros waved them in. "I could

see through the side and rear windows that no one was inside, and when I found an open one I thought I'd spare us the trouble of breaking down the door."

It took less than a minute for them to check out every room. The place was even smaller than it appeared from the outside. Two tiny bedrooms, a bathroom, and one large living room open to the kitchen.

"I thought this family had money," said Kouros. "It looks like the sort of place rich people give their house-keepers to live in."

There was a fireplace in one corner and photographs on the mantle above it. Andreas pointed at a photo. "That's Petros with what looks to be his sister. My guess is the one with them is the other brother."

"Well, at least we know they live here," said Tassos.

"If you call this living," said Kouros.

"I can understand why Trelos spends so much time walking the island if this is what he gets to call home," said Tassos.

"Any ideas on where they might have gone?" said Andreas.

"Not a clue," said Kouros.

"My guess is the sister ran to whomever she passes along the information she picks up in the bar," said Tassos.

"That means if we find her we just might find our shepherd," said Andreas.

"But where's the brother who lives with her?" said Kouros.

"Who knows?" said Tassos. "Probably out wandering the island. Neither bed looks slept in. I'll get the local cops to cover the house and grab him when he comes back," said Tassos.

"While you're at it, ask them to keep an eye on Petros. He's not convinced me he's clean, just that we don't have enough yet to hold him. He'll probably try to connect with his sister. Better have them watch the Polish girls, too, but tell them to make it obvious. Even if they complain it puts a crimp in their business. We want to discourage anyone who might be thinking of getting rid of them."

Tassos said, "Odysseus is still on that holiday Spiros ordered him to take, and the lieutenant covering for him is a real pencil pusher. I can almost hear him bitching about how our crisis-mandated cutbacks mean we're asking him to tie up half the Tinos police force on a case he must know the minister wants closed."

Andreas shrugged. "Once you point out the potential downside implications to his career if the robbery of the century takes place in his backyard, under his nose, on his watch I'm sure he'll find us the people."

"You have such a high opinion of our brethren," said Tassos.

"Only most of them." Andreas yawned. "Time to get some sleep. Tomorrow we've a lot of hunting to do."

"For what?" said Kouros.

"Answers."

FIRST THING THE next morning Tassos and Andreas stopped by Eleni's office while Kouros went off to make sure the local police were providing the requested surveillance.

"I certainly hope you're here with good news, uncle. August 15th is the day after tomorrow and if you still think something might happen to the *Megalochari* I'm very uncomfortable at keeping that from my boss."

"Don't tell him yet. We think we're on to someone who may have the answers we're looking for," said Andreas.

"Who's that?"

"Meerna, the sister of Petros and Trelos."

"You must be joking." Eleni paused. "If you're not, I think you're both crazy. I'm not even sure she can talk. I've never heard her say a word in all the years I've known her."

"Have you ever tried to speak with her?" said Tassos.

"Yes, many times when I was an administrator at the Foundation's old age home. She was a volunteer there and whenever I tried she simply shuffled away."

"What in the world did she do there?"

"Whatever the doctors and staff told her to do. They loved her because she had an uncanny ability to anticipate what needed to be done without being asked."

"All without her saying a word?" said Andreas.

"That was regarded as a plus. Like I said, she just did as she was told." Eleni smiled. "A rare quality among Greeks."

"Does she still volunteer there?"

"Not that I know of."

"What else do you know about her?"

"Aside from that tragic love affair I mentioned to you once before, I heard she was a terrific athlete in her youth."

"We heard the same thing. Almost a national cycling champion," said Tassos.

"She just missed making Greece's Olympic team," said Eleni.

"For cycling?" said Andreas.

"No, the pentathlon."

"Amazing," said Tassos. "Seeing her now it's hard to imagine what she once was."

"Her brother even more so, but his skill set was pure gray matter," said Eleni.

"Petros?" said Tassos.

"No, Trelos. It's said he was the smartest kid of his generation on Tinos. A certified genius."

"What happened to him?" said Andreas.

"The same thing that happens to a lot of kids who can't find stimulation in school, they find it elsewhere. He ended up hooked on heroin. His parents tried everything they could to help him. Even had him physically dragged off the island to some special clinic in Switzerland. Rumor was they did something to his brain there. When he came back he was never the same. He spent all his time with his music and computers. And after his parents died he never talked to anyone again. He just started dancing around the island and hasn't stopped."

"How did his parents die?" said Tassos.

"In a car accident on the road between here and Pyrgos. They were driving back late at night when their car went off the road and over a cliff. The police said the father apparently fell asleep at the wheel. A real tragedy."

"How come you know so much about the accident?" said Andreas.

"It was big news on Tinos. The family was quite prominent, descendants of one of our island's most celebrated heroes of the War of Independence, and zealously dedicated to preserving Tinos traditional life. They also were among the richest Tinian families and left a considerable donation to the *Megalochari*."

"You mean the Foundation, don't you?" said Andreas.
"Yes."

"How considerable?"

"I really can't say."

"Can't or won't?"

"It was one of the largest bequests ever received from a Tinian family."

"Seven, eight, nine figures?"

"I've said all I'm going to say on that subject." Her tone was sharp.

Tassos stood up. "Thanks, *kukla*. I don't think we have any more questions, do we Andreas?"

Andreas looked at Tassos and smiled. "I guess that's your uncle's way of saying I'm pushing you too hard again. Sorry. But I do have one last question. Do you have any idea where we might find Trelos?"

"He always walks the road his parents died on. If you follow that road sooner or later you'll find Trelos."

Andreas stood up. "Thanks. Anything else we should know about him?"

"Yes, I understand he's really quite harmless."

THEY FOUND A place to park on the right side of the road up against a hillside just before a hairpin turn to the right. On the left was a brilliant view of the sea, a guardrail, and a sheer drop of several hundred feet. It was impossible to see around the bend at what might be coming from the direction of Pyrgos, but this was the only spot within three hundred yards of the curve that allowed them to park off the road.

"According to the police report, they were coming in the other direction and went over the cliff right there." Kouros pointed from the back seat of the police cruiser straight ahead between Andreas and Tassos. "There was no guardrail then."

"Did you find anyone at the station who knew any-thing more about the accident than was in the report?" said Andreas.

"By the time you called and asked me to get the re-port the only two who might have known anything more were out doing our surveillance. I left word for them to call me when their shifts were over."

"What makes you think they might know some-thing?" said Tassos.

"The accident happened about a dozen years ago, and those two are the only ones still on the force who were here at the time."

Andreas started drumming his fingers on the steer-ing wheel. "You know, your niece is right. If we had to say out loud what makes us think Trelos and his sister have anything to do with whatever is going on here, we'd be giving Spiros grounds for certifying us as crazy."

"Speaking of crazy, Chief, look who's coming down the road."

Dancing toward them in the oncoming lane, wear-ing a black tee shirt, black running shorts, a black waist pack, and black tennis shoes, was Trelos. He seemed oblivious to everything but what was coming through the earphones from the white iPod in his right hand. He did a pirouette-like move at the edge of the road clos-est to the cliff before backing across the road toward the hillside in a style that would make Michael Jackson fans proud. He seemed to catch a rhythm that had him strutting up to the police car. He stopped in front and spun around twice, almost like an ant searching for a way around an unexpected obstacle in its path.

Andreas opened his door. "This should be interesting."

# TWENTY-TWO

TRELOS DIDN'T MOVE from in front of the police car when the three cops got out and surrounded him. Nor did he stop moving in time to his music.

"Pandeleis, good morning." Andreas thought it better to call Trelos by his given name.

Trelos kept spinning and dancing in front of the police car.

"I said, 'Good morning.'"

Andreas thought he saw a slight nod, but beyond that nothing to indicate Trelos heard a word Andreas had said.

"We want to talk to you about your sister."

More dancing.

"Get in the car."

He didn't move from his spot.

"Yianni, put him in the back seat."

Kouros stepped forward, gently put his hand on Trelos' elbow, and led him back to the car. Kouros opened the rear door on the driver side and steered him into the car, taking care not to hit Trelos' head on the roof pillar. Kouros closed the door and went back to the front of the car.

"I thought you were going to rip off his earphones," said Tassos.

"No reason for that, he seems a gentle soul."

"Inspires your protective instincts, does he?" said

Andreas. "That's quite a gift to have. His brother, Petros, said something about it being his obligation to 'protect' him. I wonder if his sister feels the same way."

"What are you getting at?" said Kouros.

"From the way things seem to be going with this guy, I'd say nothing," said Tassos.

"Let's take him back to his house," said Andreas. "Maybe we'll find some way to get through to him there. Because we sure as hell aren't getting anywhere with him here."

WHEN THEY ARRIVED at the house a Tinos police car was parked in front.

Andreas turned to look at Trelos in the back seat. "They've been waiting for you to come home. You put many people to a lot of trouble to find you."

Kouros got out of the backseat on the passenger side and went around to get Trelos out the other side.

"By the way, since you obviously didn't come home last night, where were you?" said Andreas. "You're clean shaven, so don't tell me you were out dancing on the streets all night."

Andreas got out of the car when Trelos did. "I'll take him from here, Yianni. Please thank the Tinos cops and tell them they can leave now. And check to see if any of them know anything about you-know-what."

Andreas pointed in the direction of the house and said to Trelos, "Walk."

He didn't move.

"I didn't think you'd listen. That's your hustle isn't it? I don't buy your Peter Pan routine. So, *move*." Andreas pushed Trelos toward the front door.

Trelos paused.

Andreas pushed him again. "Keep moving or I'll ram that iPod so far up your ass you won't need earphones."

Tassos stepped in next to Andreas and whispered. "I see Yianni's playing good cop and you're playing Attila the Hun cop."

"He's moving, isn't he?"

Once inside, Trelos walked over to the mantle and touched a photograph of a man and a woman.

"Are those your parents?" said Andreas.

Trelos said nothing. He went over to the refrigerator, took out a bottle of water, opened a cupboard, took out a glass, filled it with water, drank it all, refilled the glass, and drank that, too. Then he put the bottle back in the refrigerator, took the glass over to the sink, washed it, dried it, and put it back in the cupboard.

"I see you clean up after yourself. Is that because you have no help here? Does your sister help when she's here? Or isn't she here that much? Or maybe you're the one who's not here that much? Funny, isn't it? Such a tiny place for two grown-up people, especially for someone with your peculiar habits."

Trelos went into the bathroom and started to close the door. Andreas stopped the door with his foot.

"Uh, uh. No private time for you. Don't worry, I won't watch. Just make on like you're back in the army. You were in the army, weren't you?"

There was the unmistakable sound of a stream hitting water.

"Good boy."

Andreas waited until Trelos came out of the bathroom. "You know what has me wondering. Here you are, a big time music fan, into computers for sure and there's not a computer or audio devices to be seen anywhere in here. Not even a radio. I hope you're not going to try and convince me that your only link to all the music you love in this world is that tiny little thing in your hand.

"All of which makes me wonder whether you have another place for your music. Maybe even a whole house somewhere else. Is that where your sister is now, at your other place? You know we're going to find it sooner or later. So why don't you just tell me now. It will save us the bother of ripping up this place looking for clues. It would be a shame to make a mess so unnecessarily?"

No answer.

Kouros stuck his head inside the doorway. "Chief, may I speak with you?"

Andreas looked at Tassos. "Keep an eye on him," and went outside.

He was back in two minutes, walked over to the mantle, and picked up the photograph of Trelos' parents.

"Lovely looking people. Your mom and dad?"

No answer.

"You know, my own father died when I was very young. I never really got over it. But I did get on with my life. Why, I wonder, haven't you?" Andreas smiled.

No answer.

"I just found out that it could have been a lot worse for you. Your sister was with them the night they died. She went with them to dinner in Pyrgos, but she didn't come back with them. Said she wasn't feeling well and stayed over at a relative's house. My, weren't you lucky? You almost lost your only sister and your parents in one night."

Trelos didn't move.

Andreas studied the photograph. "Interesting, looks like it was taken right around here." He walked over to the window on the north wall and held the photo up to the light. "You know, the church in the background of the photo looks an awful lot like that one over there." He pointed at the church in the distance. "Could that, by chance, be your family's church? Perhaps where your parents are buried?"

No answer.

"Tassos, why don't you and Yianni take a walk over to that church and check it out. And while you're at it, take a look inside the other structures in the area." He stared at Trelos. "Just in case his sister might have gotten lost in one of them."

Trelos hadn't moved from where he'd stopped after coming out of the bathroom, but his eyes trailed after Tassos leaving the house.

"You know, Pandeleis, all this talking to myself has given me a mighty thirst." Andreas put the photograph down on the kitchen counter by the window. "I assume you won't mind if I help myself to some water?" He reached for the refrigerator door handle.

"Not at all, Chief Inspector Kaldis. But please, call me Trelos, everyone else does. By the way, your friends are wasting their time. They won't find a thing."

Trelos walked across the room to where Andreas was standing, took off his earphones, and put them and the iPod down on the counter. He picked up the photograph of his parents, kissed it, and carried it back to the mantle.

Trelos turned and smiled at Andreas. "No one will. Ever."

ANDREAS GRIPPED THE door handle for a few seconds, opened the door, took out a bottle of water, closed the door, opened the cupboard, took out two glasses with one hand, shut the cupboard with the back of the same hand, turned, and set the glasses and bottle on the countertop across from Trelos.

"Is this where the master-criminal divulges his secret plan to his noble adversary knowing that it cannot be stopped?"

Trelos smiled. "Not at all. There is nothing left to stop. My plan is simple and underway. My only desire is to give choices to those who would like to change their lives for the better. Give them the chance at finding honest work they truly enjoy, an opportunity I never had. I support them financially until they are able to support themselves."

"So, you're the Shepherd."

"I have taken an oath to tell only the truth or speak not at all."

"I'll take that as an 'I'm not going to tell you.' And what happens to those who talk too much, death?"

"I do not understand you. We are dedicated to bringing a better life to those desiring it, not death."

"'Revenge or Death' is a rather catchy slogan for an organization claiming such lofty goals."

"That is not our slogan. Yes, we are modeled on *Filiki Eteria*, for it too brought great change to Greece in very difficult times, and in no small measure because of the dedication and commitment of foreigners. But those words are the creation of one who does not understand our goals or purposes."

"And who would that person be?"

"I have no idea. But surely not one we embrace in the brotherhood."

"Why all the secrecy?"

"There are those who do not share our goals. Help-ing the foreign born and outcasts of society to attain better lives directly challenges many who would like to keep them down, akin to slaves."

"I can't argue with you there."

"And then there are those who would simply like to rob us of the riches we use in place of empty promises and prayers to make the lives of others better."

"Where's the money come from?"

"It is my family's. I spend only what is ours. I do not seek to raise funds."

"Or compete with the Foundation?"

Trelos smiled.

"And your sister, what about her and your brother? Are they also part of your 'brotherhood.'"

"No, Petros would not understand. He is of the sort that sees no value beyond the euro in non-Greeks. And she is far too fragile for the stress of working with the world's most difficult souls. She just informs me of those who pass her way who are in need, and I do what I can to help them."

"You mean she tells you what she overhears in the bar?"

"Not just in the bar. She, as I, is virtually invisible wherever we may go. It is as if we do not exist. In time you learn to accept that as a rare luxury."

"What about the others in your organization? Are they also 'invisible.'"

"I have sworn an oath never to reveal another mem-ber. But, believe me when I say they are good souls, who care only to do good."

"Like murdering five other souls?"

Trelos reached for the bottle and filled his glass. "I know of three deaths here, not of five. But of those three, I know little more than I do of the other two. And what I do know is certainly far less than you."

"Did you know the Carausii brothers who died here?"

"Yes, they came to us along with their *tsigani* clan."

"Did you know that they were planning to expose you to the Albanians?"

"No, but I was prepared for that day to come. Everyone has a Judas. Don't you find it strange that wherever you find good intentions massing, jackals come in packs to devour them?"

"You're getting a little heavy on me, Trelos."

"Albanians are a unique force in our country. Whether or not Greeks wish to admit it, many trace their roots back to Albania, and Orthodox Albanians assimilate easily into our culture. At least those who want to do so. But for those ruthless few who persist in their historic criminal ways, one cannot reason with them. They will take by violence what you are willing to give in peace.

"I could not risk allowing them into my house, for fear they would pillage and burn it to the ground."

"And the *tsigani*? Do you actually think you're going to change their ways?"

"It's worth the effort. Tinos offers a unique opportunity at succeeding with *tsigani* for they revere the holy icon and are accustomed to behaving when on our island.

"But Tinos is only our beginning. This island can handle a population five times its size, and Greece offers many more places where we can do our work. All Greeks know that past governments have banished those they labeled 'undesirables' to the islands. We only seek to modify that practice by offering the unwanted incentives for finding a better way of life. We wish to make them part of the solution and not treat them as the problem."

"Is that why you excluded Albanians? You were afraid they wouldn't stay with the program."

"You could put it that way, but I realized in denying them what others were offered so freely would most certainly attract their attention. In time, one or another of them would likely attempt to do us harm."

"And just what do you plan on doing when that time comes?"

"It's already been done. We've built an army of *metanastes* who have found a better, honest life. They will not allow the exploiters to take it away from them."

"That might work. The Albanians wouldn't want to go to war with the rest of Eastern Europe, unless there's a mighty big profit in it. But what's going to prevent someone from some day putting a bullet in your head, or a hit and run driver taking you out on one of your daily jaunts."

"I do not fear death. But nor do I wish to hasten it. That is why I keep my role in all of this secret. And why I am telling you all of this."

"Not sure I get that last part."

"You would not stop until you found me. I could see that. And in so doing would undoubtedly reveal my identity to the world. I judged it better that I confide in you my secret, show to you that I am not the 'master-criminal' you seek, but only one who seeks to better the lives of the unloved and anonymous. This could change the world."

"Great, but now that I know, what's to keep me from telling the world who you are?"

"Nothing, but what have I done to justify your betraying my confidence? Not turn over my sister to you? How could I do that? The stress you would bring into her life would surely cause her to try and take it again. Besides, it's hardly worth the trade to you. Exposing me to the wrath of the Albanians will only return all those we are helping back to a life of crime."

Trelos smiled. "Lastly, who's going to believe you when you say, 'Trelos the madman is behind it all'?"

Andreas pulled a silver-color digital recorder out of his pocket. "Surprise."

Trelos shrugged. "It's been scrambled since you came into the house. Like I said, 'I do not wish to hasten' my demise."

Andreas checked the recorder and put it back into his pocket. "You do realize this is not going to end here."

"I should hope not. The killers of those poor people must be found."

"There's more involved."

"Are you talking about the Foundation and the 'robbery of a church' that's supposed to happen here this week?" He accented his words with finger quotes.

"How do you know about that?"

"As I said, we are invisible. Many people talk. We listen. But don't worry, I can assure you that will not happen."

"How can you be so sure?"

Trelos picked up his iPod and earphones. "Because it's already happened." He put on his earphones. "I have no more to say." And began to dance as Kouros and Tassos came through the front door.

"We didn't find a thing, Chief."

Trelos did a quick pirouette, ending with a wink that only Andreas could see.

# TWENTY-THREE

"THAT'S ONE SMART son-of-a-bitch. He made sure to put you in a 'your word against his' situation over a supposed conversation between you and a notorious whack-job who never talks," said Tassos.

"And how the hell do you scramble a recorder?" said Kouros from the backseat of the cruiser heading toward town.

"You're asking me?" said Andreas. "I'm still trying to remember what he said."

"You remembered enough for me to have a chat with my niece. Unless one of us talked where we shouldn't have, Eleni's the only other person who knew about the robbery."

"And what was all that about the robbery having 'already happened'?" said Kouros.

"Another question for Eleni," said Andreas.

Kouros shook his head. "What I don't get is why does everybody in the sister's family think she needs protection? She's the one going face-to-face every night in that bar with the hard-ass customers her brother is trying to save. And from the way she got away from us last night, she just might have the biggest balls in her family."

"I think Trelos has a pretty good size pair," said Andreas. "Let's not forget he's been playing chicken with the Albanians."

"I'd say leaving dead bodies all over Greece qualifies as more than a game of chicken," said Kouros.

"But who's doing it, and why?" said Andreas.

"Isn't Trelos the obvious 'who'?" said Tassos. "I can't see him personally doing that sort of heavy-lifting dirty work, but for sure there's a hell of a lot of guys in his brotherhood who could. Like he said, that's why the Albanians don't want to mess with his 'army.'"

"Great, so what's the 'why' answer?" said Andreas.

"He's sending a simple message. 'This is what happens to anyone who tries to fuck with me,'" said Kouros.

Andreas gestured no. "No, not 'fuck with me.' That can't be the message. As far as we can tell the only threat the victims posed to Trelos was to expose him as the Shepherd."

"Sounds like a difference without a distinction to me," said Tassos. "Once he's exposed, the Albanians would do the fucking."

Andreas nodded. "Which is precisely why it makes no sense that, if he's responsible for eliminating those he thought posed a threat to exposing him, he simply out of the blue decided to announce to me who he was."

"Like he said, he thought you'd find out sooner or later, so he's trying to con you with misdirection," said Kouros.

"Bullshit. If he was behind the intricate planning that went into arranging the murders of those five men, plus getting that package to me, and his reason for doing all that was to keep his identity a secret, I can't imagine that less than an hour of my busting his balls would break him. He knew that even if I suspected who he was there was no way I could prove it. All he had to do was keep playing dumb and wait for the chance to take me out.

"No, we're definitely still missing the 'why.'"

"Aren't you forgetting the 'robbery'? He could have said what he did to distract you from discovering what he's planned?" said Kouros.

"Only if the robbery hasn't already happened. For if it has, even the murders make no sense."

"Which is precisely why we're seeing my niece."

Andreas pulled into the lot behind the Foundation's offices. "Who gets to play bad cop this time?"

"She's my niece, my turn."


"WHAT DO YOU mean you have good news and bad news to tell me, uncle?"

"The good news is, we understand from a reliable source that your church won't be robbed. At least not this week."

"That is good news, but I never really thought anything like that was possible."

"The bad news is, you've already been robbed."

"*What*? That cannot be. Who told you that?"

"No, the question is, 'Whom did you talk to about a possible robbery?'"

"No one."

"You're the only one on the island other than the three of us who knew."

"Honest, I didn't tell anyone at the Foundation. I kept my word."

Andreas raised his hand. "Excuse me, but possibly you mentioned something in passing about it to a girl-friend, a boyfriend or—"

"I'm not a gossip." Her tone was sharp.

"Enough already with that dismissive tone of voice of yours. I don't like it and it's not working. I want to know who you told and *I want to know now*." Tassos was shouting.

"Stop, uncle, you're making a scene."

"Not nearly as big a one as I'll make if you don't tell me what I want to know."

"Okay, okay. After we met at the taverna, Dad called to ask why the private meeting. I think he was hurt that you hadn't included him. I told him it was 'police business.' That made him worry I was in some sort of trouble, so I told him it wasn't about me, but the possibility of someone planning to rob a church on Tinos. But I swore him to secrecy before telling him."

Tassos smacked his hands on his thighs. "Swearing your father to secrecy is about as good as telling a hungry kid not to touch the cookies. God knows how many he told."

"And considering the source of the information, it wouldn't take much guesswork to figure out the church was the Foundation's," said Kouros.

"Well, at least we have our answer to that part of the puzzle. Now on to the grand prize question," said Andreas. "When was the last time the Foundation was robbed?"

"And we're not interested in one-hundred-seventy-year-old stories," said Tassos.

"We've never been robbed."

"Is that your final answer?" said Andreas.

"Yes."

"Good, where's your boss's office?"

"Are you threatening me?"

"Of course not. It's just obvious you're not included

in the Foundation's 'we've-been-robbed' loop. There's no doubt in my mind that over the last one-hundred-seventy-years the Foundation's been robbed. The only question is when and how much was taken."

"My boss will not see you."

"Yes he will. I'm Chief Inspector of Special Crimes for GADA, and I've reason to believe a robbery has occurred at the Foundation, an institution under the direct supervision of two government ministries. If your boss refuses to see me I'll be duty bound to present a full report to the appropriate ministers. And by the way, if that's not enough to convince your boss to see me, suggest that he begin preparing to accommodate all the media that will be joining the pilgrims and *tsigani* camped out around the Foundation. In my experience, government ministers have a harder time keeping juicy secrets from the press than daughters do from fathers."

Eleni swallowed hard. "I'll be right back."

As soon as she left the room Tassos said, "I thought I was supposed to be the bad cop."

"Sorry, force of habit."

"What do we do now?" said Kouros.

"Wait," said Tassos.

Andreas looked at a photograph on a bookshelf behind Eleni's desk. It was of Eleni with her father and probably her mother. "Yianni, did that cop you talked to about the accident that killed Trelos' parents remember anything squirrelly about it?"

"No, he said it was straightforward. The father fell asleep at the wheel."

"Did they check the brakes?"

"Yes, and all the other systems. Everything was in working order."

"What about toxicology?"

"Only tested for blood-alcohol levels. Nothing out of line there either."

"Why are you asking?" said Tassos. "Do you think the kiddies did away with mommy and daddy for the family fortune?"

"It's happened before. And their deaths probably gave Trelos what he needed for his save the world project," said Andreas.

"And if he'd been able to catch his sister in the car with them it would have increased his share of the estate," said Kouros.

"What's happened to your 'gentle soul' take on Trelos?"

"I've learned to be flexible in my thinking. It comes with maturity."

Andreas flashed an open palm at Kouros just as the door to the office swung open.

A pudgy man with a neatly trimmed salt and pepper toothbrush mustache stepped inside and shut the door. He was about Kouros' height and Tassos' age. He went directly to Eleni's desk and sat down in her chair.

"I asked Eleni for permission to use her office. She's using mine for now. I understand you want to speak to her boss about a robbery at our Foundation. As I am responsible for overseeing the protection of the Foundation and its treasures, the vice-president asked that you kindly direct your inquiries to me. Please, call me Dimitri. Now, how can I help you?"

"Thank you for being so concise and to the point. I shall be the same. My name is Andreas, and I'm GADA's Chief Inspector of Special Crimes."

"I know your boss."

Andreas smiled. "Everyone seems to. Then I'm sure

you appreciate the delicate nature of the situation as I have not yet brought the details I intend to share with you to his attention."

"Why did you come to Eleni with your questions and not to her superior directly?"

"She is my colleague's niece," he nodded toward Tassos, "And we came to her only for a recommendation of the appropriate person to approach at the Foundation."

"Did you tell her what you're about to share with me?"

"Only that it concerned a possible robbery at the Foundation."

Dimitri nodded. "Good. This is the sort of thing that can spread harmful unnecessary gossip. We can't have things getting out of hand, can we?"

Andreas nodded. "No, but nor can we afford to have more bodies turning up. Five dead and counting is a pretty good indicator that things are already out of hand."

"I'm sorry, but I don't see how any of those deaths could possibly have anything to do with the Foundation."

"All I'm saying is that bad guys tied into the murder victims seem to know that the Foundation has been robbed. It's only the good guys who are in the dark."

"Five dead souls." Dimitri crossed himself. "How can you be sure their deaths are related to the robbing of our church?"

"Shall I take that as a 'yes' as to whether you've been robbed? Because believe me, there are three murders on Tinos and two in Athens tied into it." Andreas let his words sink in.

Dimitri seemed lost in thought. "We noticed the first one about ten years ago."

"The first one?" said Andreas. "How many have there been?"

"That's hard to say?"

"What do you mean, 'hard to say'?"

"They're not wholesale thefts of treasures, just one here, one there, hardly noticeable except when we take inventory."

"How often do you take inventory?"

"Depends. For some items it's done once a year, for others not so often."

"Are you saying you're still being robbed?" said Tassos.

Dimitri nodded. "With each inventory we're missing more things."

"And you never tried to catch the thieves or at least stop them?" said Andreas.

"Of course we tried. We suspected everyone, still do, even ourselves. We installed security cameras wherever we could, but the thieves found ways to get around them and things kept disappearing."

"Why didn't you call the police?" said Andreas.

"As you said, Chief Inspector, it is a situation of an extremely 'delicate nature' and new donations more than replenish what is lost. We've come to accept it as God's way of tithing us for the many contributions we receive in the Holy Virgin's name."

"Wow, that's some way to look at being robbed, tithing!" said Kouros.

"Tithing means ten percent. Are you saying you've been loosing ten percent of donations every year for the past ten years?" said Tassos.

"I see no reason to put a number on it. You get the idea."

"Now that's what I call a very serious motive for murder," said Andreas. "I want a list describing every stolen item. If we can find one missing item we might have a shot at tracing it back to the thieves."

Dimitri shook his head. "I'm sorry, but although we log in every item before it's sent off to storage, the description is no more than the weight of a 'gold ring' or the size of 'diamond earrings' and that sort of thing, except for the most precious of items and those have never been stolen."

"What do they steal?" said Tassos.

"Simple things of value, but not valuable enough to be unique. Gold jewelry, gems, items like that."

"All portable?" said Kouros.

"Yes."

"Great," said Tassos. "We've got thieves acting like careful mice, taking only what they can carry away in their cheeks."

"Where did the robberies take place?" said Andreas.

"There was no one place."

"What do you mean?"

"Our main vaults are here, in caverns and rooms underneath this complex, but we have other places for safekeeping all over the island."

"A sort of 'not keeping your eggs in one basket' approach to security?" said Kouros.

"Yes, but once we thought we'd secured one location things would disappear from another."

"And you've been robbed at all locations?" said Andreas.

"Yes."

Andreas put his right elbow on the desk, and his forehead in the palm of his hand.

"I know just how you feel, Chief Inspector. It is a burden I've carried for the Foundation for many years."

Andreas looked up, "You mean the Foundation's commission doesn't know about any of this?"

Dimitri said nothing.

"I want a map showing every site where you've been robbed," said Andreas.

Dimitri gestured no. "I cannot possibly do that. The locations are top secret, known only to a handful of persons completely above suspicion. And that includes the few longtime, trusted employees who inconspicuously transport items from the Church to our places of safekeeping."

"Plus, let's not forget the thieves. They seem pretty well informed. Dimitri, that was a non-negotiable request. You've left us no other place to start. Either I get the list from you or I start asking government ministers to get it from the Foundation for me. And believe me that most definitely will '*burden*' the Foundation's commission."

"But—"

Andreas cut him off. "How you choose to deal with all those robberies is your own business. Frankly, unless you force my hand, I don't want to get involved in any of that or go public with your 'delicate' decade of details. But how I choose to deal with solving five murders is my business. Do we understand each other?"

Dimitri cleared his throat. "Very well, but promise me you'll not share what I give you with anyone outside of this room."

"Agreed."

"So help you God?"

Andreas looked at Tassos and Kouros.

"So help us God," they said.

# TWENTY-FOUR

THE THREE COPS stood by their car in the parking lot behind the church and across the street from a grassy, tree-shaded park running up a hillside. "What I don't understand is how Dimitri possibly could have kept something like that secret from the Foundation's commission for ten years," said Tassos.

"You're assuming that he did," said Andreas. "And isn't just taking one for the team. After all, Eleni said he's dedicated nearly his entire life to the Foundation."

"But why keep a robbery secret in the first place?" said Kouros.

"The 'why' I understand," said Tassos. "I don't know if you remember, but the Foundation once announced a public auction to convert some donated treasures into cash to fund its projects. Supporters went wild. They didn't want their gifts to the *Megalochari* sold off to strangers. Can you imagine how those supporters would react if they knew how much of what they've donated has been stolen?

"I think the 'why' is nothing more than our traditional Greek 'cost of doing business' attitude. You must give up to get."

"But if we're talking about tithing that's a hell of lot of money disappearing every year," said Kouros.

Andreas opened the driver's door. "Guys, I'd prefer if you'd come up with another 'why' theory."

"How about a conspiracy between the supervising government ministries and someone at the Foundation?" said Kouros opening the driver side rear door.

"Another Greek trait," said Tassos. "When all else fails, find a conspiracy." He walked around the car and opened the passenger side front door.

"It would also answer your 'how' question," said Kouros sliding onto the back seat.

"Can't we come up with something else, like biblical justification for all this? After all, we are talking about a church here," said Andreas.

Tassos sat down next to Andreas. "You mean like not cutting to the edges of your field so that the poor may live off of what is left?" said Tassos.

"That'll work," said Andreas.

"But it's Old Testament," said Tassos.

"Still works, I'm just looking for someway to justify to myself why I'm willing to ignore a ten year cover-up."

"Come on," said Tassos. "You don't actually believe that no one at those ministries knows about the robberies?"

"I see, we're back to conspiracies," said Andreas.

"Yes, but let's not look upon it as one premised on an opportunity to corruptly profit, but instead evolving out of a genuine desire to protect the victim from further harm by adopting a 'let sleeping dogs lie' approach."

"Wow, you make it sound as if something like that could actually happen in this country," said Kouros.

"Enough already. Let's leave it at if we find the thieves we'll find the killers. And screw whatever else happens." Andreas started the car and handed Tassos a document. "Here's the secret map. You navigate. Just tell me the first stop on our treasure hunt."

"Eleni's father's taverna."

Andreas looked at Tassos. "You're joking. The Foundation has a secret vault at his place?"

"No. I'm hungry."


THE FATHER PUT them at a large table beneath a sprawling tree and placed a bottle of water on the table together with what he called the "the yield of their shade," ripe, freshly peeled figs. Tassos thanked him, and took him aside for a few moments of private conversation.

By the time he returned half the figs were gone. "Hey, you're eating them all."

"No, only our half," smiled Kouros.

"What did he have to say?" said Andreas.

"No more than what Eleni told us." Tassos popped a fig into his mouth. "Plus, the part about him 'only telling a few people.'"

"Anyone we know?"

"Nope. But enough to say it probably got back to Trelos through him or possibly indirectly though Trelos' sister. Eleni's father mentioned it to a *metanastes* who works here and hangs out at her brother's bar."

"Maybe we should ask Eleni's father if he has any idea where the sister might be?" said Andreas.

"How would he know?" said Kouros.

"Because gossip goes two ways," said Tassos. "And, I already asked him. The only places he could think of were where we already looked. He said that whole area over by Trelos' house belongs to their family. It covers practically everything for a quarter mile north of the sea between Aghios Fokas and Aghios Sostis, except for that prehistoric settlement."

Tassos took another fig. "He did have a bit of interesting gossip on the sister. It seems that fellow who jilted her wasn't all to blame. He came from a very traditional family but he wasn't from Tinos and not someone her parents approved of. Her parents were outraged when the couple became engaged without obtaining their consent and refused to give her a dowry. That killed the deal for the boy's parents. No dowry, no marriage."

"How long after that did the parents die?" said Andreas.

"You and your patricide-matricide theory. She was jilted about a decade before, so that would have given her a very stale motive."

"Anything else?"

"She'd tried to get the Foundation to give her a dowry, something they did for girls in need of that sort of help. But the Foundation said that since her family was very rich they couldn't do it for her. No one has heard her say a word since."

"That's probably when she tried to hang herself," said Andreas.

"Did he have anything to say about Trelos?" said Kouros.

"Nothing more than we already know."

Andreas reached for the map in front of Tassos. "Since you're busy with your figs, let me take a look at this." He spread the map out on the table. "And, Yianni, keep an eye on the father. I don't want his curiosity costing me my soul oath to God."

The map was a common tourist map, marked with eleven bright red circles. Starting with a circle in the port town around Panagia Evangelistria, five more ran roughly north centered on Kechrovouni Monastery, the ancient Xobourgo fortress, a Catholic Jesuit monastery, a place outside Greece's finest basket weaving village of Volax, and a spot on the sea off to the northwest just east of Makrisia Bay. From west to east Dimitri had circled five more sites, beginning at the island's artistic heart in Pyrgos and moving east to Katapoliani Monastery, the island's livestock breeding capital in the Steni-Potamia-Myrsini villages corridor, the church of The Prophet Ilias on a western plateau of Mount Tsiknias, and a promontory just west of the Bay of Livada. Within each circle were delicately drawn crosshairs, also in bright red.

"Here comes pappy," said Kouros.

Andreas quickly folded over the map.

"May I get you anything?"

"Yes," said Andreas. "Undisturbed solitude."

Tassos raised his hand, "Sorry, *filos*, my friend has had a very bad time of it recently. His wife went off on their honeymoon without him. So, let's just give him his space. I'll let you know if we need anything."

The father hesitated as if wanting to say something, but turned and walked away.

"I appreciate what you did to cover for Eleni, but couldn't you have been a bit nicer to her father? He's like a brother to me."

"But he's not mine, and I made a promise to God not to let anyone but us see this."

"You know, Yianni, maybe there's some truth to what I said about the reason for our friend's mood."

"I've got no dog in this fight. You two work it out," said Kouros.

"Okay, I'm sorry if I offended him. Does that make everyone happy?" Andreas unfolded the map and spread it out on the table. "Now, would you please take a look at this to see if we can come up with a clue as to how thieves pulled off so many robberies for such a long time without getting caught."

"My God," said Tassos. "Those sites are all over the island. It will take us ten more years just to get to them all."

"And places like Xobourgo have been used for concealing treasures for centuries. How the hell did the thieves ever find where the stuff was hidden inside that massive rock?" said Kouros.

"Or any of the other places without a map like this one, with crosshairs precisely drawn over treasure rooms," said Tassos.

"This is starting to sound like an *Indiana Jones* film," said Kouros.

"Let's just figure out what these places have in common," said Andreas.

They stared at the map.

Andreas was the first to speak. "The church in town and that convent where the nun's dreams led to the discovery of the *Megalochari* are obvious hiding places for Foundation treasures. Not so obvious are the monastery outside of Kardiani and that church in the middle of nowhere on Mount Tsiknias. But I'd say the cleverest move was getting the Catholics into the act by using their Jesuit monastery."

"So, we have five church related sites," said Kouros.

"Six, if you take a close look at where the crosshairs meet at that spot over by Steni." Tassos pointed with his finger. "Right by where the crosshairs meet is a small church. Care to bet whether there's a tunnel running between the church and whatever is at the 'x'?"

"Okay, so now we have six likely places within church control. What's that mean?" said Andreas.

Kouros said, "Just like the fortress at Xobourgo, the church on Tinos has always used its properties for concealing treasures from marauders and pirates. I'd bet there are secret passages and hidden rooms for just that purpose at all those locations. The thieves probably knew the same thing."

"What about the other five?" said Andreas.

Tassos pointed to the map again. "Xobourgo is a no-brainer. It's a stone honeycomb of secret places. And that spot outside Volax is filled with volcanic thirty-foot high monoliths and bizarre-shape boulders covering a plateau of natural hiding places. As for Pyrgos, it's home to some of Tinos' greatest marble sculptors and the crosshairs are fixed on a place filled with some of the finest examples of their craft, entombments in the Pyrgos cemetery. Another not so unusual hiding place for treasure.

"But what I can't get a fix on are the two along the coastline. There's nothing there but shoreline."

Kouros took a paperback book out of his back pocket.

"What's that?" said Andreas.

"A guidebook to Tinos."

"You're kidding," said Tassos.

"How do you think I've been able to find my way around this island on my own? Or know how to pronounce 'Xobourgo'? Don't knock it, it's been very helpful."

"So, we've got nine obvious hiding places and two that aren't. How—"

"Chief, I've got it!"

"I haven't even asked the question?"

"I mean about the other two. According to the guidebook those spots marked by the sea are caves! The one up by Makrisia Bay is called *Mygospilia* and the other cave is *Spilias*, over by the Bay of Livada."

"Very good, Yianni. Put that guidebook on your expense account."

"I have an expense account?"

"Back to my question. How did the thieves possibly figure out all eleven hiding places without someone on the inside tipping them off?"

"Anything on that in your guidebook?" said Tassos. "Check out those suggested day long excursions to places of interest around the island. Perhaps it's listed under 'Follow the yellow brick road to secret hiding places.'"

Kouros shot Tassos the middle finger.

"That just might be the answer," said Andreas. "They 'followed' the Foundation's 'inconspicuous' couriers when they transported valuables from Panagia Evangelistria to the other storage sites."

"But how would the thieves know who to follow?" said Kouros.

"Because the couriers are 'longtime' employees of the Foundation. Do you care to bet how many locals could tell you right now who the likely couriers are if you put the question to them?"

Tassos said, "That still doesn't explain how the thieves found the hiding places, let alone got inside. They would have had to follow the couriers into the middle of nowhere to find some of those places. They'd be spotted in a minute. Even a helicopter would be noticed."

Andreas rubbed his eyes. "Not necessarily."

"What the hell are you talking about?" said Tassos.

"I can't remember the name of the book, but it had some pre-historic man character with a unique way of hunting dangerous prey far quicker than he was. He'd start out by stalking his quarry as far as he could before losing it. Then he'd wait at that spot until the prey passed by another time, and track it from there as far as he could again before losing it. The hunter did this for as many days as it took to find the quarry in its lair."

"Nice story, but that would take a hell of a lot of time," said Kouros.

"And patience. Especially since we're talking about eleven sites," said Tassos.

"Not really," said Andreas. "Panagia Evangelistria is obvious and you could easily follow the couriers to Kechrovouni Monastery and the Jesuit Monastery without being noticed. The same for Xobourgo and, depending on the time of day, Katapoliani Monastery, as well. And with Pyrgos being such a popular place for tourists, couriers wouldn't be likely to notice anyone trailing them unless their stalkers were dumb enough to follow them into the cemetery. That left only five storage sites requiring more time and ingenuity to pinpoint. But why would the thieves care how long it took to find the others, or for that matter, however many more secret sites there were? They'd already struck it rich with six locations to rob at their leisure."

"Uhh, Chief, there's another explanation," said Kouros.

"Which is?"

"They put a tracking device on the courier vehicle and followed its signal to the sites."

"I like Andreas' theory, it has a more traditional flair to it."

"Whatever way they did it, it could have been done without the thieves being tipped-off by someone on the inside," said Andreas. "So, that leaves us with three open questions aside from who they are. How did they get in, how did they transport the items, and where did they take them?"

"To repeat myself, it would take a lot of time and patience to case those sites before finding the best way to get in and out undetected," said Tassos.

"And specialized electronics help to get around the alarms and cameras," said Kouros.

"But evidently the Foundation didn't start to put in that sort of security until years after the robberies began. And by the time it did, I'm certain the thieves had stolen more than enough to buy whatever brains and equipment they needed to get around anything the Foundation installed," said Andreas.

"It's a no-brainer how they transported the stuff," said Tassos. "In their pockets, and not a soul would notice. They could have used motorbikes or even walked away. We're talking gems and small pieces of gold, not tea sets and paintings. As for 'where the stuff is,' how about anywhere in the world by now? And if any is still on Tinos, I think you guys realize by now that this island is nothing if not one big hiding place."

Andreas took a drink of water. "It seems to me that we're looking for a person or persons capable of spending extensive amounts of time patiently locating and carefully reconnoitering eleven sophisticated hiding places, and of circumventing elaborate electronic surveillance and security systems once they do. And who are smart enough to realize that by committing tiny burglaries they're not likely to draw the sort of heat they'd do with big ones."

"A 'don't kill the golden goose' approach," said Tassos.

Andreas nodded. "It's almost as if the bad guy doing all this hasn't had anything better to do with his life for the last ten years or so."

"You're saying Trelos?" said Kouros.

"He's always been the obvious choice, and he sure as hell fits the profile, even knew how to scramble my recorder," said Andreas.

"Plus, as he said to you, he's 'invisible.' No one on the island ever notices him, and everyone expects to see him in the craziest, out of the way places," said Tassos.

"But didn't he tell you he only gave away his family's money?" said Kouros.

"Are you suggesting he wouldn't lie?" said Andreas.

Tassos rocked his head from side to side. "Frankly, I'm not so sure he'd have thought of himself as lying even if he is the thief. Do you remember Eleni saying that when Trelos' parents died they left one of the 'largest bequests ever' to the Foundation?"

"Are you're saying he considers himself to be recovering his family's money from the Foundation?" said Andreas.

"Who knows what he thinks, but the timing works," said Tassos. "The parents died a dozen years ago, the first thefts were noticed two years later but, considering the Foundation's inventory practices, there's no telling when the first robbery occurred. Under any scenario, though, Trelos had more than enough time dancing all over the island between his parents' deaths and the first robbery to figure out how to pull it off."

Andreas said, "What doesn't fit is how he found killers disciplined enough to do his dirty work and keep quiet about it. He doesn't seem the type to inspire confidence or loyalty in the breed that does that sort of work. And I definitely don't see that happening if he never talked to them."

"But he obviously knows how to get followers," said Kouros. "He does have his 'priests.'"

Tassos shook his head. "As far as we know he's paying them to act as recruiters at so much per soul. They would never have to know a thing about the nasty side of his business. And as long as his priests and their recruits are paid on time, everyone's happy."

"I think it's time to bring Trelos in for some serious questioning. Not that I expect him to talk, but I don't want him out there arranging more murders while we're running around trying to nail him. It makes me anxious, and that makes me prickly." Andreas smacked Tassos on the arm.

"Oh, so that explains it. And here I thought it was just your missing Lila and Tassaki," said Tassos.

"That too."

"So, do we wait for him at his place, or on the road by the spot where his parents died?" said Kouros.

Tassos looked at his watch. "I think it's too late to catch him on the road. There's probably a better chance at his house." Tassos pointed south toward the town. "That's where he lives, over there to the left of the town just beyond and across from the prehistoric acropolis."

Andreas stared. "From up here, the *Vriokastro* looks a lot like the tip of Tinos' new port on the other end of the bay between them. Interesting how two very different places, separated by a mile and a half of shoreline and five thousand years of history end up with the same designer."

"Why mess with Greek perfection?" said Tassos.

Andreas smiled. "Spoken like a true Greek god. But before we leave our lofty perch to go down and mingle among the mortals, let's stop by police headquarters and borrow some ballistic vests. Just in case our boy might be expecting us and has made some welcoming arrangements, I don't want to make it easy for him."

"Are you trying to make me anxious, too?" said Kouros.

"Make that 'us.'"

"It's good to share."

# TWENTY-FIVE

TWENTY MINUTES LATER they were back in the port, headed east along the sea toward Trelos' house. On the right was the stretch of sandy beach they'd seen from the taverna. It lay separated from the two-lane paved road by a nearly unbroken line of *almirikia*—salt cedars or tamarisk—painted around their trunks with white lime to keep away the pests. To the left were mostly empty fields and an occasional shack or business just off the edge of the road. The only thing resembling anything modern was the Tinos heliport, but even that was not much more than a concrete pad and bright orange windsock on a tiny patch of land between the road and the sea, close-by the base of the *Vriokastro*.

The road turned left at the ancient mound and wound to about halfway up its backside. At the eastern edge of the *Vriokastro* they turned left into Trelos' driveway and parked next to the house.

There was nothing to suggest anyone was home. No vehicles, no lights, no sounds.

"It's still early," said Kouros. "Only nine."

"Let's do it again the same way. Yianni around the back, we take the front. But this time, if you find a way in let us know before you try it. No heroics."

"Aye, aye, Chief."

Two minutes later, Kouros opened the door for them.

"I told you no heroics."

"What heroics? The place is empty. The guy doesn't even have a cat."

Andreas waved his hand at Kouros. "Just sit over there by the window and keep an eye on the road. Tassos, watch the back."

Kouros turned on a light.

"What are you doing," said Tassos.

"What's the matter, do you think a police car sitting in front of the house won't be enough to alert Trelos or his buddies we're inside?"

"No, I just wanted to know what you're doing, wise-ass," said Tassos.

Kouros reached into his back pocket and pulled out the guidebook. "Reading."

"Terrific."

An hour went by with nothing more happening than Tassos and Kouros going back and forth at each other in an effort to kill the boredom.

"What time is it?" said Tassos.

"Five minutes later than when you asked me the last time," said Kouros.

"Big deal. What in that book could possibly be more important than keeping me well informed?"

"Caves."

"Great. Sort like the one we're in now." Tassos went back to looking out the window.

"Whoa, guys, take a look at this," said Kouros.

"I wouldn't think a Tinos guidebook would have that sort of picture," said Tassos.

"Just listen. 'A mile and a half east of the town is the prehistoric *Vriokastro*. Little is known about this site as the Greek government has refused all requests for permission to conduct archaeological explorations there. On its southern edge, centered on the apex of the mound, is a cave open to the sea to a depth of fifteen feet and accessible by foot or by boat.'"

"Do you think…" Tassos let his words trail off.

"That our suspect is living next door to what could possibly be the best hiding place on all of Tinos?" said Kouros,

"Accessible by land and boat," said Andreas.

"And only a few hundred yards from the heliport," said Tassos.

"His family has lived here for generations. He must know more about that mound than anyone else on the planet," said Andreas.

"And they own all the property around it. Who's to say what they've been doing with it over the last couple of centuries?" said Tassos.

"It would explain why there's not a piece of electronic equipment in this place," said Andreas.

"And where the sister is," said Kouros.

"I think it's time we take an evening stroll," said Andreas.

"The good news is it's practically a full moon out there," said Tassos.

"Good news for whom?" said Kouros.

"Whoever shoots first," said Andreas. "Check your vests and weapons. And easy on the flashlights. If we're right about this, no way he'll be happy to see us."

Tassos shrugged. "Unless he's been expecting us."

THEY HID THE car behind a tightly clustered row of bamboo about a quarter mile further east down the road from the *Vriokastro* and Trelos' home. They walked back past the house to a sign on the left side of the road

marking the official entrance to the historical site. A
low stonewall of stacked flat stones ran along its border with the road. It would be easy to jump the wall at
any point, and not just for goats and cats.

At the sign, a three-foot wide break in the wall
opened onto an uneven dirt path lined by two-foot high
stonewalls. The path was trampled down in the middle
to no more than a foot-wide of packed dirt, bordered on
each side by a foot of brush.

"Doesn't look like this place gets a lot of traffic,"
said Kouros.

"At least not of the two-footed kind," said Tassos.

"Isn't Tinos known for snakes?" whispered Kouros.

"That was the island's name in antiquity, 'the place of
snakes,'" said Tassos, "But a miracle drove them away."

"I don't believe in miracles."

"Then watch where you walk," said Tassos.

"Keep it down, you two, I was kidding about this
being a stroll."

The path widened and narrowed erratically as it
climbed amid what seemed endless rows of more low
walls of flat stones. Some walls ran straight up the hill
as if barriers to the sea, but most ran horizontal, creat-
ing plateaus of dirt that once were crop-yielding soil.
Today those walls retained what bore little more than
thistle and lizards.

The top of the mound looked to be twenty-five feet
of solid stone, and the way up there was lined with a
haphazard array of wind carved sculptures of unnatu-
ral shapes. Or so they appeared in the moonlight. By
day they were boulders.

"We're not going up there, are we?" whispered Kouros.

"No," said Andreas. "If there's a way into this thing

from up there we'll never find it in the dark. I'm heading to the sea. I want to see that cave. We might get lucky and find some way inside from there."

"As if that will be any easier to do at night," said Tassos.

"Why don't you stay here and we'll pick you up on the way back?" said Kouros.

"Not a chance."

"As a matter of fact, that's a good idea," said Andreas. "Find a spot up the hill to keep an eye on us, and anyone who might come along while we're inside. We'll be sitting ducks in there."

"More like fish in a barrel," said Kouros.

"Okay," said Tassos.

"Don't fight so hard to come with us," smiled Kouros.

"Stay safe guys. I'll be here waiting and watching."

Andreas handed Tassos a communicator. "I borrowed a pair from the Tinos boys, just in case."

The moonlight made it easy to see, and the walls between them and a straight march to the sea were simple to get over. The most difficult part of the hike for Andreas was keeping his eyes on the ground in front of him so as not trip. It was hard to focus on the path with the Aegean spread out across the horizon, ablaze in shimmering silver. He wondered what Lila was doing at the moment. They'd not spoken all day.

"Chief."

"What is it?"

"Off to the right, it looks like a goat path leading out to the rocks above the sea. The cave should be out that way, and if it has fresh water like the guidebook says some do, goats would know that."

Andreas followed the path out onto the rocks. Tinos

was legend for its constant winds. Thankfully, tonight was relatively calm, with no wind driven waves to soak the rocks.

"Yianni, I think it's over there." Andreas pointed down at an indentation about thirty feet away at the edge of the sea. "Careful going down, I don't want to have to carry you back."

The two crept along on what seemed no more than a ribbon of stone across a cliff face.

"The more I do this the more respect I have for goats," said Kouros.

"Don't make me laugh, it's slippery."

Andreas jumped the last five feet down to a stone shelf just outside the cave. "Careful when you jump."

Andreas stopped at the mouth of the cave to wait for Kouros. He shone his light inside. The cave was broad and tall enough, and the floor deep enough below sea level, to easily accommodate a fast boat capable of making it to Athens, or anywhere else in the Mediterranean for that matter. Andreas inched inside the cave along a slippery ledge that led into a tiny alcove barely larger that a double-size phone booth. He shone his light on the roof, walls and ledges, and down into the water. Kouros stepped in next to Andreas and did the same inside the alcove.

"I don't see anything that looks like an entrance," said Andreas.

"Or a ventilation duct," said Kouros. "In fact, I don't see anything that looks unusual at all, not even a hole."

"Yeah, isn't that unusual. You'd think if the sea took such trouble to carve this cave into solid rock it wouldn't suddenly stop its work right here. The water must beat the hell out of this place when the wind is blowing, but there's not even the hint of a crevice beyond where we're standing. And what about that fresh water you talked about? Those goats must be pretty disappointed after making the trek down here to come up dry.

"I think we better come back tomorrow with some people who know about caves and see that they think. I've a feeling this one's been tinkered with."

"That will really piss off all those archeologists trying to get in here. Why do you think the government is keeping them away? This seems an obvious spot for a dig."

Andreas shrugged. "Who knows, but hopefully not because of Trelos' influence."

"More likely it's the Foundation's juice. Maybe it doesn't want attention drawn away from its church? After all, this place probably honored ancient gods."

"I doubt that's why. You've got the excavated Temple of Poseidon on the other side of town, and that was pretty important back in the days of the gods. Doesn't your guidebook say pilgrims stopped there to prepare themselves on their way to Delos?"

Kouros nodded. "Then what do you think is the reason?"

"An alien spaceship that our government doesn't want anyone to find. Like the one the United States has been hiding for decades in one of its western states."

"Mexico?"

"No, New Mexico," said Andreas.

"Let's get out of here."

Andreas laughed.

THEY'D JUST STEPPED off the narrow goat path leading back from the cave when Andreas caught a glimpse of a figure in the distance highlighted against the sky. It was coming toward them quickly. Andreas motioned for Kouros to move forward and downhill. Andreas went off at a similar angle up the mound, staying as low as he could so not to silhouette himself against the horizon. They'd keep whoever was coming between them.

The figure abruptly turned and headed up the hill toward Andreas. Andreas crouched beside a wall, and waited until the figure was ten feet away before standing up. "Fancy meeting you here."

Trelos stumbled backwards. He seemed surprised and clutched his iPod to his chest. Andreas walked down to him as Kouros came up from below. They met on a narrow plateau, with Trelos in the middle.

"Rather late for you to be out and about here, wouldn't you say?"

No answer.

"Oh, we're back to that again. It's not going to work this time. So start talking." Andreas reached over and pulled the earphones off Trelos' head.

Trelos stepped back as if trying to protect his iPod and Andreas leaned forward to grab it.

That was when Andreas heard the buzz fly past his head, the crack of a rifle shot, and the sound of Kouros stumbling back and falling against a wall behind him.

"*Yianni*," Andreas screamed. He grabbed Trelos by the throat and dragged him as a shield toward Kouros' body. "Move from that spot and I'll kill you myself." He reached down, grabbed Kouros, and rolled with him over the wall. Andreas felt the bullet hit him in the side before he heard the sound of the shot.

"*Stop! Stop! What are you doing? This is wrong!*" Trelos was screaming but Andreas didn't look to see at what. He was too busy trying to find where the bullet had entered his buddy. Kouros' forehead was covered in blood.

Andreas heard another shot, this one from a pistol. He grabbed the communicator and yelled, "*Tassos, what's happening? Yianni's been hit and we're pinned down. Where are you?*"

No response.

# TWENTY-SIX

ANDREAS SLID ALONG the wall until he was between Kouros' head and the shooter. He couldn't see Kouros' wound. All he saw was blood. He brought his flashlight close to Kouros' head and, blocking the reflected light as best he could with his body, gently ran his fingers along his friend's head until he found the wound: an ugly jagged cut high above the right temple. Andreas pressed his fingers against Kouros' neck and felt for a pulse. He tore open the front of Kouros' shirt. The bullet was caught in the vest.

Andreas dropped his head and said a prayer. That's when he sensed the pain in his own side. It felt like a broken rib. He ran his right fingers along his vest and found a second bullet.

He wanted to look over the wall to see if Trelos was still there, but didn't dare. The shooter was too good.

"Trelos, are you there?"

Nothing.

"*I said, 'are you there*?'"

Andreas heard a very weak, "Yes."

"Who's shooting at us?"

Andreas heard something, but couldn't make it out. "What?"

"He's coming," said Trelos.

Andreas spun around and crawled along the wall toward Trelos' voice. Whoever was coming probably was focused on where Kouros went down. If he moved away from that spot he might be able to get off a shot before the shooter could target him again. It was his only choice. He couldn't just sit there waiting. Instinctively Andreas drew in a deep breath to calm himself, but a sharp pain at the broken rib stopped him. Instead, he closed and opened his eyes, crossed himself, and prepared to shoot at the first human sound he heard.

They were footsteps, but erratic, of a person moving quickly from one place to another, as if stopping to hide or listen. Andreas waited until the sounds were directly in front of him before jerking his gun and head together above the wall to fire.

He didn't.

"*Tassos*!"

Tassos slid over the wall and dropped down next to Andreas. He was out of breath. "Thank God you're okay. Where's Yianni?"

"Over there." Andreas nodded toward Kouros. "He probably has a concussion from hitting his head on the wall. But his pulse is good. The vest likely saved his life."

Tassos drew in and let out a deep breath. "I was up near the top of the mound where I could keep an eye on what was happening down by the cave. I watched you come back up and around to where you saw Trelos. We saw him at the same time so I didn't need to warn you."

"I tried to reach you on the two-way after I heard the pistol shot," said Andreas.

"I couldn't tell for sure where the first rifle shot came from but I knew it was below me and to the left. That's when I turned off the two-way, so it wouldn't give me away."

Tassos paused to catch another breath. "I got as close as I could to where I thought the shooter was. When I saw the muzzle flash on the second shot, I knew where to go. It came from inside a cluster of boulders. The pistol shot you heard was mine."

"You took out the shooter?"

Trelos sat down on the wall above them and stared up the hill.

"Not sure, I heard a scream but when I got there the shooter was gone. The rifle too. I found blood but no telling how bad the wound. My guess is the shooter is still out there. That's why I didn't try you on the two-way. Didn't want to risk giving away your position."

A groan came from Andreas' side of the wall.

"Watch him," said Andreas pointing at Trelos. He crawled over to Kouros.

"How are you feeling?"

"Like I rammed my head into a concrete wall."

"Close. It was stone. Someone took a shot at me but the bullet missed when I leaned in toward Trelos. You caught it in the middle of your chest and it knocked you back to where you fell and hit your head on the wall."

Kouros pushed himself up on his elbows. "Where's Trelos?"

"Over there, sitting on the wall like he's at a picnic watching butterflies."

Kouros tried to get up.

"Hold on there, fella, you've taken quite a hit."

"I've had worse." Kouros stood up and stared at Trelos. "And given a lot worse."

Andreas pulled Kouros back to the ground. "Careful, we haven't found the shooter yet."

Andreas looked at Trelos staring up the hill. "Who's shooting at us?"

Trelos didn't move.

"Did you hear me?"

Trelos nodded but said nothing.

"Asshole." Kouros tried to lunge for him, but Andreas held him down.

Trelos shrugged. "I don't care what you do to me. It doesn't matter anymore."

"Yianni, forget about him for now. We need better cover. Can you walk?"

"Yeah, I'm fine."

"How about that building down there?" Tassos pointed at a small concrete shed at the bottom of the hill, adjacent to the eastern edge of the mound and across the road from Trelos' house.

"It's windowless," said Trelos without turning to look. "You'll be trapped inside with no way out but the door. We built it on top of a streambed running out of the mound to bring power and ventilation into the *Vriokastro*."

"Who's 'we'?" said Andreas.

"My sister and I."

"What about your brother?" said Tassos.

"No, Petros never comes here anymore. Not since our parents died. He lives up on the mountain. He has no idea what we've done here."

"Does he know how to get inside the mound?" said Tassos.

"Some of the ways, not all of them."

"Like through the cave?" said Kouros.

"That's one, but we rarely use it. Tourists kept coming there trying to find a way inside the mound. A few years ago a young American couple almost found the entrance."

"What happened to them?" said Kouros.

"A storm came up and they drowned in the cave. That's when I decided to seal off anything suggesting there might be something more than the front of the cave. I also mounted a camera so we could see whoever came inside. It looks like part of the stone roof. And I put in a sensor that sets off an alarm if something heavier than a goat stands in the alcove inside the cave."

"Guess that's how the shooter made us," said Kouros.

"But that means the shooter had to be inside the mound when we were in the cave." Andreas looked at Trelos. "Who else knows how to get inside?"

"No one but my brother and sister."

"And anyone interested enough in your activities to have followed you," said Andreas. "Sort of the same way you found the Foundation's secret hiding places. By trailing Foundation employees."

Trelos shrugged. "It's all over now."

"What I can't figure out is how you managed to find your way inside all those places once you located them?" said Andreas.

"It wasn't very difficult. Much of what I needed was in old records, mainly in the Archeological Museum just down Megalochari Avenue from Panagia Evangelistria. Those records were my roadmaps into most of the places. Getting into the others was like solving elaborate puzzles, and I like puzzles."

"Weren't you worried about getting caught?"

Trelos gestured no. "I was careful. I never went to the same location more than twice a month, and I always took only what I could carry in the pack around my waist. Did you notice that I always carry my iPod in my hand, even though I have a waist pack?" He shook his head. "No one ever noticed that."

"How did you handle electronic security?" said Tassos.

"It was a challenge at times, but they never installed anything sophisticated and I had all the equipment I needed to get around whatever they tried."

"Where's your equipment?" said Tassos.

Trelos pointed at the ground. "Here."

"Speaking of 'here,' I think it's time we get away from here." Andreas pointed up the hill to the boulders where Tassos last saw the shooter. "My guess is there's a way inside the mound from there." Andreas looked at Trelos. "Am I right?"

Trelos nodded. "But I don't think you'll find anything. Anyone who knows how to get inside the *Vriokastro* could be anywhere by now."

"Wounded and with a gun," said Tassos.

Andreas nodded. "More of a reason to get moving. I'd rather be the hunter than the hunted."

FOR THOSE WHO believed in ghosts the evening was theirs. The figure that emerged from the very top of the ancient site was shrouded in black and moved like a cat. It held a broomstick in one hand, or at least something long, and found a perch on the east side of the peak. It watched four others making their way up the hill. The figure didn't budge, just sat quietly holding the broomstick.

"UP THERE, TO the right," said Tassos.

The spot was a group of boulders about sixty feet

from the peak. "They look like a coven of witches," said Kouros.

"Just worry if one starts to move," said Andreas. "Trelos, where's the entrance?"

Trelos pointed to a dark oval about the size of a front door and ringed by the boulders.

"That's where the shooter was, inside that hole," said Tassos.

The four men made their way to the opening.

"Yianni, stay out here with Trelos. Tassos come with me."

"You'll never find the entrance without me," said Trelos.

"He's right," said Tassos. "I couldn't find it when I was looking around inside and it's a rather obvious spot for tourists to explore."

Andreas took Trelos by the arm and pushed him through the opening. "Fine. But don't even think of pulling something."

"I have no reason to. I've done nothing wrong."

"How about killing five people?"

"I know nothing about any of that."

"What about robbing a church. Does that count as 'wrong' to you?"

"I didn't do it for the money, my family is very rich. I was recovering what my parents had given away to strangers, so that I could do God's work in a better way and, in the process, redeem my parents' souls for all the grievous harm they'd done to me. And to my sister."

"Yeah, I heard all about her broken engagement," said Andreas.

"That is only part of what they did to her. She suffered much more difficult and tragic pain than that."

"Frankly, I'm more worried about the pain the shooter's causing us." Andreas turned on his flashlight. "Just get me inside your mound."

Five paces in Trelos stopped at two abutting boulders. To the left was an alcove filled with goat crap, candy wrappers, and empty water bottles.

"The leavings of visitors, I see." Andreas shone his light on the ground in front of the two boulders. "Blood stains. And they end here."

Trelos reached up, pressed his hand into an opening between the boulders, and fidgeted with something for a moment. He shook his head. "The release won't work. It's locked down from the inside. We can't get in from here."

"Where's the next nearest entrance?"

"It won't matter. If one's locked down they're likely all locked down."

"How do we get in?"

Trelos shook his head. "We don't. Unless whoever's inside wants to let us in."

"Terrific, a siege."

"We could get in if we found the entrance used by the last one to get out."

"Then there'd be no one left in there to catch?" Andreas pointed toward the outside with his flashlight. "You first. I wouldn't want you getting lost on the way out."

Outside, it was Yianni and Tassos who'd disappeared.

Andreas whispered, "Yianni? Tassos?"

"Above you, behind the boulders," said Tassos.

Andreas pushed Trelos ahead of him toward Tassos' voice.

"What are you doing up here?" said Andreas.

"The boulders give us cover on the east from a shooter below. And those—" Tassos pointed at stonewalls to the left and right "—give us at least some to the north and south."

Andreas looked up the hill. "What if the shooter's up there?"

"Then we've got a problem," said Tassos.

"Add it to the list," said Andreas. "We can't get into the mound, everything is sealed from the inside, and whoever's still in there could pop up anywhere. I better check out the peak, just to be safe."

Andreas pointed at a boulder and said to Trelos, "Sit over there."

"Be careful, Andreas," said Tassos. "But don't worry, *if anybody shoots you, I shoot Trelos.*" Tassos said the last words loudly and pointed his gun at Trelos. "*Just in case anyone up there is listening.*"

Andreas shook his head and started up the hill. It wasn't as easy a climb as it looked. The path was off to the left but Andreas headed straight up toward the peak and the last twenty-five feet was on solid slippery rock. Twice he stumbled, once almost losing his gun.

Just before reaching the top he thought he heard a sound. Like fabric brushing against stone. He froze as his eyes darted about for the source of the sound. A pebble tumbled down the hill on the other side of the peak. It could be a goat or a lizard or a bird. Or the shooter. Andreas took a deep breath, winced at the pain in his rib, and charged the last few feet to the top.

There was nothing waiting for him. Thank God.

He did a three-hundred-sixty-degree scan down the mound. There wasn't a living creature to be seen. Damnit.

The way back was easier. He took the path down the hill.

"Nothing up there that I could see," said Andreas.

"Maybe the shooter is holed up inside the *Vriokastro*, bleeding to death from my bullet."

"Aside from praying that you're right, what do we do until then?" said Kouros.

Andreas sat down on a footstool-size rock at Trelos' feet. "I think it's time you give us some answers. Let's start with why you killed the Carausii brothers?"

"I already told you. I don't know anything about that."

"My friend over here is very upset with you. You almost got him killed. So, unless you want things to get very nasty for you very quickly, I suggest you tell us everything you know about the Carausii brothers."

"He doesn't know." The voice seemed more to mimic than be human speech.

Andreas swung his head around in the direction of the voice. Thirty feet to his left a shrouded face stared at him from behind a stonewall. And a rifle barrel pointed at his eyes.

ANDREAS SWALLOWED. His gun was on his lap, but he didn't dare go for it. "I guess if you wanted to kill me you'd have already pulled the trigger. Is there something you want to say?"

The shooter's focus did not stray from the riflescope. Nor finger from the trigger.

"I guess you're the executioner part of Trelos' secret society," said Andreas.

"He would do honor to Greece in a way no one has in a very long time. He would make life better for many, and bring change not just to Tinos, but to places all over the world desperate to make immigrants a productive part of their societies."

"And what part were you supposed to play in all this? A Manto Mavrogenous sort of heroine?"

"She was never appreciated during her life and deserved a far better end than she received."

"Is that why you learned to shoot? To be like her, a warrior for your brother's cause?"

Trelos spoke before his sister could answer. "Meerna mastered her Olympic skills long before any of this."

"What do pole vaulting and hurdling have to do with shooting?" said Tassos. He and Kouros sat frozen in place about ten feet up the hill from Andreas.

"You're thinking of the decathlon. Her event was the pentathlon."

"So?" said Tassos.

"The pentathlon covers five sports, swimming, cross-country running, an equestrian event, fencing, and…" Trelos paused. "Pistol shooting."

"The skills of war." Andreas swallowed again. "Strange training for a woman, don't you think?" He hoped the more they talked the better the chance of working something out before Meerna pulled the trigger.

"Our parents did not think that way," said Trelos. "Our family's ancestors were military heroes and there is history on Tinos tied back to Manto Mavrogenous. Meerna's skills were a source of great pride to Mother and Father, but when our parents prevented her from marrying the man she loved she refused to compete again. She did that to hurt them, but I think her decision harmed her much more than it did our parents."

"How did your sister feel about your parents' deaths?" Andreas held his breath.

Meerna kept staring straight down the barrel at Andreas' head. Her only movement was a slight flick of her trigger finger.

"It was an accident," said Trelos, still sitting on the ground.

Andreas looked up at the moon. "It's a beautiful night to be outside. I know you love being out in the dark, Trelos. Bet it doesn't even matter if there's moonlight. You've come here so often I'm sure you could find your way blindfolded.

"Sort of makes me think of your father driving along a road he must have taken thousands of times, not having had a drop to drink, suddenly falling asleep at the wheel. And your poor mother. Hard to imagine she wouldn't sense when her husband of more than forty years was getting sleepy, and wouldn't do whatever it took to make sure he stayed awake for the rest of their brief trip home. Or make him pull over.

"Then again, maybe your mother fell asleep first? But she didn't have anything to drink either, and somehow I think your parents had a lot to talk about on their trip back home. For instance, how concerned they must have been that their only daughter was so sick she couldn't even lay down in the back seat for the short trip home. Can't you just imagine what they must have been saying about her?"

Trelos leaned forward. "They wouldn't have been talking about Meerna. They would have been talking about me. They considered themselves pillars of Tinos' society, protectors of island traditions, and they insisted on us being nothing less than perfect children. But perfect to them did not include a daughter who disobeyed traditional practices or a son whose vision was broader than their own myopic ways."

Trelos got to his feet. "They were going to send me back to that clinic in Switzerland. She was afraid for me. She cried for weeks after I came back from there the first time. She promised me she'd never let anyone hurt me again."

"Are you saying your sister killed your parents to keep them from sending you away?" said Tassos. "What did she do, drug them?"

"I have no idea what happened. At their funeral she made me promise that each of us would always protect the other, because there was no one else in the world we could trust to keep us safe."

Trelos looked at his sister. "But not like this, Meerna. Not like this."

Trelos stepped between Andreas and Meerna. "Put down the gun or kill me." He walked toward her and reached for the rifle.

The shot came from another direction.

TASSOS' LEFT HAND had been holding his gun by his side from the moment he heard Meerna's voice. But he couldn't attempt a shot at the tiny target she offered while her rifle was fixed on Andreas. When Trelos reached for her rifle Tassos brought up his gun and began firing one-handed up and down in line with Meerna's head. She flinched at the spray of stone and splattering lead, and swung her rifle in Tassos' direction, but by then Andreas had grabbed his gun and was firing at her too. She ducked down behind the wall.

"*No!*" shouted Trelos and he flung himself over the wall onto his sister.

Andreas was right behind him and stepped on the rifle barrel, pinning it to the ground. Meerna struggled to pull it free but Andreas pointed his gun at her head. "Like your brother said, '*It's over.*'"

Trelos sat on the ground by his sister, holding his hands over his eyes, shaking his head, and repeating, "What have you done…"

"Handcuff her, Yianni," said Andreas.

Kouros cuffed Meerna's hands behind her back. She didn't struggle.

Andreas reached down, took Trelos by the arm, and pulled him to his feet. "Turn around." Andreas handcuffed him and led him back to the spot where a moment before Andreas had been his sister's target. "Sit here, with your back to the boulder." But before Trelos could sit Andreas whispered in his ear, "Thanks for what you did."

Andreas looked at Kouros. "Put her over here, next to her brother." He whispered no words to her.

# TWENTY-SEVEN

ANDREAS HADN'T NOTICED the crickets before. Now they seemed to be everywhere. It was just a take-it-for-granted little thing, but not so at that moment. Andreas stood with his back to everyone, closed his eyes, and said a prayer.

He turned and looked at the prisoners. They were sitting handcuffed on the ground between Tassos and Kouros.

"Which of you is going to tell me about the Carausii brothers?" said Andreas.

"She's bleeding." Trelos nodded toward a red stain on Meerna's left shoulder.

Andreas shrugged. "I don't care."

"She's my sister."

"Same answer."

"But she could bleed to death."

"Nah, she's just in pain." Tassos leaned over and pressed on Meerna's shoulder.

She screamed.

"And there's nobody out here but us to hear the screams," said Tassos.

"Or gunshots," said Kouros.

"If you want to help her, let's start with why and how you incinerated the two Carausii brothers?" said Andreas.

"How many times do I have to tell you I don't know anything about that?"

"What about you, Meerna?"

She said nothing and her eyes stayed focused on the ground in front of her.

"Or do you prefer that I make a murder case against you *and* your brother?"

Meerna shifted in her spot but kept looking down. The voice came again. "They were going to expose Trelos. He was doing such great things to make the world better and those two pieces of garbage were going to destroy him."

"How did you know what the Carausii brothers planned to do?" said Andreas.

"Like always. I listened. The two Polish tramps were talking to each other about how their boyfriends were going to make a lot of money because they'd found the '*cioban*.' They didn't know I knew *cioban* meant shepherd."

"And on the basis of that you murdered those two boys?" said Kouros.

"No, of course not. I knew of two Ukrainian women who were also prostitutes. I contacted them and made arrangements."

"What sort of arrangements?" said Andreas.

"That they would deliver the two *tsigani* to me unconscious."

"And did they?"

"No, but others did. It was not as I desired, I wanted no Greeks involved in whatever bad had to be done to protect Trelos' good works. But I had no choice."

"Where did they deliver the brothers?"

"At the house I'd rented for the prostitutes."

"How did you get them from there to where their bodies were found?"

"I'd stolen a van from where drivers liked to park their trucks by the port overnight and left keys in ashtrays or under floor mats in case the trucks blocked another and had to be moved. I drove it to where I could watch the house for the prostitutes to leave on the brothers' motorbikes. When they left it meant the brothers were unconscious. I went inside the house, dragged the brothers and the nitrous oxide cylinder into the van, chained the brothers together, and drove to where I knew we would be alone. I waited until one started to regain consciousness and got him to tell me what he knew. In his condition it was easy. That's when I learned they'd discovered my brother was the Shepherd and that he was taking from the church."

"How could you possibly know that?" said Trelos.

"Because you were careless in your dealings with their *tsigani* leader. You met with him even though I said you should not. You thought he would not recognize you."

"It was necessary. He was the first *tsigani* leader willing to commit his people to our brotherhood. He'd taken the money I'd offered him to move his clan to Tinos, but he was refusing to cooperate further unless I met with him."

"I understand, brother, but he was not dealing honestly with you. He had the Carausii boys follow you. They saw you going in and out of places you should not have been and later disappearing into the *Vriokastro*. Their instincts told them there was money to be made on what they knew, but their greed kept them from telling their leader. Instead, they were going to the Albanians. If I had not stopped them the Albanians would have killed you."

What with the voice, the story, and the setting, Andreas was beginning to wonder whether there might not actually be an alien space ship inside the mound. "Why the Greek flag and the words 'Revenge or Death'?"

"I wanted there to be no doubt in the mind of the *tsigani* clan leader that my brother was to be feared. He knew my brother patterned his brotherhood on *Filiki Eteria*. He would not miss the message in my note and the flag."

"And after you had your answers?" said Tassos.

"I put inhalation masks back on them. At the old age home where I once worked, a woman tried to kill herself with nitrous oxide from a dentist's office. I overheard a doctor say that had she used pure nitrous oxide she would have succeeded, but the gas she used was mixed with oxygen. I did not make that mistake. I waited until they were no longer breathing, wrapped them in a flag that would not burn, chained a cylinder containing my note to the steering wheel, and sent my message in flames to any who might think to harm my brother."

"How did you get away?" said Tassos.

"On the bike I'd brought with me in the van."

"A motorbike?"

"No, a collapsible bicycle. It was small enough for me to carry on my motorbike so I used it to get me to where I'd left the motorbike."

"And what about the third brother?" said Andreas.

"His death came because the fates were with us."

"What are you talking about?" said Kouros.

"The Carausiis' clan leader sometimes came into Petros' place to try to sell him chairs and tables. He had no idea we were related to Trelos. One day he came in a bit drunk. He said he was celebrating because he'd just learned that the police were about to catch the killers of his 'two boys.' He said someone had called him from a taverna outside of Athens to say that you—" she nodded at Andreas "—had just been talking with the dead boys' brother."

"And that's what justified your killing him?" said Tassos.

"I couldn't take the chance. Could I?"

"You're who killed the brother's assassin," said Andreas.

"I did not plan to. I went to kill the brother in case the assassin did not appear. I told Trelos and Petros I wasn't feeling well and had to see a doctor in Athens." She turned her head toward Trelos. "He was so concerned about me."

She went back to staring at the ground. "I killed that man only because your people captured him. You gave me no choice. I had to protect Trelos."

"How did you arrange for the third brother's assassin?" said Andreas.

"A lot of very bad people come into the bar. And they talk about what they've done and who they know who does bad things. They sometimes even mention a name or a phone number. I remember that sort of thing. It was only a matter of making the call and delivering the money."

"How did you know where to find the brother?" said Tassos.

"I asked a *tsigani* woman I knew if she could find out where I could have a religious gift delivered to the brother of the two murdered boys. 'To help ease his loss,' I said. She had the answer for me within an hour."

Tassos shook his head. "You've got quite a sister here, Trelos. If you wanted to change the world I think you should have started at home."

Andreas stretched his back until he felt the pain at his rib. "Why did you kill the Pakistani?"

She stared at Andreas. "You had put me to a great deal of trouble planning how to eliminate the possibility of the third brother leading you to Trelos. Planning is very important. When things go according to plan good things happen. Planning was how I won my races." She looked away. "Two nights after I arranged for those two men to die in Syntagma so that you would never find Trelos, you walked into Petros' bar. I had not planned on that. I was frightened. I do not like being frightened. And when I overheard the Polish girls talking about the Romanians saying that the Pakistani had talked to you about the *cioban*, I knew what I had to do."

Andreas cleared his throat. "How did you find the Pakistani?"

"I listened at the other tables until I heard someone say where he was. He'd gone to another bar. Probably because he was afraid you might come looking for him in Petros' bar. I left early and took Petros' car, as if looking for Trelos. I often go looking for him. It's not unusual. I must protect him. I have a duty to—"

Andreas interrupted. "When you left your brother's bar where did you go?"

"I went to the bar where the Pakistani was supposed to be."

"What was your 'plan' for him?" Andreas struggled to keep his voice professional.

"A few weeks before, a drunken customer in Petros' bar was bragging about having pills that, if you dropped one in a drink, made resistance impossible. When he showed them off to his friends one pill fell on the floor. He didn't notice, so I picked it up and kept it. I took it with me to that bar.

"I knew the Pakistani drank too much and what he liked to drink. When I saw he'd almost finished his drink, I bought another at the bar, dropped in the pill, walked it over to his table, and exchanged it for his old one. He never even noticed. Probably because he was used to me bringing him drinks and was so out of it by then that he didn't know what bar he was in.

"I went outside and waited for him. When he came out he could hardly walk, and someone was helping him to his motorbike. The stranger left him there. For a moment I thought God would arrange for him to die in an accident. But, instead he fell asleep on the ground next to the bike. I waited until I was sure no one was watching and pulled him into my car. I drove to the dump out past Livada. It was as far away and as deserted a place as I could think of. But one where the body would definitely be found the next morning."

"And your reason for writing 'Revenge or Death' on my card and sticking it in his mouth was to send me a message?"

"I wanted you to know how quickly and horribly people died who presented a risk to my brother. I wanted to scare you away."

Meerna seemed to sigh, but Andreas couldn't be sure.

"But I knew I'd misjudged you when my brother told me of your colleague's threat to the *tsigani* clan leader to banish all of my brother's followers from the island if he did not meet with you." She nodded toward Kouros. "That was when I decided you would only abandon your efforts to destroy my brother's destiny if you realized to continue meant your son's life."

"That was you in the jewelry store on Mykonos with the doll and Andreas' card," said Tassos.

"Yes. I found the card on the Polish girls' table. It was as if the fates had again intervened knowing I would later need it to deliver my final warning."

"I'd say they used it to curse you," said Kouros. "If you hadn't put the card on the doll we'd never have come back to your brother's bar to find out how it got there."

Andreas reached up and rubbed his eyes with his hands. He felt something come off on his face. He looked at his hands. They were still covered in Kouros' blood. He stared at the mad woman in front of him.

Andreas knelt down in front of her as if to pray. He whispered, "May you rot in hell."

# TWENTY-EIGHT

ON THE POLICE boat taking Meerna and her brother from Tinos to jail on Syros neither said a word, but as soon as they arrived in Syros Trelos demanded to see his lawyer and the prosecutor. In their presence Trelos said, "I have taken an oath to tell only the truth or speak not at all," and proceeded to recount every word of his and his sister's confessions. He then told his sister to do the same. Whether judged mad or sane Meerna would never be free again. Or so Andreas hoped.

Andreas made it back to Mykonos just in time to catch a charter flight to Naples. He couldn't wait to surprise Lila. He'd never been to Capri, but Lila called it the deep blue Tyrrhenian Sea's "most famous rock." At the Naples airport he caught a taxi to the port and made his ferry connection to Capri with plenty of time to spare.

Andreas tried not to think about how close he'd come to being dead, but his aching cracked rib wouldn't quite let him forget. He wondered what would happen to Trelos. Even if his sister were telling the truth about him having nothing to do with the murders, and Trelos named those who'd helped him convert what he'd stolen into cash, he still faced serious jail time for the robberies. That was *if* the Foundation were willing to risk publicity and prosecute.

As for the future of Trelos' brotherhood, Tassos was

right about him paying his priests for their loyalty. They were the ones who saw to it that the brothers were paid their proper additional compensation. No money, no priests, no brotherhood. End of story.

In Andreas' experience, that was the fate of most grandiose plans for changing the world both good and evil. They ended not with a bang but a whimper.

Andreas smiled. He realized he'd just twisted all out of shape Lila's favorite line of the English language poet, T.S. Eliot. *This is the way the world ends / Not with a bang but a whimper.*

I guess we Greeks just see things differently, he thought.

Tinos had harbored no grand conspiracy. Just a whacko Wizard of Oz, and his psychotic sister dutifully paving her brother's road to good intentions with horrific harm. There had been no massing of bigots seeking to rid the world of those that their intolerance judged unwanted or undeserving, and yet, five human beings still died. Yes, not five thousand or five million, but how many more killings could Meerna have justified if Trelos had found a broader stage?

There was no doubt about it: Andreas definitely preferred the whimper end for world changers.

Andreas shook his head. Anything else on the subject was now officially someone else's problem. He'd done his job and closed the case. Unless, of course, you believed the Athens media's headline story: "Minister Spiros Renatis kept his word to the Greek people by spearheading a daring investigation into the Tinos murders and apprehending the craven killer of five innocents." Buried in the story were congratulations from the Minister of Culture to Spiros for preventing the "attempted" desecration of a national historic site.

I wonder what's really inside the *Vriokastro*? Screw it. Screw it all.

"*And fuck you, Spiros.*" Andreas looked to see if anyone heard him curse, but realized he'd sworn in Greek. He was now a stranger in a strange land and liked the feeling.

The boat was underway. It would take an hour to get to Capri but, no matter, soon he'd be with his wife and son. "My wife." He said the words aloud and smiled. He'd have to buy her a big present. They'd been virtually incommunicado since she left for Capri. He tried calling her that morning to tell her he'd kept his promise to catch the "bastards," but Marietta answered and said she was out sailing. He looked out the window. Lila might be out there right now.

Andreas tried to nap but couldn't. He looked across the water toward Capri and saw what seemed to be a necklace strung back and forth across a broad, green-capped tower of stone soaring out of the sea. As the boat drew closer, he could make out beads of different colors and sizes along the necklace. Then he noticed the beads were moving. The necklace was a highway anchored to the face of the cliffs, winding surreally all the way to the top.

The ferry docked at Marina Grande, Capri's main port. Old homes ran up the hillside from the harbor toward the best-known part of the Island, Capri center, a playground and shopping Mecca for the world's rich. It was where world-class jewelers and couture fashion shops endured day-trippers from Naples and Sorrento while awaiting the evening's bounty of strollers from the island's world-class hotels and anchored yachts.

Andreas asked a cop in English where he could catch a cab to the Capri Palace Hotel. A minute later he was in a Fiat taxi with a stripped canopy for a roof winding its way through narrow streets up toward Capri center. At an intersection where the entrance to the town was off to the left the taxi did a counter-clockwise nearly full circle swing around a monument and headed out onto the necklace. What had seemed surreal from a distance was distinctly real up close.

The road was a narrow two-lane slab clinging to a cliff. Cars, motorcycles and the occasional bus whizzed past them coming down the mountain in the traditional devil-may-care manner of Italian driving. Andreas winced as a bus came by on a turn just a little too close for comfort. He shot a look at the taxi driver but the man seemed unconcerned, so Andreas decided to look out to sea and let the driver worry about the road. It was a good choice. There was the bay of Naples and its islands opening up to Sorrento and the Amalfi coast. Peaceful Italy.

At the top of the mountain of stone he'd seen from the ferry, the island seemed different. More relaxed. This was Anacapri. The road ran past ancient giant trees and mansions overlooking the sea. It ended at a small square by a funicular taking those who wished to an even higher level.

The driver motioned for a bellman to take Andreas' bag and Andreas followed him through a linen-draped walkway bordering a glass-sided pool. He thought he recognized two pairs of toes dangling in the pool.

At the top of the path Andreas stopped to catch a

glimpse of the sea over the treetops of the town. Ahead of him was a row of bushes setting a grassy pool area off from the rest of the hotel. He walked to a break in the bushes and looked for the owners of those toes. But the toe people saw him first, jumped up, and hurried hand in hand across the grass in his direction. Andreas lifted Tassaki in the air and kissed him, and holding him in one arm, kissed Lila and hugged her with his other. He accepted the pain from his rib as worth the price.

Lila kissed him again. "I have missed you, my darling. Please don't ever again leave me alone to this sort of life."

Andreas smiled. "I can imagine how you suffered."

"No you can't. Just me and a million Italian men on the hunt."

"Where are they? I'll shoot them all."

"Save your bullets darling. I'm a Greek woman, I'm used to it."

"Good thing I'm not the jealous type."

She pressed her index finger into the middle of his chest. "Well, I am, mister, so your late nights of running around deserted Aegean island venues chasing after wild women are over!"

"So you heard, huh? Damn it, you can't trust anyone to keep a secret these days."

"I got the message you called when I got back from sailing with Tonino—"

"Who's Tonino?"

Lila smiled. "I thought you weren't jealous. He's the owner of the hotel. You'll really like him. Anyway, I couldn't reach you and so I called Tassos. He told me what happened and said to tell you, 'Yianni must have hit his head harder than we thought, he's actually being nice to me.'"

"Anything else?"

"Yes, 'Eleni said to thank you for everything you did for her.'" Lila put her finger back in the middle of Andreas' chest. "Who's Eleni?"

"Her father owns a taverna. You'll really like her."

"Bastard."

"Freedom or Death."

Lila laughed. "Choose wisely, my love. One might prove unexpectedly more painful than the other."

\* \* \* \* \*

# Get 4 FREE REWARDS!

## We'll send you 2 FREE Books
## <u>plus</u> 2 FREE Mystery Gifts.

**Harlequin® Intrigue** books feature heroes and heroines that confront and survive danger while finding themselves irresistibly drawn to one another.

**FREE**
Value Over
**$20**